JILL WAGNER

The Mother Killer Series
BOOK 2

JANE'S
PUNISHMENT

Jane's Punishment
Copyright © 2023 Jill Wagner

https://www.facebook.com/jill.wagner.author
Book design by www.delaney-designs.com
Cover image by Shay

Acknowledgment

I want to acknowledge the absolute best readers a writer could hope for. Your encouraging comments and positive reviews are what keeps me motivated, and on track.

Thank you all!

Chapter One

Ionia State Penitentiary
April 2011

Studies have shown that long term isolation causes anxiety, depression, and paranoia. Being locked in a small, windowless cell, alone for 23 hours each day has also been attributed to a psychosis in the inmate, causing an almost feral madness in most men when they're finally reintegrated to the general population. But I am not like an ordinary inmate. I am more intelligent than any of them and am always in control. I am, by self-admission, a narcissistic psychopath, and I feel joy only when I'm engineering the end of a life or controlling the actions of others. Hell, the authorities don't even know how many lives I've ended, or those I've had a hand in ending.

My name is Tad Wilkins, and I am known to most as The Mother Killer. My protégé, Lloyd Tally, was arrested for serial murder in October, and for six months, while the FBI chased their tails around trying - and failing - to connect him to me, I was sent to isolation. His killing spree was brief, but the former FBI agent was a perfect choice because he satisfied the real reason I chose him, and that was to put me back into my daughter Janey's head. I knew Tally's kills would be recognized as a copycat to mine and would bring the best team in the Bureau on for the hunt. Janey was a new part of that team, and to help Tally mess with Janey's mind, I directed him to engage another agent on her team: Adrian Sanchez. Sanchez was ripe for my special brand of mind control and was an unknowing partner in the game. He was arrested with Tally and I initially pegged him as a disappointment, but then he contacted me on the morning of their arrest and I knew he would one day be of service to me. An unwilling ally perhaps, but useful.

Ruining Janey's FBI career has been my focus since I learned she'd gone against me to join their ranks. I know she would not have flipped on me if I had had the chance to complete her grooming. I was only months away from beginning the final stages of Janey's programming and of becoming the most prolific father-daughter killing team in history. My end game now is to infiltrate her every thought and to question my involvement in every one of her cases, because I know that her cushy upbringing has given her a false sense of morality. I do realize the game I'm playing is a long one, but I am certain she will eventually realize that a lot of innocent people have lost their lives because of her. By then it'll only be a matter of time before she admits to herself that, like her father, she loves having that control over life and death.

The only ounce of forgiveness I'll allow is that I know she would not have chosen that path if I had been able to complete my grooming. I believe nature is stronger than nurture, so despite the nurturing she got at the hands of her aunt Judy Newell after my arrest, I know that if I stay the course and remain patient, Janey will realize her true nature and become the partner I so richly deserve.

When they were arrested, I was abruptly, and without explanation, hauled to the isolation ward of the prison. The Feds thought they could make a case against me for facilitating Tally's kills, dubbed by the press as The New Mother Killer, but I wasn't worried because as an expert puppet master I was certain that no strings would lead back to me. I snipped them all, and not even the team's brilliant analyst, Abbey, was able to burrow through the walls I'd erected. I will give her props, however, for ferreting out my safe haven and leading Janey's team to Tally. My anger was so intense when I saw my own daughter, on live TV, desecrating my hallowed spot with the arrest, that it felt like I'd been buried beneath a ton of wet concrete. I didn't lash out irrationally, though; instead, I began to germinate the seed that would give life to a new plan that would bring Janey back to me.

Patience plus planning equals success. That's the mantra I've applied not only to my killing life, but to the calling I found when I made this place my home – a controller of lesser minds. I knew the first thing I had to do when I went into isolation was to find a way to communicate with my disciples that lived outside the walls that imprisoned me, and since unfettered access to an attorney is my constitutional right, I had my solution. Jacob Ray, the lawyer I chose was a man who, before I was arrested, thought he was smarter than me and tried to fool me out of a scam that bilked millions of dollars from unsuspecting investors. My brilliant strategy not only protected me, but it also provided the foundation of a financial portfolio most people never even dream about. I was an architect by trade. We build more than just buildings, and if you're as talented as I that mindset can build an empire. I didn't end Jacob then. I didn't even freeze him out of a financial windfall. I knew that the information I had would be like a cloud that hovered over him for the rest of his life, and I love that kind of power. He knew I could end his cushy life at any time, so when I requested his representation he had no choice but to agree.

Before my isolation, with the help of guards and other inmates, I was able to engage in some very intimate communication from men and women around the globe. That, of course, was impossible during my exile, and knowing how I'd be watched when I got out, that method was no longer an option. Undeterred, though, I was able to narrow down to five those I felt would be most susceptible to the subliminal messages I planned to deliver through Jacob. The three women and two men I chose had repeatedly professed their undying love and devotion to me, so I was certain that at least one of them would absorb my personal pain, and as a gift, would pay homage to me through their actions. Again, as a master puppeteer, I would enjoy complete and total anonymity.

However, formulating my thoughts and mentally drafting letters that would help put the next chink in Janey's armor only occupied a part of my confinement: I also spent a lot of time allowing my hatred for a reporter to fester and grow like a slow, erupting volcano. Candace was just an intern with a local news station when I was arrested, but she seemed to show up like a dirty penny everywhere either my daughter or I was taken. I was livid when I saw her on my hallowed ground the day of Tally's arrest because I realized she was the one who coined the Original and New Mother Killer monikers. I decided then that Miss Candace's glory days as an up-and-coming household name would have to end. Allowing myself to be called the Original Killer would be like admitting that Tally was actually a Mother Killer, and he was not. The acronym, OMK works, but only in the sense that I am the *Only* Mother Killer. As always, I'm certain my patience will pay off and the timing of Candace's end will present itself.

Chapter Two

Sunday, May 15th, 2011, 6:00 AM
SILVER LAKE STATE PARK- MEARS, MI

Maureen didn't have to rely on sight to know that she'd reached the cool down phase of her morning jog along the shore of Lake Michigan. The sound of her footfalls atop the hardened, damp beach sand seemed to harmonize with the crescendo of the waves an instant before they broke shore. Despite the pre-dawn misty fog, she was able to visualize the froth that would settle briefly in the impressions her feet left in the sand before the wave would recede, and another swell would break.

Standing in the sparkling white sand, between the beach trees and the Little Sable Point Lighthouse, the head ranger at Silver Lake State Park stopped her run and began the process of regulating her heart rate and breathing. There was a majesty about the 115 foot tower that helped start her days with a calming feeling of gratitude. Touched only by natural elements, the quiet beauty of her morning stop was a moment in time she treasured, and would find herself visualizing often. The Lighthouse would open to the public again on Memorial Day weekend, and while she understood and appreciated the public's desire to see the magnificence of it all, a part of her enjoyed having it to herself.

Bent at the waist with her hands on her knees, Maureen focused on deep breaths in through her nose and the slow release of oxygen through her mouth. When the hypnotic sound of her huffing and the breaking waves was interrupted by a grunt and a thud, Maureen stood up and tried to focus her sights through the fog and the condensation of her breaths. About 200 yards ahead of her she could faintly see the silhouette of a large person trying to gain purchase in the sand. It looked to her like someone was clodhopping with a couple of lead feet.

"Hey," she hollered, "do you need help?" But when the figure looked back, then found his footing and moved quickly down the beach, she added authority and shouted for the man to stop so she could speak to him.

Before the message from her brain that said to go after the stranger could put her feet in motion, something dripped from above and plopped on the toe of her shoe. She took a step back and tilted her neck so she could see the top of the tower. The fleeing man forgotten, Maureen turned and ran toward the door that led to the spiral staircase up through the inside of the lighthouse. When she saw what was hanging over the iron rail, on the ledge just below the copper lantern. she bolted through the door and took the steps three at a time. Realizing that what hit her shoe was a drop of blood, she paid no attention to the fact that the door was hanging open, and held in place by only the hinges at the bottom.

A park ranger by choice, Maureen had been through the State Police training academy, and knew she was breaking every safety protocol in the book by not waiting for back up to secure the scene, but she didn't care. There was a body hanging over that ledge, and if there was a chance of saving a life, Maureen was going to take it.

Chapter Three

Sunday, May 15th

FBI Headquarters – Quantico, VA

Jane Newell stopped by the breakroom for a fresh cup of coffee before meeting her mentor, training agent, and best friend Kate Jenkins at her cubicle. Jane was excited for the team meeting, and hoped it meant they had a new case. It had been six months since they closed her father's copycat case. Dubbed The New Mother Killer case, it was believed that Jane's father, Tad Wilkins, engineered the men from his prison cell to copy his kills with the goal of reconnecting, and ultimately destroying her FBI career ambitions. His plan did not deter Jane from her goal of hunting and caging monsters just like him, but admittedly, he did manage to get inside her mind and risk the career she'd worked so hard to attain.

Once Jane began receiving cryptic text messages from an anonymous person that included private knowledge of her childhood, she began her own off-the-books investigation that included an unsanctioned visit to her father in prison. Once the lines between Tad's kills and the new ones began to intersect and her family was threatened, Jane knew she needed to share what she'd done with her team. Instead of firing her on the spot, her unit chief and team leader Bill Jacobs allowed her to see the case through. The day they arrested Tally and Sanchez gave Jane a natural high that she knew she'd spend the rest of her life reliving. She was fully prepared to pay the consequences of her actions with the Bureau, but knew that in some capacity, she would become a part of the law enforcement world because it was her calling to stop other men like her DNA donor from ruining lives. She thought of it as a living amends to all the lives her father ruined.

When Jane came up behind Kate, the piping hot coffee she carried sloshed over the top and burned her hand when her friend, startled out of some sort of mind trip, yelped when she spoke.

"What the hell, Kate," she asked, "where were you just now? I told you I'd grab us some coffee and meet you at your desk for the meeting." With her freshly painted, hot pink for spring fingernails, Kate used a tissue to wipe the coffee off Jane's hand and apologized.

"I'm sorry, I was thinking about seeing my family tonight and must've zoned out for a second. Are you ready for the meeting, rookie?"

"Yes, I'm very ready. For the last six months I've been back in the classroom, reviewing the lessons on protocol, and how much our lives, and the success of our cases depend on teamwork." Kate tipped her neck back so she could train her eyes to the top of her six-foot-tall trainee's eyes and waited for her to finish her thought because she knew that with Jane there was always more.

"I know that the time out of the field was ordered by the director as a requirement for staying with the Bureau, but I really learned a lot. I'm glad he sent me because after putting that go-alone thing to the test, the risk I took with the Wilkins case really sank in." Still not finished with her epiphany, Jane said, "And the Krav Maga dojo you sent me to has helped tremendously with my street fighting skills."

Jane's physical strength and proficiency in the field was already superb, but she knew that adding Krav Maga to her arsenal would make her better, and beyond all else she wanted Kate, and everyone else to know they could, without hesitation, trust their lives with her. Kate smiled at Jane, and as they stepped into the meeting room, Jane had her final word. "How long do you plan on calling me rookie?" Kate tipped her head back and chuckled as the two women entered the meeting room.

Any of the fears she had that this first meeting would be awkward were immediately put to rest when she saw Bill and Seth engaged in lively conversation around the table. Their leader and calming voice of reason, Bill, smiled and nodded while Seth, their seasoned mince-no-words agent railed loudly against the road closures and detours he had to deal with just to get to work. Seemingly grateful for the interruption their entrance caused, Bill stood and greeted the women.

"Good morning, Kate. Jane, it's great to see you. The reports I've gotten in the last six months have all been great. I trust you took advantage of the training you were offered?"

"It feels great to be back sir, and yes, everything I learned on the first go around was reinforced and I can say without hesitation that this time, it really sank in. I'm ready to be a contributing part of this team again and appreciate the second chance." As they took their seats, Abbey's zippy entrance into the room had the group smiling.

"Good morning family, how are my lovelies today?"

Jane resisted the urge to stand up and hug their lively technical analyst and noticed that her platinum blonde hair was vibrantly highlighted in a violet that seemed to match the big, oval stone atop a wide silver band on her pointer finger.

"Abbey, it's so good to see you again," Jane said, "Your hair looks awesome, and I love how it matches your ring."

"Oh, you sweet, conventional lady in khaki, it's quite clear you've had no exposure to a hippy. This is an old school mood stone ring. Violet is the color for excitement, but will most certainly change before we're finished."

Seth greeted Abbey with a smile, and then added, "My first ex-wife had one of those, but the color rarely changed from the unhappy, bitter color of amber."

Jane settled in and pulled the notebook she was never without from the messenger bag she carried crossbody. Her sense of belonging didn't start to develop until she was 15 when Tad was arrested and she moved in with her Aunt Judy, but she knew this team was exactly where she belonged. Reflecting back as she often did, Jane was reminded that her journey was more like a winding, gravel path that oftentimes led to barriers she had to break through, but with the help and patient guidance of Aunt Judy, Dr. Isles, and even Kate, that path was starting to smooth out. Just the motion of getting ready to take notes at a team meeting felt right to Jane despite the fact that all of her senses were tuned in on Kate. Being the empath she was, Jane knew something heavy was on her friend's mind and wondered if perhaps it had anything to do with her scheduled speaking engagement this evening.

Bill returned to the room with a tray of fresh coffee for everyone, and started the meeting. "First on the agenda, Tad Wilkins has been out of isolation and back in general population since the middle of April. He doesn't have all of his old privileges back and is being watched, but we're a little concerned because he hired a new attorney who will have unfettered access to him, and to the outside world."

The group turned to look at Jane, but one of the lessons she did learn from watching her father was how to frame a facial expression to hide a feeling you may not want others to see. Of course, Tad's masks all hid evil, and Jane's did not, but she did sense they were waiting for a response, so she asked, "Does that mean we couldn't find any connection to him and Tally"?

Abbey knew that was her cue to start, so she flipped open her laptop, and with a fuzzy, bendable bumble bee wrapped around her stylus, began to scroll through her report.

"I have mad hacking skills," she proclaimed, "and as much as I loathe to admit defeat, that mad man has built an intricate web of mazes around himself as entangled as a hunk of weeds and roots buried deep underground with not even enough of a gap a grain of sand could get through. Even for me, it's impossible to find even the teeniest of an end loose enough to tug on."

"Don't get down on yourself, Abbey," Seth told her. "We all underestimated the power and control he still has on the outside." Seth's comment about Tad's power and control triggered a flashback so intense that the group noticed a glazed look in Jane's eyes.

"You okay, rookie?" Kate asked, "it looks like you left us for a second."

Jane's eyes roamed around the table as she processed the recollection, because she knew she wanted to share it, but needed to find the words to articulate it in a way that made sense. And since fresh coffee always helped clear her head, she took a drink from her cooled brew and spoke to the group.

"When Seth told Abbey that we all underestimated the power and control Wilkins still had, a memory from my childhood came back." Later she would realize that her path was about to take another turn and evaluate what made her nervous about sharing the memory, but for now, she looked at Kate for silent encouragement, and continued. "Our den was his office and he kept it locked at all times. I was never allowed to go in, but one day, not long before he was arrested, I came home from my friend's house and he was in it. The door was open a crack, so I crept up and peeked inside."

My benign, childhood memory was about to turn ugly, so I paused just long enough to remind myself of how far I've come since then. "He was closing a leather notebook, but he had this freaky gleam in his eyes, and an almost villainous smirk on his face." Jane cringed and then continued, "He reminded me of The Joker from Batman comics, and it scared me, so I quickly backed away, but he saw me. He locked the notebook in a metal box, then locked the box inside a drawer and came out into the hall."

Jane had the rapt attention of everyone around the table when Kate broke the silence.

"How did he react?"

"I expected him to be mad," Jane answered, "but he put his arm around me and told me not to worry, that one day soon I'd understand it all."

In the sing song voice Jane loved, Abbey said, "Well, there you have it boys and girls, he didn't keep anything on a computer. All is right in my world again." Her perfectly timed levity helped bring the meeting back into focus.

"Well, it's obvious he had a connection," Seth said, "yet very clear that we're not going to prove it, so let's move on and quit wasting our time on him." Jane appreciated Seth's direct, spare no feelings approach and nodded in agreement with the rest of the group.

Bill set his coffee cup down and asked Abbey if she had any information on the RICO case she helped build against Wilkins' shady ex-lawyer and his financial firm because they were certain it played a role in The New Mother Killer case, and in Tad's ability to fund his network.

As Abbey turned her computer screen around to give her report, Jane noticed her mood stone had turned a dull gray in color and made a mental note to learn what all the colors meant.

"On that part of my search, my brilliance did not fail, but I'm afraid the information is not going to be of much help." Abbey looked down at her ring, tapped her violet, sparkly fingernails on the table and went on. "The sleezy lawyer is still missing, and the case isn't set for trial until October, but the suit's like an airtight case, and since their whistleblower is in Witness Protection, it's taking a little longer."

"Is Sanchez still locked up on suicide watch?" Kate asked.

"Oh, the bonus creep you arrested is no longer on suicide watch but is serving his time in what some refer to as Club Fed in Prince George County, southeast of Richmond. He'll be lucky to find a job flipping burgers when he gets out. The scuttlebutt I'm picking up is that the folks with the pocket protectors and calculator brains are in the process of divesting him of the fortune he stole, and the best part of it is, when they get it all figured out, his family will get their money back."

That news made Jane happy because he was an integral part of her father's mind games that almost cost her the career she loved. She knew Bill had asked Abbey to dive into her former boyfriend's life for a connection to the communications she'd received during the case and decided to ask about it.

"Did you find any connection to Nick Richards?" Abbey's ring color seemed to be changing as she formulated her answer and appeared almost a dark brown when she spoke.

"What I uncovered there is like a riddle wrapped in mystery, because there is not now, nor has there ever been, a Nick Richards who resided in Virginia, or enrolled at VSU."

Jane was as dumbstruck as she'd be if she walked headfirst into a concrete wall, but tuned back to the group when Abbey responded to Seth after he questioned her findings.

"Oh, my favorite Italian gray fox, will you ever learn to trust how proficient I am with a virtual shovel? I tried every possible variation on his name, and dug to the deepest depths of the earth, and there is no one that matches."

Jane's train of thought finally cleared enough to respond. "That can't be possible. I met him my first year there, we were together for two years. I spent time with his family."

Bill's voice, while firm, was very soft when he said, "Jane, it's very possible he was planted by Wilkins for the sole purpose of getting close to you. With his obvious connections on the outside, it's not out of the realm of possibility that the family you met wasn't even his."

"No disrespect, sir, and I suppose anything is possible, but I was there, and he was real. We were real."

Kate offered a different explanation to there being no trace of him or his family.

"Is it possible," she asked the team, "that Wilkins got to him after the relationship began with some sort of threat? Maybe he is the whistleblower."

Abbey told the team that she did consider that possibility, "because the only way a person and their entire family can be completely obliterated off the grid, is if they're in wit sec and the U.S. Marshals cleared it all off. And before you ask," she continued, "it is impossible, even for me, to track down someone in the witness protection program."

Following Bill's cue, Jane realized her first meeting back was over and as she gathered her things, Bill told her that it would likely be another six months before she knew if Nick was the whistleblower, and then strongly encouraged her to leave it alone until then.

"Let's all take advantage of our down time right now and get caught up on our paperwork and reports," he told them. "Jane, you still owe me a couple, and since you've been officially reassigned to my team, it's best to stay on top of it all because our next case is always just a heartbeat away."

Jane's takeaway from her unit chief's last statement was that she was officially back on his team, and did not try to hide her smile when she assured him that all she had left of her reports were just a few finishing touches. Her long stride had her walking beside Kate out of the room and back to their desks, but she seemed so distant that Jane wasn't even sure Kate knew she was there.

"Hey, earth to Kate," Jane said, "you seem very distracted. I know you're a guest speaker tonight, but I've never known you to stress out about public speaking. Are you worried about it?" Jane could almost see Kate's wheels turning, and while she had an idea of what Kate might be sharing at the meeting tonight, she wasn't sure.

"It isn't so much about actually speaking," she said. And then in true Kate fashion, she immediately deflected the conversation away from herself, and added, "I'm really thinking that Nick could be the whistleblower."

"How did you come up with enough dots to make that connection?" Jane asked.

"First of all, your instincts are usually spot on, and I trust them. You're still kind of like a baby bird and might flop around a bit, but you've done a lot of work on yourself, and in so doing, are flying stronger than ever. You believe what you had with Nick was real, and I trust that. I know you really loved him, and you said yourself that his reaction to your acceptance into the academy at Quantico was totally out of character for him."

Jane stopped at her desk, and thought again about Nick's anger, and that he actually tried to forbid her from going.

"And he did move to New York right after that, so you're suggesting that possibly Tad got to him, but why, and how? The only thing he ever knew about my sadistic father was what I told him."

Jane took the bag off her shoulder and sat down, more confused than ever because she too had thought a lot about her relationship with Nick and had a hard time reconciling his actions at the end of it. He helped her as she struggled with being the adult child of a mad man and serial killer, and never judged her, blamed her, or accused her of being a part of her father's sick, killing world. Jane put the idea that she was still in love with him to the back of her mind, because the rest of the day and night were Kate's. And while it's impossible to uproot a seed once planted, she needed to be totally present for her friend because if her hunch was right, Kate was about to reveal details she'd long kept buried. The lost memory she'd recovered at the meeting was enough to make her realize that facing the past isn't always easy.

"Aunt Judy, Isabelle, and I will be in the front row tonight. I assume the whole litter of siblings will be there? I'm excited to see them and your parents again."

The faraway glaze in Kate's eyes was back when she replied simply that they would all be there.

Chapter Four

Sunday, May 15th

Kate

I know I made the right decision to share the details about the night of my assault, but I feel bad about blindsiding Jane and my family. When Wilkins was arrested and her Aunt Judy became her permanent guardian, I was a grad student, and Judy was my advisor. When I was assaulted, my former advisor and dear friend became my therapist, and was the only other living soul who knew the whole story. When Jane was finishing up her criminology/criminal justice degree at VSU, Judy arranged a meeting between us because she hoped I could offer some guidance to her niece on career choices. The two of us made an immediate connection, and after seeing how Jane absorbed every detail I was able to share about life in the FBI, I started to believe that she'd make a hell of an agent. Her skills at the firing range were second to none, and if not for my Krav Maga skills, she probably could've brought me down when we'd spar at the gym. I was also impressed by how she always seemed hyper-alert to her surroundings, and with her head on a swivel, seemed very aware of the people in her orbit, so my recommendation to apply for a spot at the training academy at Quantico was easy.

Jane is also an empath in every sense of the word. She attributes that sensitivity to finding her way out of the shadow of a sadistic murderer. She told me once that she didn't always feel what others felt, that it started after hearing the names of 15 women her father murdered. "I felt their intense pain, and cried for every one of them," she told me.

That sense she's developed over the years is why I know that she senses there was more to my assault than I shared, but she respected the boundaries of our friendship enough not to push it.

In the ten years since my attack I've been successful at locking the trauma away. I was even able to convince myself that my job was the only real relationship I needed, or had time for. The brief encounters I had with men were for my physical release only, and having shared no intimacy with them, cutting ties before any feelings developed, seemed natural. And then I met the tall State Police commander, Patrick Murphy, and I started to realize that I am capable of having real feelings for a man; I just had to figure out how to open myself up.

Patrick and I met in Michigan, during The Mother Killer case, and seemed to be drawn to one another. We have spent the last six months getting to know one another on the phone, and the attraction has grown. As Judy so simply stated, I protected myself inside something like bubble wrap, and until Patrick with his unassertive, quiet way started to pop those bubbles, I was unaware that I torpedoed every relationship I was in before I allowed myself to face any real feelings I might develop. I inadvertently hurt a lot of very nice men when I closed myself off from them. Once I admitted to myself, and Judy that I might be developing real feelings for Patrick but was afraid I'd hurt him, she convinced me that the real healing process couldn't start until I was honest about - and shared - what really happened that night.

After Patrick invited me to spend Memorial Day weekend with him in Michigan, instead of panicking and closing myself off I told Judy about it. She has a way of leading you to make the best possible choices for yourself without telling you what to do, and I knew it was beyond time to do what I needed to do in order to heal.

The assault is what led me to my clean and sober lifestyle, and tonight I will proudly accept a ten year coin from my program sponsor at a meeting where I've been asked to speak. I invited my whole family, and of course Jane, to come and share this milestone with me. Judy knows that I am going to tell my story and I have some concerns about the people I love the most hearing it for the first time, but I can't change the choices I made in the past. Life is about learning and growing, and the only way I know how to do that, is one day at a time.

Chapter Five

Sunday, May 15th, 7:00 AM
Pentwater, Michigan

I was glad when my cousin fell asleep almost the minute we left the State Park, because I needed to process how a night that started so good may well have turned ugly in a hurry. His unguided, hasty decision to hesitate after we left the dead whore in the lighthouse's tower took away our chance to nonchalantly leave the park. I didn't think that whoever grabbed his attention was in pursuit, but didn't want to take a chance, so I grabbed his hand and pulled him to the truck. Reminding myself how careful I'd been with the others helped me regulate my quick, nervous breaths. From the grab to the disposal I was careful, and certain there would be no trail back to me. I'll admit that my first couple were done without much thought, but between the second prostitute in January, and the little tramp in April, I discovered that I did indeed have a just mission which intensified the sweet release I felt. I also knew that in order to complete my mission, careful planning was called for.

Junior woke up when the truck hit my gravel driveway, and as we pulled into the garage, I turned to him and asked, "What the fuck happened out there? You looked like you were trying to do the hokey pokey in big ass clown shoes."

"Um, I, I got my feet, I mean my feet sunk in the sand and my legs got all twisted up. Then that lady yelled at me, and I got scared."

"That's my point, Einstein, if you would've stayed with me like I told you to when we were coming down the stairs of the lighthouse, you wouldn't have gotten all hung up." I softened my tone when he dropped his chin to his chest, and clasped his hands together which was a quirk he developed as a kid and he had to endure a beating from my drunk mother. When it got really bad, he'd rock the upper half of his body, and twirl his thumbs around one another like a helicopter blade.

"I'm not trying to bust your balls, Junior, but that hesitation could have ended us. I know you understand that our mission is necessary, and why we do what we do. I've protected you since we were kids, but to continue doing that, I need to know that you're going to follow my instructions, to a tee, every single time."

Junior lifted his head and nodded, and as we got out of the truck I told him to go into the kitchen, that I was going to have coffee but would make him a cup of hot chocolate.

"Can I, uh, will you, um, with tiny marshmallows?"

There were times when his simple, man-child demeanor riled me up, but at other times, when I remembered what we'd both faced as kids, my attitude toward him became gentler. He was, after all, just an unintended consequence and a by-product of his drug addled parents, and then after their death, just another punching bag for my drunken parents. Some people, like me, are made stronger by abuse, but not Junior.

As I took the marshmallows out of the cupboard, and put them on the counter, I took a softer, but firm tone with him and said, "Junior, I need you to think really hard." When I knew I had his attention, I asked, "Do you know who the person was on the beach?"

He clenched his eyes closed tight, like he does when he's really thinking about his words, and said, "I couldn't see her too good cuz it was so foggy, but when she yelled at me to stop, she sounded kinda like that nice ranger lady at the state park."

Well shit, that girl knows us, but if he couldn't see her, she probably couldn't make out who he was, either. "Do you think she saw you?" I asked him.

Junior didn't even hesitate when he said no that it was still dark, but it was also very foggy, and that tracked accurately. He was also dressed head to toe in black, and I knew he had his hood up, so we were probably okay.

"We're probably safe, but I'll keep my eye on her just in case. If you see her, do not for any reason tell her you saw her, or ask if she was on the beach this morning. Do you understand?"

With a chocolate mustache he nodded that he did, so I continued with his duties for the day, which included scrubbing out the bed of the truck, including the attached toolbox.

"I have a few appointments today and need to shower, so once the truck is done, you can reload it. What I'll need for the day is piled in the corner of the barn. Once you're done there, check your chicken coop and get some rest because I have already chosen the next sinner, and we have some prep work to do."

Once he walked out of the kitchen, I headed toward the shower and thought about the tramp who would soon be sacrificed for my mission. She didn't quite fit all the attributes of my surrogate, but it was just a cosmetic issue, and simple to fix.

Chapter Six

Sunday, May 15th, 6:00 PM
Aquia Episcopal Church - Stafford, VA

When Jane walked into the basement of the church and smelled the bitter dregs of coffee long past its prime, she was grateful she'd brought her own. As tall as she was, Jane was able to look over the heads of the people who'd already taken their seats. She used Kates's dad in the front row as a guidepost because his strawberry blonde hair sat head and shoulders above those behind him. In contrast to Kate's towering dad was her mom, a Jamaican native who was as dark as her dad's Irish complexion was fair, and in her highest of heels could still be tucked up underneath his arm. Jane smiled when she looked down the row at her best friend's six siblings, because when she saw them all together, she was reminded of their neighborhood nickname. They were affectionately tagged as the piano key family because the seven offspring of the biracial couple ranged in shades from ebony to ivory.

Jane reached the row and took the seat they saved for her, between her Aunt Judy and Kate's dad. After she greeted them all, Jane watched Kate as she smiled and accepted congratulations from the people with whom she shared her recovery journey. Her friend's congenial motions would make anyone who didn't know her as Jane did believe she was excited to take her ten-year coin and be a guest speaker, but Jane felt, and sensed at her very core, that the exact opposite was true. As Kate's dad took her hand, Jane looked down the row at Kate's brothers, and she knew the family felt as she did and had united together in a physical show of support. That demonstration of unconditional love eased Jane's concerns because it was clear that whatever Kate was about to reveal would be met with support from her very close family. To keep the chain going, Kate reached for her aunt's hand, and watched her friend take her place at the podium.

Jane noticed Kate's nod and followed her eyes as she scanned the front row, then took a deep breath, and began.

"Hello, my name is Kate, and I'm an alcoholic." While the others in the room automatically answered with "Hi, Kate," she motioned for her sponsor to join her at the podium.

"I owe so much of my sobriety to my sponsor, Linda, and am thrilled to accept my ten-year coin from her." As the group applauded, and Linda left the stage, Jane watched as her friend turned the coin with what looked like a badass female on the front over in her hand, and read what she knew to be the serenity prayer on the back of it. For as long as Jane knew Kate, she'd been listening to her recite either all, or just the beginning of it, *God grant me the serenity,* whenever she needed a boost of courage, or confidence. When she set the coin down and stepped up to the microphone, Jane was certain she had silently recited the entire thing.

"By a ten-year birthday, most people have already shared what brought them to these rooms, the point when they decided they were at their bottom and didn't want to dig any deeper. I haven't shared what led me here yet because I thought it would be either too painful or too shameful, but the truth is, I wanted to bury it so deep I'd never have to remember, but every one of us in here knows that like a dead fish always floats to the top, so does what we're trying to hide from."

Already Jane felt like she had a peach pit the size of Georgia in her belly, and found it hard to swallow around the lump building in her throat. She looked down the row at the worried expressions Kate's family wore, and felt like they too were anticipating life changing information. Kate's mom had her tiny, racoon-like hands clenched together at her chest, and before she continued, Kate made eye contact as if trying to tell her that it would be okay.

"I thought my 20 weeks of training at the FBI academy at Quantico would be the hardest thing I'd ever face, but it was not. Ten years ago, I, along with about 8 other survivors of the grueling program, decided to celebrate how we'd all defied the odds by going out for drinks on the night before our graduation." Kate took a drink from her bottle of water, looked at her family, and continued, "I couldn't decide if I was most happy about surviving the 20 weeks, or of seeing my family the next day at graduation. I wasn't ready to leave with my academy-mates because I had a lot more to celebrate than they did." That comment got a few chuckles from the other healing souls in the room, but not so much from Jane or Kate's family.

"I assured them all that I'd stay for one more drink and take a taxi back to the dorms. Well, how many that one drink actually turned into is still a blur, but I knew they were getting ready to make the last call announcement, so I settled my bill and stepped out the front door."

Jane was now certain that she was about to hear what actually happened to Kate so many years ago, she just wasn't sure she wanted to and as she watched Kate's dad's and brothers' hands clench and relax, she knew they weren't either.

"There was a canvas portico attached to the building, but just outside of it, attached to the building was an enclosed copy of the menu, but also the numbers of local cab companies, so I stepped toward it and rifled through my purse to my find my phone. You'd think that someone who was about to graduate from the world's most renowned law enforcement training program would know better than to step out from a well-lit, crowded building into the dark night, to make a call that could've just as easily been made indoors. First lesson learned that being intoxicated leads to bad decisions." Kate hoped she'd be able to dissipate some of the quiet tension that hovered over the room like a dense fog, but she couldn't so she took a cleansing breath and continued.

"While my focus was on rifling through my bag, a great big, oily hand clamped over my mouth. He wrapped his other arm around my head to hold it still, and I tried to break his grip, but my arms were suddenly pulled up over my head, and my ankles grabbed by another man. I was carried away by what my drunk mind calculated as three men, and I was powerless to stop it."

Jane looked at Judy, and when she handed her a purse-size packet of tissue, Jane realized that her aunt knew what was coming, and came prepared to do what she'd always done, which was to help her to deal with a sudden onslaught of feelings. Jane took a tissue out and looked down the row at Kate's family, then wiped the first tear from her cheek. Her dad's fair complexion was so red that Jane was afraid he hadn't taken a breath, and her sweet mom was quietly wiping raisin sized tears off her cheeks, but it was Kate's six brothers Jane was most concerned with because their faces, and their body posture read pure rage.

"The front of the bar was on a main road, but behind it was an alley, and that is where my attackers carried me. The fresh night air, and of course the shock of being grabbed by three men and carried into a dark alley had me starting to sober up, so I started kicking with everything I had, and it worked. The thug dropped my feet, but the oily man who had my mouth clamped shut, let go of me and then hit me hard on the back of the head. I was knocked hard enough that my world went dark, and my body limp."

When Kate paused, she looked over at her and Judy, and Jane knew she was digging deep into the well to finish her story. When their eyes connected, both she and her aunt gave Kate the strongest look of solidarity, love and support they could with just their eyes. It seemed to work because Kate continued.

"I don't think I was out for very long, but when I opened my eyes, one of the goons held my arms above my head, oily was unzipping my pants, and the third hoodlum was unzipping his pants and calling first dibs. So many thoughts raced through my pounding head, but the loudest one screamed at me to remember my training, and fight like hell because what these street punks were after could not, would not happen to me. I remember shouting, "Not tonight punk," as I lifted my hips off the ground to gain the leverage I needed to kick the bastard standing over me out of the way."

While Kate paused for a drink of water, Jane dabbed at the bubbles of perspiration on her forehead and looked at the family. The boys' jaws hung open, but with their fists clenched in what could only be rage, she knew they were thinking about the many ways they could exact their revenge. Kate's dad, while clearly enraged, focused more on his one arm embrace of his wife, whose chest heaved with her sobs. Jane wiped her own raisin tears and attempted a telegraphic message of strength to her best friend.

"My kick certainly wasn't strong enough to do any harm, but it did distract the man holding my arms enough that I was able to break free and get to my feet. I was under no delusion that I'd be able to fight off all three, but hoped I'd sobered enough to at least neutralize them long enough to run away. My knee to the groin of the man standing over me was at least forceful enough to drop him to his knees in agony. He was the jerk calling first dibs, so I was happy to see that the organ the idiot was using as a brain, would be out of commission for a while."

The audience seemed to relax just a bit with Kate's levity, and when the rustle of the crowd calmed, she began again.

"I couldn't really enjoy his pain though because the man I kicked away charged me like a bull. I didn't have a lot of time, but knew if I waited until he was close enough, my elbow strike would deliver enough impact to at least get him to back away. The immediate projectile of blood spewing from his nose proved to be more successful than I'd hoped for because as he cupped his gushing face in his hands, he crab walked backward and away from me. My reprieve was brief though, because before my feet could gain enough purchase to run, oily pulled a gun from his waistband. With surprising quickness for a mostly intoxicated person, I executed a side kick, hoping like hell I'd connect with something. When oily man yelled out in pain and grabbed his knee, I took the opportunity to run. It was pitch dark, but in the distance I saw faint rays of light, so I headed in that direction. I'm not sure if it was the booze, or the knowledge that it's harder to hit a moving target with a bullet that made me zig and zag through the alley. He never fired, so I don't know if it would've worked, but I don't ever want to put it to the test again."

Jane realized that she was literally perched on the edge of her chair, and that at some point she'd taken Aunt Judy's hand. The Jenkins boys had formed a fraternal huddle from their seats, and Jane could see the angry animation in the oldest boy as his hands flailed in concert with his moving mouth in what she assumed was a verbal tirade against the men who'd hurt their only sister. Kate's mom practically disappeared in her husband's hug, sobbing as he gently rubbed her back and stroked her hair with his bear sized hands.

This pause of Kate's was the second time Jane noticed her reach into her pocket for just a quick look before she continued her share, but she could see a change in her facial expression and that troubled her.

"I must've looked like a ghostly apparition, when breathless, I stepped out of nowhere and faced the patrons congregating under the portico I'd been hauled away from only moments before. My hair looked like a strand of frayed cable, all but one of the buttons of my wrinkled, untucked blouse had been ripped off in the struggle, and my pants, while still on my hips, were wide open. At the time I wasn't sure what was smeared all over my face, but when the tissue I used to wipe it off turned burgundy in color, I figured out it was a mixture of watered down motor oil, and blood splatter."

Jane heard the Irish accent that only presented in Kate's dad when he was excited, say, "Bloody hell, those fuckin' bastards."

Kate almost grinned when she heard it because she loved when her dad's Irish came out, but instead she went on.

"Only seconds after I appeared, the two couples asked if I was okay and told me they had my purse and wallet. One of the men said he was going to call the police, but I told him not to because I was okay, that it was just a couple of kids, and they ran away. I was clearheaded enough by that time to think of my hard earned graduation ceremony the next day, and my future as an FBI agent that I was certain would be adversely affected by my assault." Kate's attention was drawn back to her pocket, and Jane knew that whatever she saw was the reason she concluded her share so quickly.

"That is my story, friends, because it's the night I threw away my shovel and quit digging. My drinking affected not only my ability to make good choices, but it also slowed my ability to react, and that could've cost me much more that night, including my life. I've kept it boxed up for ten years, but I finally feel like I'll be able to live my best life. I owe an amends though to my family, and to those who, but for the lack of shared DNA, are also family, for the pain I've caused them tonight." Kate wiped her eyes, and then stopped long enough to make individual eye contact with everyone in the front row, starting at the end with Judy, and ending with her oldest brother.

"I also owe an amends to any woman who may have been attacked by those three men because I selfishly failed to report it to the police. You know, people who are robbed aren't ashamed or afraid to go to the police, so why should a female feel ashamed, or be afraid of how an assault and near rape would affect her career? In my ten years of law enforcement I have never judged a victim, or felt they asked for, or deserved what happened to them, and in sharing this tonight, I've finally realized that I deserve that same consideration. Thank you all for coming."

Kate's family seemed more composed as she walked off the stage toward them. Jane had also regained her composure and sensed that Kate had another mission beyond the tears and embraces she was sharing with her family. Although she stood off to the side talking with Aunt Judy and her partner, Isabelle, Jane was once again grateful she was tall enough to see over the tops of the heads of people lined up to hug Kate, because she knew as soon as she could, she'd break free and join her.

"You noticed her distraction with her right pocket, too, didn't you?" Aunt Judy asked Jane.

"Yes, I did, and as much as I'd love to talk with you about all that I learned tonight, I feel pretty certain that I'm about to be pulled into a new case." Jane broke away and headed toward Kate who was finally coming toward her.

"We have to get to Quantico and call the team," Kate said as she dialed her phone, "I got three '911' texts from Patrick. His sister found a dead body in a lighthouse on a Lake Michigan beach, and it looks like a serial. He wants us on the case."

"Let me go tell Aunt Judy," Jane replied, and then asked, "what about your family, are they okay with you leaving? They were pretty shaken up."

"Yes, they're okay because I assured them that I was. Had to talk the boys down from a vigilante hunt, but I promised them we'd all, including you, get together for a big ass barbeque when we got back."

Chapter Seven

Sunday, May 15th-8:00 PM
Petersburg, VA

Judy was happy to be home, and with the lemongrass tea Isabelle brewed for her, she settled in and got comfortable in her office. One of her earliest, and most comforting memories from childhood was her dad's study. On two walls were floor to ceiling bookcases filled with books that ranged from first edition classics and romantic suspense fiction, to his medical journals and biographies of anyone worthy of immortalization. If Judy breathed in deep enough, she could still smell the aromatic potpourri of worn leather, the lemon polish that was used to keep the old wood shiny and supple, and pipe tobacco. Sometimes she could even see herself tucked under his arm on the overstuffed couch and her baby sister, Hannah, tucked up under the other arm, both silent as he weaved tales of princesses battling evil forces to maintain peace in their kingdom.

Judy loved those memories but tonight she had to be alone with her own thoughts, so she queued up her classical music playlist, lit her calming, vanilla-lavender scented candle, and processed the night. She was so proud of Kate and how she'd finally found the courage to share what happened to her so long ago. For ten years, that incident defined almost every personal decision she made and Judy felt good that having shared it, she would be able to move on from the trauma. Judy had come at it from numerous angles over the years, but then Kate realized she could possibly have developed real feelings for Patrick, and finally heeded her advice. Judy always held

Kate in high esteem professionally, but tonight she smiled at how blessed she felt at having her as a friend, and more, that she'd become a mentor, and friend to her niece, Jane.

Judy made a promise to Jane's mom, Hannah, before she died that she'd help her daughter learn about the power, the love, and the strength of the princesses their dad talked about. As a psychologist, Judy began reviewing the nature vs nurture debate when Jane was eight and Tad banned her from his daughter's life, and learned that non-shared environmental factors outweighed genetics when it came to personality traits. She only hoped that after having no contact with her for seven years, that it wasn't too late for nurture to prevail. Judy recognized that to the 15-year-old whose life had just been rocked, the distrust she felt in her world would only intensify because as far as she was concerned, her Aunt Judy abandoned her when she was only eight years old. Judy knew, from the minute she heard about Tad's arrest, that it would take time, and a great deal of patience to earn the girl's trust. That she eventually also won her love was the best gift either one of them could've hoped for, and when Jane chose criminology and criminal justice to study in college, it gave weight to the nature vs nurture studies she'd read and introducing her to Kate seemed logical.

Judy knew she was on the precipice of the rabbit hole she called Tad Wilkins, but she had to complete the report she'd been contracted by the FBI to do after The Mother Killer case resulted in the arrest of two agents. Her job was to re-evaluate, and make changes to the current protocol they used in their psychological profiles that helped determine a recruit's risk factor before they were accepted into the program. Her proposed changes would include an interview with her, in addition to their written profile, every five years. As she stated in her report, an individual whose psychopathy is already bordering on abnormal is intelligent enough to anticipate the desired response and answer accordingly. However, a face-to-face interview will provide certain tells by the candidate, making it harder for them to slip through the cracks.

After the report was electronically sent to the FBI director, and printed for her records, as always happened when Judy spent time trying to understand the mind of a psychopath, her thoughts turned to Tad Wilkins. He was one of the most prolific, cunning, and manipulative psychopaths she'd ever encountered, and she had known there was something off about him from the time she met him when Hannah was at Michigan State University. Hannah fell in love with what she called his dreamy blue eyes, but when Judy looked into them, she saw nothing but ice looking back at her. There was no depth to his glare, almost like he lacked what separated humans from wolves: a soul.

When her sister traded her active social life for quiet nights at his apartment, and Judy warned her against giving up her own identity for him or anyone else, Hannah began to pull away. With both of their parents dead, Hannah was all she had so when she married Tad without even telling her, Judy was both devastated and worried. And while she was always wary of how his charming charisma gave way to his chameleon-like cloak and afforded him the ability to be whomever he felt he needed to be, Judy never imagined he had the propensity to torture and kill as he did.

Hindsight did give her a view of how things changed after Hannah refused lifesaving treatment for her brain tumor in order to preserve the life of her unborn daughter. She seemed less susceptible to his expertly manufactured allure, perhaps because a simmering rage seemed to lie deep inside his icy blue eyes. Judy was a psychology professor at Virginia State University but took a leave of absence to help care for three-month-old Jane and sister Hannah during her final days. Tad was mostly away on business, but when he was home, he spent his time with contractors he'd hired to build an in-home office. Judy was relieved that he wasn't hovering, so she paid no attention when she learned the contractors' work orders included fortifying the new office with a fireproof door or modification to the inside walls that would house a safe.

Once she'd finally gotten full parental rights of Jane, Judy was tasked with clearing out the Holly, Michigan home to get it ready to sell. It was then that she realized why Tad had taken such care to fortify his office, and when Tad began insinuating himself back into Jane's world in an effort to harm Jane's mental stability, she started questioning the decision she'd made so long ago to protect her niece from what she had discovered.

It was with that thought that Judy blew out her candle, turned off her iPod, and left the cozy confines of her office. She wanted to spend the rest of her evening with Isabelle and a cup of sleepy time, chamomile tea.

Chapter Eight

Sunday, May 15th – 9:00 PM
FBI Headquarters – Quantico, VA

Jane was happy when she and Kate walked into their meeting room and she saw the commercial sized Bunn coffeemaker dripping her liquid nirvana into a pot because she sensed it would be a long night. She felt conflicted because she realized someone had been murdered, yet after six months out of the field she was happy to have an active case to work. She and Kate left the church in their own cars, so Jane used the quiet of the drive to do what she knew her mentor would do and would expect of her. She processed Kate's share enough to put it aside, because once they walked into their briefing at Quantico the case would get their entire focus. The victim deserved nothing less.

Jane stopped for coffee, but she heard Bill tell Kate that Patrick called him when he couldn't reach her. The Mayor of Hart had called to formally request their help on the case. When Jane reached the group, she put her notebook and coffee on the table and her brown leather satchel on the floor just as Bill was getting ready to address the team.

"Thank you all for getting in here so quickly. Abbey will be here in just a minute. She's in her office printing off the crime scene photos, but Seth is going to walk us through what we have so far."

"I hope you all heeded Bill's advice earlier, and made a dent in your paperwork because we're heading back to Michigan. All we have so far is the short version, but the State Police commander we worked with on Tally's case, Patrick Murphy, received a panicked call from his sister, Maureen, at around 9:00 AM, after she stumbled on a dead body."

Kate, having spoken with Patrick on the ride over, added that Maureen was the head park ranger at Silver Lake State Park, in Mears, Michigan, and was responsible for overseeing the nearly 3000 acres of mature forest land.

"It's about three hours north of Holly, between the shores of Lake Michigan, and Silver Lake, and is a tourist destination because of the nearly 2000 acres of sand dunes topping 70 feet tall." The attention of the team was drawn to the door and the expressive lilt of Abbey's voice.

"Good evening crime fighters, and now that Kate has painted such a beautiful picture, allow me to ruin that serene visual with the crime scene photos." With a face that looked like she'd just taken a gulp of curdled milk Abbey handed them the reports.

She gave the group a couple of minutes to shuffle through the packet, and then continued: "What you're looking at is The Little Sable Point Lighthouse. Built in 1874, it stands over 100 feet tall and has a spiral staircase inside of it that is about 130 steps."

As gently as he could, Bill prodded Abbey to move it along.

"I'm sorry," she told them, "I have pink, purple and rainbow bobble heads that surround me in my cave of magic to offset the ugly I see, but they're not here so I was trying to fill my brain with the beauty of sugary sand and Caribbean blue waters before I got into the ugly." Abbey looked around at her family, and apologized, "I'm rambling again, I know. Okay, here's the 411 that I've been able to gather so far."

There wasn't much to report on because the female victim was at the Medical Examiner's office in Hart, a larger but still small town about four miles from Mears, awaiting the autopsy and identification. The naked woman was displayed with her arms draped over the iron railing around the ledge, just beneath the copper lantern of the lighthouse, and her legs were threaded through the bars and hanging down. It was quite clear that her death had been a violent one.

"Look at all those gashes on her bare back," Seth pointed out. "They look pretty damn deep. This poor woman was tortured badly before she died."

While they were still looking at the gruesome photos, Kate added, "Patrick's sister had just finished up her morning run underneath the lighthouse where she always stops when she saw what she thought was a man, about 200 yards up the beach. She called out to him but he ran off, and before she could make chase, a drop of blood dripped on her shoe."

Before he put his packet back in the folder, Bill directed their attention to the last photograph, which was a crudely painted sign propped up behind the victim.

"For anyone who curses his father shall surely be put to death" Leviticus 20:9 ESV

"This sign, coupled with the brutality on the back of the woman, is a clear indicator that this guy has either done this before, will be doing it again, or both. In either case, it has the hallmark of a serial. Abbey, you're going to check ViCAP with the markers we do have, right?" The Violent Criminal Apprehension Program is a national repository for violent crimes available to law enforcement agencies at the local, state, and federal level.

As Abbey grabbed her paperwork to leave the room, she told the group that she did have an opportunity to research the Bible passage the killer wrote. "He actually had the nerve to mis-quote the bible," she said, seeming incensed when she told them that the actual quote included the mother. "Not that I think anyone should die for misbehaving, but who in the world would have the nerve to misquote the Bible?"

"Get some sleep everyone," Bill told them. "We fly out at 4:00AM from Regan International. We have to go commercial this trip because another team has the plane in Mississippi. We'll fly into Grand

Rapids, and then drive the three and a half hours to the Michigan State Police Post in Hart."

As Jane put her notebook back in her bag and got ready to leave, Kate told the group that Patrick would meet them in Hart, and that his sister, Maureen, was standing by for interviews. Jane did not point out the faint blush on her friend's caramel colored cheek, but instead, just nodded at her with a playful grin. Kate just shook her head and told her she'd pick her up at 3:00AM.

Chapter Nine

Sunday, May 15th - 9:00 PM

Pentwater, Michigan

I had grown used to walking into my house to the earsplitting noise of cartoons on the television, in full stereo at a decibel level that seemed to make the floors vibrate and my ears pound inside my head. I usually just yelled at Junior to turn it down, but not today, because the simmering agitation that had been stewing since lunch seemed to morph into a full rage and I blew my top. When Junior began rocking his upper body and twirling his thumbs like a helicopter, I realized that my anger was not over the blaring noise of Bugs Bunny chomping on a carrot, nor was it Junior's fault, so I walked out of the room to gain some control. The man child had suffered so many angry beatings for transgressions he was totally unaware he'd committed, and while I'd never beat him, his fear of what may come caused him to check out of his reality. I got the same beatings and more, but I always knew what they were for and seemed to grow stronger because of them.

When I got into my bedroom, I turned the shower to hot and stepped out of the functional Carhart pants and green plaid flannel that I wore to call on my rural customers. The hot steam from the shower helped me clear the anger out of my head and allowed me to think about my mission. While I wasn't exactly sure of my end game, I had a clear picture of my objective and believed I would know when my quest was complete. I also knew that once I discovered my true purpose, the release I felt every time I ended one of the sluts was stronger than the most intense climax a man, or woman would ever experience. I also knew I was a long way from being done, so keeping a cool head while also adjusting to the things around me over which I had no control, was critical.

Small towns are notoriously adept at spreading breaking news quicker than any media outlet could, and if you're a local no one tries to shield you from their conversations. When I heard that Maureen from the state park found a dead body at the lighthouse that morning I was not surprised, but when I learned that her brother is a State Police commander downstate, and is the same man who worked with the FBI to catch The New Mother Killer last October, my ears perked up. I ignored the buzz about him being involved with one of the agents because that just seemed like gossip, but tuned in when the table beside me reported that he had made a call and the exact same team was heading to town to work on the beach killing case. I listened in for just another minute, and when the chit chat turned to the planned Memorial Day activities I paid my bill and left because my anger was radiating up my neck and I didn't want the townsfolk to see the red heat on my face, lest I become the next headline for Sally and her newsies.

I hated that team, in particular their newest agent Jane, and not because they caught a killer, but for the way she tried to connect a man already in prison to the murders; when I found out she was his only daughter, I was enraged. How dare she forsake her very own father whom I knew to be a loving dad. I also knew that she never even wrote to him or visited him in prison, which is unforgivable. I chose to see the arrival of the FBI and Jane in my town as a divine intervention of sorts, and decided to change my timetable because it would be a great way to discredit the high and mighty Jane if I took someone on her watch. Once I was dressed in yesterday's jeans and a clean flannel, I headed back to the living room to talk to Junior who hadn't moved from the couch.

"Junior, come here for a minute," I requested as I took a beer out the fridge and patted the seat next to me at the kitchen counter. "We have a change in plans, and I really need you to focus on what I'm saying. Can you do that for me?"

Junior nodded, and with a smile on his face, asked, "Will I, um, can I, um, will you make me some hot chocolate?" If that's what it took to get his mind off my earlier tirade and focused on what I had to tell him, it was worth it.

"With tiny marshmallows?" I asked, and was rewarded with a big smile and definite nod of his head.

I became almost hypnotized by the spinning turntable inside the microwave as I considered how to simplify the words I'd use to explain the necessity of the change to our schedule. The phone call I took while I was mixing the Swiss Miss into the boiling water gave me my talk path, so as I handed the cup and the bag of tiny marshmallows to Junior, I told him, "Pour your drink in a cup to go. That was Sam Richardson. His heifer is having a hard time calving. He figures it's a male and too big for the birth canal. He needs our help."

It took him a second to process and respond to my words, "That's Millie, ain't it? Poor girl."

"Get your boots on. I'm going out to the barn to get a couple of syringes ready in case she needs to be calmed, and grab a jacket, because it's going to cool down tonight and we'll be out for a while."

Already planning for the fun part of my night, which will begin after I get Millie squared away, I cleared away the remains of my day's delivery from the oversized, locked tool chest in my truck and prepared a couple extra syringes that I carefully placed in the tackle box I kept on the front seat.

"We have another job tonight, but it's a fun one," I told Junior when he stepped up into the truck ."While I was at The Pink Elephant for lunch, Sally and the town newsies said that the FBI would be in town by tomorrow to work what they're calling the beach killing case."

When it became clear that I had his undivided attention, I went on. "I'm moving up our timetable because I want this next bitch's disappearance to fall in with their arrival."

Junior closed his eyes tight, so I knew he was looking for a string of words to form a complete sentence.

"Maybe we should wait till they leave. It might be, what do they say on TV, too hot to move around?"

"No, it's perfect because we can dump this one, and take another one from under their cocky noses, and teach the biggest bitch of them all, Jane, a lesson once and for all."

"But I, um, what about, um, what if I'm not ready?" Junior asked.

"Hey dude, don't worry, you got this. My choice this time is Alicia Singleton and she's seen you with me enough that she won't feel threatened when you offer your help. I know that she has a sex date tonight at The Viking Arms, in Ludington, but parks clear over on Diane Street. I'll drop you off, then park at the campground where I'll have a clear view of her car."

I relaxed then because I could see on Junior's face that his muscle memory was at work, and that he'd do his part. "When she can't start her car, I'll walk up and offer help, which is when you'll coast up in the truck."

"Good job, buddy. Have I ever led you wrong? Hell no, I haven't, and remember, we're doing the right thing. Now buckle up, we have a calf to coax out, and then we need to hit the Dollar Store outside of town. Alicia needs a bit of work before my fun can really begin."

Chapter Ten

Sunday, May 15th – 10:00 PM

Ionia State Penitentiary

I am very good at cutting loose threads, and eliminating potential threats to my underworld. Adrian Sanchez could prove to be trouble for me because he is the only one still alive that can tie me to Lloyd Tally's killing spree. His arrogance when he unearthed my involvement was his downfall. If he hadn't been so cocky, and contacted me on the day they were arrested, I would never have known he was the only living person savvy enough to make the connection, so I took immediate counter measures to prevent blow back. I put the threats in motion through one of my handlers on the outside before I was hauled off to isolation. Being the smartest man in the business might get tedious to some, but not to me because my mind never stops. I am proud that I've always been steps ahead of those who would either try to take my place on the top of the pyramid or, in most cases, stop me altogether from my life's work.

It's been six months and Sanchez hasn't chirped, but being the forward thinker that I am, I decided I needed to fortify that loyalty. One of Jacob's first assignments was to gather as much information on Sanchez's pathetic life as he could. I've always known the little scoundrel was a coward, but now I know the feds have seized all the money he stole so he's broke and will be virtually unemployable once he is freed. I also know that his younger sister is very beautiful and a high-end escort, which she's keeping secret from her uptight, staunchly religious parents. When Jacob first approached Lacey with a financially beneficial offer to visit her brother monthly and deliver messages and to fund his commissary account, she adamantly refused. She hated him and what he did to her family, and never wanted to see him again. I give credit to Jacob's persuasiveness, though, because after threatening to expose her lifestyle to the parents she so clearly adored, he was able to convince her that not only would the extra money she made help the family, but in a small way she'd get some retribution from her brother because her visits would not make him happy.

I may be a man without a soul, but I'm fair and not unreasonable, at least not to those who stay in line. Sanchez's first message from Lacey was to remind him that he was not, nor would he ever be free of me, but as long as he remained the compliant, spineless jellyfish he'd always been he would have funds in prison, and once he got out was guaranteed a decent, well-paying job. The fact that'd he also retain all his limbs and appendages was implied, and while he was a gutless worm, he was not stupid. As further proof of my superiority, using his sister as the contact would throw up no flares, and would of course offer me complete and total anonymity.

The next message I'm going to have Lacey deliver will be about a certain whistleblower in the Witness Protection system. I am all but certain I know who it is, and while he can't do any legal damage to me, he really pissed me off when he betrayed the few men in that firm capable of cleaning and moving my money around. He also forced me to end the attorney I used as a go between with that poor sap Luke Johnson, and Lloyd Tally, because he was the only one in the firm who could be tied back to me. As I said, Adrian Sanchez may be a namby-pamby cad, but he is probably the only person who could confirm his identity, and further, uncover where they have him hiding.

Chapter 11

Day One – Monday – 2:00AM

Ludington, MI

Sam was right, Millie's calf was a male, and just a little too big, but once I was able to sedate her, she gave birth without too much added stress. The timing of it all worked in my favor because it aligned perfectly with Alicia's walk of shame back to her car. I was pumped so full of excited adrenaline that it was hard to keep my foot still on the accelerator pedal of my truck. The exact opposite was true for Junior though, because he crashed almost the minute the truck pulled off the dirt road. I was okay with him resting, though, because I was confident enough in my plan and his role in it that I didn't feel the need to repeatedly harp his instructions.

As my truck neared the late night, deserted streets of Ludington, Junior woke up and with his normal groan, stretched his arms toward the windshield, and his feet out straight in the footwell. He'd banged his knuckles enough times on the roof of my truck that he finally learned to stretch forward, and not up.

"Have a nice nap?" I asked him, "you ready to right a wrong and have some fun?"

Junior grinned like the man child he was, and stammered, "I uh, have you, uh, I mean, did you unhook the battery already?" As confident as I was in my cousin's ability to take care of his end of the plan, I was relieved to hear him ask that question because it told me that his mind was in the right place.

"Yes, already done. I'm going to drop you off on the corner of

Dexter and N. Stafford, head toward Diana Street because that's where she shamefully parked her car, and will be walking up from E. Ludington. I'll park at the campground where my truck will blend in and I will be able to see you."

When Junior plunged his fists into the pockets of his dark black hoodie, I turned the truck around and drove over to the campground. Fate was on my side when I found a spot that would give me the perfect vantage point, because my timing would be critical. Through my windshield I could see that Junior stopped just long enough when they met on the street to say hello, and without turning back continued to walk slowly while Alicia unlocked her car. Go time was mere seconds away, my headlights were off, but I knew I wouldn't be able to prevent my brake lights from going on when I put the truck in gear, so with a slow and steady pressure, I pressed the brake pedal down. The dead silence of the night seemed to be broken only by the noise of my pounding heart, because the success of my plan now hinged on Junior and his ability to get the target where I needed her to be.

When the interior light in her car went on, I slowly dropped the truck into gear and watched the scene play out. I knew she'd called out to Junior from outside her car because he turned around and walked back toward her. The two of them stood together for just a minute, during which time I'm sure the adulterous vixen was using sound effects to explain what it sounded like when her car wouldn't start. I was already creeping along without headlights when Alicia reached into her car and popped the hood. When I opened my tackle box and removed a pre-made syringe, I slowed my heart rate down with deep cleansing breaths. I couldn't afford the wired up feeling I had when my adrenaline spiked, I needed to be alert and methodical for this next part of my plan.

With both of them hunched underneath the hood of her car, I pulled up directly behind them on the off chance she sensed trouble and tried to run. I hoped Junior was speaking loudly, or even stumbling enough on his words that Alicia would be distracted and not hear the thunk of the transmission when I put the truck into park. The dome light inside my truck had long been disabled, so I was able to open the door and step out unnoticed. With the syringe loaded and ready, I reached her with a single stride and jabbed the needle into her neck, then quickly plunged until the barrel was empty.

Before her hand reached her neck to shoo away what she probably thought was a bug, she began to collapse. Junior was ready and caught her under her arms before her sagging body crumpled in a heap on the concrete. The whole process took less than 60 seconds, but I scanned the area again to confirm we weren't being watched. With only the light from under the hood of the car to guide us, I stepped up into the bed of my truck and unlocked the oversized silver, toolbox.

"Toss her in," I ordered my cousin. "Get those battery cables hooked back up and take off. Don't forget, you need to take Monroe Road where there's less chance of someone seeing her car." I've learned from taking care of Junior all these years, that it's most effective when I pause and confirm his understanding of one instruction before I give him another one. Once I heard the thud of her limp body hitting the bottom of the container, and then the click of the padlock when he locked the lid down, I knew Junior was focused on his job.

"Don't forget to toss her purse and phone into the swamp you pass on the way. Remember where it is. Do you remember where to leave the car?"

"Yes, um, I remember, and then I walk back to you. Don't, um, I, um, ah, I won't let you down," he stammered.

"Hey dude," I said as I got into the truck, "I know you won't. I'll see you soon."

Once I got to the still deserted main road, I turned my headlights on and took the first full breath I'd taken since I parked at the campground. And then I smiled with my whole face, from ear to ear, and started to feel the familiar jitter I get when my adrenaline spikes. To settle the excited bounce in my legs I went through my mental checklist which allowed the euphoric buzz I felt to remain, but focused my thoughts enough to calm what felt like electrical charges flowing through my system.

I knew she would be starting to wake up when we reached the shack at the edge of the Manistee National Forest. Her level of alertness would also awaken, and her abject terror would take over. I was certainly strong enough to overtake her, but my job would be much easier if she at least shuffle-stepped while I dragged her through the gravel. Carrying her would've been a pain in the ass and would require more than one trip, so I loaded my bucket with the hair dye I'd bought at The Dollar Store, my heavy-duty flashlight and a couple bottles of water. The darkness of the night was so complete it reminded me of the charcoal soot I cleaned out of my grill, and without even a moonbeam to shed a light I stood in the glow of my headlights to rip four long strips of duct tape off my roll. One was for her mouth: not because anyone would hear her screams, but because I couldn't stand to hear the wailing; the others were to bind her wrists.

As predicted, by the time I unlocked, and opened the lid to the metal box she was confined in she had become almost feral. Her hands still weak and shaky from the shot came up like claws, as if she'd be able to save herself with those slut-red fingernails. I laughed when I grabbed them both in one hand, and with the other crossed her wrists and wrapped the tape around them. When I grabbed hold of her shoulders and pulled her to a sitting position, she was as floppy as a rag doll which is a residual effect of the drugs, but worked in my favor.

"We're going to jump off the bed of this truck and walk. You'll fall on your ass if I let you go which would be fun to watch, but it's late and we have some grooming to do."

She fell to her knees when I let go of her at the door, and as I pressed the key into the heavy-duty padlock, she tried to crawl away. But ragdolls can't walk, or crawl, so she fell forward. Her bound hands in front of her were the only thing that stopped her from a literal face plant. I decided it was as good a time as any for the next phase of my plan, so I shined my flashlight on her inert form and grabbed my knife out of the bucket. I preferred to do most of this fun stuff inside the shack alone, and knowing Junior was probably hiking back here by now, I needed to hurry. I knelt down on one knee beside her and yanked her head up by the hair at the nape of her neck. Her muffled screams, and terrified eyes only provided more incentive for me to continue.

"Don't get too excited, bitch, it isn't going to end out here, I just want to relieve you of your clothes because I know how much you like to be naked." She shook her head frantically back and forth as I grabbed the fabric of her dress at the neckline. My dagger slid through her dress, and sliced it open as easily as a knife spreading margarine. I took the red, fuck-me pumps off her feet before I dragged her to the open door, and shoved her inside. I left my flashlight on because it would help me, but I also wanted her to get a glimpse of her accommodations. Once the light went off, she would be plunged into perpetual darkness, and I wanted her to recognize the rancid odor from the moss and mold growing on the dirt walls and floor. If she spotted a mouse scurrying away, all the better.

The only piece of furniture in the rathole was an old kitchen chair that I threw her naked body into before I grabbed the jug of water and bottle of brunette hair dye that I'd brought with me.

"That bleached blonde hair of yours has to go, so tip your head back like the good girl you want to be, and let me get it done." Once I had her hair sufficiently wet, I grabbed the arm length, plastic gloves I sometimes used for work, and put them on. The off brand, dollar store deal of the day hair dye in Indus brown would likely stain my hands and clothes so I wanted them protected. I wasn't too worried about a perfect blending, or how it looked cosmetically; she just needed meet the criteria of my surrogate, and brown hair was a part of that.

Once her mane was rinsed as thoroughly as it was going to be,

Jane's Punishment

I put the jug down into the brown puddle at her feet and ripped the duct tape off her mouth. She started to scream, but I grabbed her cheeks, and told her, "You can scream all you want, but you are in the middle of nowhere, so all you'll do is wear yourself out." Her ear-piercing screams gave way to quiet tears, so I continued. "Look around because it is the last time you'll see light. Notice there is not a window, or even a crack in the wall, so escape will be impossible. Now, to show I'm not completely heartless, I'm going to leave you with what is left in that water jug. I'm keeping your legs free, and since your hands are restrained in front of you, you'll have use of your fingers, which you may want to use to grip the jug. The rats and mice will chew right through that bottle if it's left on the ground. Oh, and another pro-tip, if you keep moving, the nasty critters that live here will probably stay hidden."

The look of panic on her face as I gathered her clothes and shoes and walked to the door was all the release I needed, at least for tonight, and as I replaced the padlock, I smiled at the timing of it all because Junior was just reaching the truck.

Chapter 12

Day One-Monday-6:00 AM

Gerald Ford International Airport, Grand Rapids, MI

Once the plane came to a complete stop, Jane wasted no time retrieving her messenger bag from beneath the seat in front of her and the go-bag she kept ready for out-of-town assignments from the overhead compartment. At times, when Jane was in what she thought of as her quiet space, her thoughts would be occupied by the years she spent adjusting to her life after her father's arrest; sometimes, even to the years before that. Many of what she used to call her dad's quirks, like how he was always happier and seemed more relaxed when he got home from one of his business trips, or the long hours spent in his locked office, made more sense now that she knew they weren't business trips at all. She didn't spend any of this flight ruminating on the past, though; this morning she realized that the empathy she felt for the victim and her family and the excitement she felt at being on the job again were not exclusive of one another because realistically she couldn't stop the murder, but she could damn well stop the murderer.

"We only have one vehicle waiting for us," Bill said as they stepped out of the jetway and into what seemed like a deserted airport, "but we'll have access to another one once we get to Hart."

No one had checked luggage, and since as federal agents they have the necessary credentials to board the plane with their weapons, they proceeded directly to the area of the parking lot reserved for law enforcement vehicles and located the Chevy Tahoe the Grand Rapids field office had provided for them.

"We're going to stop at the crime scene in Mears," Seth said. "The victim is with the Medical Examiner, but the rest of the scene is intact, and I'd like to see it."

It was common knowledge in the bureau's violent crime unit that Seth Thomas had an almost sixth sense when he walked a crime scene, and Jane, having seen it the last time they were in Michigan, was happy to repeat the experience. After almost throwing it all away during her first and only case she understood what a gift she'd been given to learn from the very best, and was determined to absorb their knowledge every opportunity she got. As she settled into the backseat with Kate, Jane appreciated that while her journey to get here started out with boulders the size of mountains, and craters that seemed bottomless, the trek was well worth it. This is where she belonged and stopping evil from touching innocents was her calling.

"I'm going to text Patrick and have him meet us there," Kate said, "he's already been there so he may be able to point out details we missed by not seeing it fresh."

Bill pulled the Tahoe into the staging area at Golden Sands Drive and N Lighthouse Drive, where the other law enforcement and crime scene vehicles were parked, at the same time Patrick arrived in his State Police cruiser. Jane smiled when she saw Kate looking at her reflection in a purse size mirror in what seemed like an attempt to fix a flaw only she could see. To Jane, and actually to the world at large, Kate always looked like she just stepped off a catalog cover. It didn't seem to make a difference if her day started at 3:00AM as it did today, or if she'd had the time to unhurriedly prepare for it. Her natural caramel complexion was the envy of many women who spent a small fortune trying to replicate the skin tone with high priced products.

"You'd make a fortune if you could bottle your skin color," Jane said as Kate folded up her mirror, "but relax. You look as good as you did when you got on the plane this morning and you're certainly as fine as you were six months ago. Now let's go and greet the handsome Commander Murphy."

Jane stepped away from the vehicles and joined Bill, who, as always, stood out in the crowd because of his impeccably tailored suit with a dress shirt obviously starched and pressed, and a necktie that paired perfectly with it all. Seth had stepped up to speak to the officer tasked with keeping the log of authorized people before lifting the yellow tape for them to duck under and proceed toward the crime scene. He was also easy to pick out in a crowd because the coal black of his wavy hair and closely trimmed beard was starting to give way to what he referred to as his silver streaks of wisdom. Jane couldn't explain it, but seeing Bill in his trademark suit, and Seth in his freshly pressed Levi jeans and collared polo shirt topped with a tweed sport coat, comforted her as he joined them.

"We're going to have to hike in from here," he told them, "and a good portion of it will be along the beach." With a snicker he added, "I'm guessing none of us keep flip flops in our go bags." Jane felt like that was an invitation to razz Kate about her choice in fashionable, yet impractical footwear, but held her tongue in deference to her friend's obvious feelings for Patrick.

"It's easiest if you carry your shoes and socks, and roll up your pant legs," Patrick said as they joined their circle. "It's a very scenic trail to the lighthouse, but hard to cordon off."

After they signed the log and ducked beneath the tape, they took Patrick's advice and carried their shoes and socks. Kate was predictably in a skirt, but the rest of them rolled up their pant legs and as Jane crouched down on the sugary white sand and saw the deep blue color of Lake Michigan, another childhood memory invaded her thoughts; this memory was a happy one, though, so when she stood up she shared it with her group.

"I'd forgotten how beautiful it was here, forgot I was ever here come to think of it, but I came once with my best friend's family. We rode our four-wheelers all around those sand dunes we saw driving in."

"Those are the Silver Lake Sand Dunes," Patrick told them, "and it's almost a rite of passage for young people growing up in Michigan to come rip it up on the dunes. Our summer vacations were always spent camping at Silver Lake State Park, and when we weren't flying around the dunes in my dad's old Jeep we were climbing them. Some of those dunes stretch 70 feet into the air."

Jane smiled at both his shared memory, and at how Kate seemed transfixed on his every word, but suddenly and without warning her mind took a dark turn. She'd long come to terms with the fact that the only good memories she had before she lost her childhood to a serial killer father at 15 were those she made with her best friend and her family. Her joyful recollection was short lived though, because she was assailed with the guilt of knowing the atrocities her father was engaging in while she was off having a great time. Jane stopped herself just short of kicking her own ass for allowing the darkness in when she had a new case to consider. The flapping sound of the crime scene tape being whipped around in the wind jolted her back to the present. The beach trees it was wrapped around didn't seem to be rooted but instead looked like moveable scenery around a toy trainset, and the thin metal poles it was attached to were planted in the sand at the water's edge and seemed to wobble precariously with the breaking waves.

There will be time, she thought, to sort out the barrage of memories she was being assailed with, after the case. The victim who was found on the lighthouse they were now standing under deserved everything she had to offer. The group followed Patrick to the hanging door that would give them access to the stairs up through the inside of it. The technicians that were trying to lift prints from the damaged door stood aside as the group stepped inside.

"It's 130 steps to the top," Patrick said as he took the lead. "Be careful: on a couple of the steps is what looks like dried blood. Samples have been sent to the crime lab, but it's a little dark in here, so don't trip on the markers."

As they climbed the tight spiral staircase, they avoided the tented crime scene markers with bold, black numbers that would correspond to the sample taken from that area.

"This is a tough path to navigate with a dead body," Bill said, "it's narrow, and a long way up."

When they stepped onto the ledge, Jane felt like she'd been gut punched by the chalk drawing on the concrete because it represented what was once a vibrant young woman. The depiction showed her body placement before she was moved, but it was clear that her legs had been jammed between two of the iron dowels. On the top of the railing, the chalk outlined where her arms had been draped and fastened with duct tape, the sticky residue of which was still present.

An angry silence fell over the group when they looked up at the space between the ledge and the lantern at the disturbing communication left by the killer. Although she'd viewed the horrific photos with her team, seeing how the hacked Bible verse was displayed made Jane's brain feel like a pinball machine with all the thoughts and theories that were bouncing around. From anger, to sorrow for the victim, and fear that this was just the beginning, she and the group were forced to focus on the entirety of what they were seeing.

Kate was the first to step closer and after raising her arm above her head, said, "I doubt the killer was able to maneuver a step stool, and a body up that staircase, so he's obviously taller than I am." Jane did not point out the obvious, that at only 5'3" tall, most everyone was taller than Kate, but she did mimic her training agent's arm stretch, and was glad she didn't make the joke out loud.

"Even Jane isn't tall enough to be able to write that," Patrick said as he stepped up, "but I am." Instead of stepping closer to the wall like the others, Seth leaned back against the railing and looked around.

"The Medical Examiner will have to verify it, but there doesn't seem to be enough blood for her to have been killed up here," Seth said, "which leads me to believe that the killer is not only tall enough to write the message, but strong enough to get roughly 130 pounds of dead weight up that spiral staircase." They all nodded because Seth's observation made sense, and would be the start of the profile they'd build as the hunt for this monster gained its momentum.

"Laura was able to determine that the message, while deep red, was not written in blood. It's spray painted on," Patrick told them, and when he noticed the downturn of Kate's head, he added, "the Medical Examiner, Laura Tibbits, is my sister's best friend."

"That he brought the sign with him indicates this is an organized killer," Seth told them.

Jane heard Bill's phone ting with an incoming text message as they stepped through the door of the lighthouse. Finished with his evidence collection, the crime scene tech waited until they cleared the structure before he padlocked the door, and then wrapped the base of the lighthouse in police tape.

"That was Abbey," Bill announced, "she was able to ID our victim through her fingerprints. Apparently she's in the system because she has a record. Let's get over to the State Police Post in Hart, and get started."

Chapter 13

Day One – Monday – 9:00 AM

Michigan State Police Post, Hart, MI

Conversation in the Tahoe on the short drive from Mears to Hart was not so much about the case, but about Kate and how she eagerly accepted Patrick's invitation to ride with him. Jane had often wondered if she was the only one aware of what she viewed as an obvious attraction between Kate and Patrick, and clearly she was not. As much as she enjoyed their banter back and forth, Jane knew she wouldn't share this ride's conversation because she didn't want to make Kate uncomfortable.

As Bill was parking the Tahoe, Jane settled her messenger bag across her chest, and when she noticed Patrick pull in beside them, grabbed Kate's briefcase as well and stepped out of the car. Their chattering about what they'd seen on the beach halted as quickly as their footsteps when they reached the end of the parking lane and were confronted by a reporter and a camera crew.

"What the hell,?" Jane muttered out of the side of her mouth, "how did she know we were even here?"

Seth heard the question, and answered, "This is probably the biggest news to hit this small town in a long while, if ever. Makes sense they'd want to be here."

Jane understood that the local media would be clamoring for a hot story but Candace was not local, so she wondered how she was able to get here so quickly. She relentlessly hounded Jane during the Mother Killer case because she was determined to find a connection between her father and his copycat killer. No matter how many times Jane refused to comment, Candace and her microphone seemed to be in her face everywhere she went because the reporter was certain that Tad had a hand in the making of the new psycho six months ago. And while it was never proven, or even reported on, Candace was unrelenting.

The group, led by Bill, hesitated only briefly when he told the news crew that they had no comment and that all inquiries should be directed to the Hart Police Department's press liaison. His dismissal of them did nothing to dissuade Candace, and with the camera man filming she stepped up, so she was almost nose to nose with Jane.

"Is this another serial killer? Your team is reputed to be the best in the violent crimes unit. Is that why you were called here? Or is there a connection to Tad Wilkins on this case, too?"

Instead of popping off like she wanted to do, Jane placed her hand on Candace's chest to back her away, and through her clenched teeth muttered, "No comment."

Kate and Jane swerved around her and the cameras and continued on, but when it became clear that Candace wasn't finished, Patrick turned back and took Jane by the elbow and continued moving.

"I know you went to the prison to visit your father during the New Mother Killer case," she accused. "What purpose did that serve? Did you make a deal with him to find the killer? Is that why his involvement in those crimes was never made known?"

Jane put her head down and focused on her walk toward the door, but before she crossed the threshold to a new case, she mentally cursed the freedom of information act that gave Candace that access.

Jane noticed that Seth circled back to Candace with Bill, the diplomat of the team, right behind him. Unsure how she should handle the last comment she stopped at the doorway and turned to Kate.

"I feel like I should address that last comment," she said. "I don't want it to look like I'm running from her, or her questions." Kate waited for Patrick to walk all the way into the building. Then with both of her hands on Jane's shoulders, told her, "For right now, you have to trust the guys to deal with it. Bill will have to smooth out the blunt way Seth has of speaking the truth, but it'll be taken care of."

"Shouldn't I be the one to straighten her out, though? I don't want anyone, especially that bitch, to think I can't stand for myself." Jane's body relaxed a bit when she remembered how her Aunt Judy used to deal with the school administrators everytime they called her in because Jane had gotten into a fight. Her aunt took the stance with them that Jane wouldn't get into the fights if they did their job in stopping the bullies, because her fights were always in defense of someone else.

"You will have that opportunity, rookie," Kate assured her, "just not today, and not under these circumstances. Now it's time to get out of your head, and into the case. Are you ready?"

Grateful as always for Kate's outspoken candor, Jane told her she was definitely ready, and then added with a smirk, "Don't think you're going to get out of a conversation about the handsome Commander Murphy."

As Bill and Seth got into the building, Patrick was shaking hands with a sandy haired, uniformed officer of about 40 years old. With his left arm, Patrick motioned for them to join him.

"This is captain Jeff Sterling, he runs this post. Jeff, this is the team I was telling you about from the FBI." Individually they all shook his hand and introduced themselves. When he'd completed the circuit, Jeff told them he was glad they were there and welcomed their help.

"Your sister is freshening up in the break room," he told Patrick, "so let's head into our conference room and I'll introduce you to the officers assigned to help you with this case. I've set up a case-board, some phones, and a fax machine. I figured you'd all have your laptops, but if you need computers, I can arrange that, too."

Jane believed that captain Sterling was sincere with his welcome, but the cordial greeting ended there. The reception they got from the officers in the room felt as cold and bitter as the smell of sludge at the bottom of their stained coffee pot, and before the introductions got underway, Jane was searching her memory for the area immediately around the station and hoping there was a coffee shop.

"These are agents Newell, Thomas, and Jenkins, and that is the unit chief, Bill Jacobs," Jeff told them. "Most of you already know MSP Commander, and our witness's brother, Patrick Murphy." The agents seemed reluctant, but did step forward when they were introduced.

"This is George Sanders, the chief from Mears, one of the officers from the Hart PD, Steve Rayburn, and from this office you'll have me and officer Dan Timmons. Of course, if you need more, we'll pull them in."

After officer Rayburn from Hart shook their hands, he looked over at Jeff and huffed, "I told you we don't need help. We can take care of our own damn town and I'll bet George and the boys over to Mears will agree."

Jane was clearly taken aback by the strained silence that followed the outburst, so Bill stepped up and told her quietly, "This attitude is not at all uncommon from local police forces; we call it a blue line of resistance, but don't let it get to you, they'll come around." After Jane nodded her understanding, Bill stepped up and addressed the group.

"We are not here to take over. This is your case and we're here to assist, but if this is a serial, and it has all the markers of one, we have resources and experience a police department, no matter how large, has and they're all at your disposal."

Jane was impressed with how he worded that statement, but wasn't sure it had the same impact on the men because Rayburn kept up with his angry spiel about Sterling's lack of confidence in his own men.

It seemed that Seth finally heard enough, and raised his voice above theirs.

"You can all put your testosterone rulers away, this is not a competition: we all want the same thing, and that's to figure out who this bastard is and stop him. We're wasting time here. We need to get the information our technical analyst Abbe, has found, talk to the witness, and get busy, because our killer won't stop until we stop him. If he isn't already hurting another woman, you can bet your paycheck that he's already chosen her."

That seemed to quiet the rumblings and as the men took seats around the table, Jane's eye caught Kate's as her gaze drifted toward Patrick who was embracing a feminine version of himself.

Chapter 14

Day One – Monday - 9:00 AM

Petersburg, VA

Judy put her teacup in the dishwasher and turned off the news program on the television. She knew Jane and her team had been called out on a new case, but did not realize it was back in Michigan. It wasn't seeing her niece that drew her in to the segment; it was the unmistakable, high pitch shrill of the reporter's voice and the way she was able to walk without wobbling in six inch stiletto heels that made her impossible to miss. She didn't even see Jane until she stepped out of the car to a microphone shoved in her face by the same reporter that covered the New Mother Killer Case.

It was more than Candace's shrill, annoying voice that put Judy on edge. The reporter seemed to be obsessed with Tad Wilkins, and by extension, her niece, and that made her very uncomfortable. She felt sure Jane would remember her from the last case because she couldn't turn around without Candace's microphone in her face, shouting questions and trying to get confirmation that her father was involved in those killings. Jane's sense of intuition was as strong or stronger than Judy's, so she couldn't help but wonder if her niece distrusted the woman as much as she did. She was very proud of Jane's poise when she handled the reporter though, because Candace was incessant about alluding to her father's connection and Jane's connection to him. Although Jane largely ignored her, she was able to do it with an air of professionalism.

Judy, and of course Jane and her team, knew that Tad Wilkins was instrumental in the copycat case, but they couldn't find anything concrete to tie him to it. More to the point, though, and what was causing Judy's instincts to ping out an internal alarm, was that she was an intern reporter when Tad was arrested 13 years before.

Judy realized, a few years after his arrest, that she'd allowed Wilkins far more control over her emotional wellbeing than he deserved. When it dawned on her that if he knew she felt his hand in every aspect of her daily life and saw his shadow every time Jane had a problem, he would be elated. Tad Wilkins got off on that kind of power over people, so she spent time with her therapist, and had a lot of conversations with her partner, Isabelle. Once she'd gotten through the period she referred to as her personal exorcism of Tad Wilkins, Judy was able to function without attributing every obstacle to a monster, who, while a gifted narcissist and psychopath, could not control her thoughts from a prison cell.

Once her demons were expelled, everything in her life, in Jane's life, and in their life together, seemed to improve and move forward. And then everything changed when his protégé, Lloyd Tally, entered their world and admitted to Jane that her father initiated the whole thing just to get inside her head.

When Candace showed up at the scenes where he tortured the women, and to the cabin where he was ultimately arrested, and started hounding Jane, it brought back some old and very dark memories of Tad's arrest. She'd grown into her career as a reporter since she was just an intern following the Original Mother Killer case, but her screechy voice, and the annoying tap her stiletto heels made when she walked, had not changed.

Candace relentlessly hounded Jane then, too, but it was easier to shield her from it because Jane was a minor, and to her knowledge Jane did not remember the reporter from back then. Now, six months after her first case as an agent, Jane was back in Michigan on the hunt for another serial killer, and so was Candace. This had

Judy wondering if there was any factual basis for the saying that there is no such thing as a coincidence, or if Tad's influence was in play again.

Chapter 15

Day One – Monday – 9:30AM

MSP

After their embrace, Jane noticed how Kate smiled when Patrick stepped back from his sister and seemed to look her over, much like a mother would do if her five year old fell off his bike. She never felt that show of compassion from her father, and until now, didn't realize just how powerful that act of love and concern could be. Kate grew up in a very large, very close family, so Jane was sure that Kate was able to relate to that tender feeling.

Patrick introduced Maureen to the FBI team, and invited her to take the seat on his left. Jane wondered if the rest of the team also noticed how she seemed to linger, and looked just a little closer at Kate when she greeted them all, but her curious meandering was interrupted by Seth, who started right in.

"It's nice to meet you, Maureen. We've read your statement, but it would help us if you would walk us through your morning?"

Almost as if she finally tuned into the case, and her job, Kate added, "If it's okay with you, I'd like to do a cognitive interview. Oftentimes they help witnesses, or even victims, recall details they either didn't remember, or never even registered, but we have found it to be a very useful tool. This is not hypnotism, but more of a guided walk through your day."

"No problem," Maureen told her. "Whatever you need to ask or do, I'm in."

Kate proceeded with the interview because outside of the

profilers, she was the best there was at helping a witness retrieve even the smallest of details. She turned her chair so that she was facing Maureen, and with a soft, rhythmic voice, began the process of relaxing her. Jane had never sat in on a cognitive interview and was happy she was going to be able to watch one unfold in real time.

Kate urged Maureen to focus on what she smelled, heard, and saw from the time she stepped out of her cabin at the State Park, through the time she stopped and began her cooling down process at the Little Sable Point Lighthouse.

"The Lighthouse is where your run stops every day, is that right?" When Maureen told her it was, Kate continued, "What I'd like you to think about now, is how it felt when your running shoes sank into the sand, and how the water sounded when it broke at the shoreline. Breathe deeply, and tell me everything you felt yesterday morning."

While Maureen was quietly recalling how hypnotic and soothing the sound of the waves were, and how the mist from the morning fog settled on her face and arms, the Hart officer, Rayburn, was on another tirade. This time about using pseudo-science to solve a crime and that they were wasting time because the witness had already told him and George from Mears everything she remembered. Seth's mean-mug look quieted the detective, but Jane knew that the agent was seething at the interruption.

"So, your cool down routine was interrupted when you heard rustling up the beach. Tell me about that."

"I really had to focus," Maureen answered, "because dawn hadn't quite broke, and the fog was really thick, but I saw a man who seemed to be stumbling, like his feet were buried in the sand but his body kept moving."

"Something stood out to you about this man. What was it?"

"His grunts. They were so deep throated that I zeroed in on his freakishly large shape to make sure it was a person and not an animal. I shouted out to him, but before I could move, something from above hit my shoe." Kate gave Maureen a minute to slow her breathing before she continued.

"You looked up at the Lighthouse and knew it was blood that hit your toe. Take us through what you saw and felt when you raced up the stairs." The room was silent, and reminded Jane of the moment in a horror film when everyone except the victim knew the monster was about to strike. Even Rayburn had settled down and, like the rest of the group, was waiting with bated breath for the final act.

"A part of me registered that the normally bolted door was hanging open, and that I should call for back up, but I didn't care. I raced up the spiral staircase because I knew there was a person hanging over the ledge and they might still be alive."

Kate took hold of Maureen's hands and leaned in toward her. "You're doing great, Maureen. We're almost there, what did you do when you stepped out onto the ledge?"

"A single leap had me at the railing, and I knew immediately it was a woman. My brain told me that her life was beyond saving and that she'd been brutalized. My chest felt like it had been crushed by my own breathless lungs when I saw that her arms had been duct taped so that they'd hang over the top of the railing. I did feel for a pulse on her neck, but of course there wasn't one."

"It seemed like forever, but actually only a couple of seconds passed until you processed what you'd seen. What did you do next?"

Jane noted that Patrick's fists were clenched when his sister's body tensed up, but he remained ramrod straight, as if he was fighting off the instinct to go to her. Kate gently rubbed Maureen's hands, and as the stiffness in her shoulders started to loosen it became clear that she was flashing back to a detail.

"I shot up to my feet and grasped the railing. I looked down the beach and through the fog, I could see that the sunrise was slowly burning it off. I focused my sights down the beautiful shoreline and on my breathing. I knew when my breaths went from rapid and shallow, to a natural sinus rhythm that the pounding of my heart up through my throat and into my ears would also regulate itself."

"What did you see once your head cleared?" Kate asked.

"It was still kind of dark and foggy, but I saw lights flash on. Not traffic lights or the lights from town, but brake lights from a vehicle. I watched them for just a second before they went dark again."

The cognitive part of the interview over, the task force started chattering amongst each other because that was the first time anyone had heard about her seeing brake lights. Patrick took his seat beside his sister and told her how great she did, and that what she remembered would be a big help.

From his seat across the table, Seth asked, "those brake lights you saw could have been the killer. Can you remember if they were big like a truck, or smaller, like a sedan?"

"Oh, they were definitely large, and spaced farther apart than they would be on a sedan, so I'm going to say it was more than likely a truck, but they went off again almost instantly." Seth repeated how helpful that information was, and then told the local officers at the table to check for tire prints, broken tree limbs, upset foliage, or even traffic cameras up to three miles away from the lighthouse.

"A person with average vision can see a flickering candle a little over a mile away, but from an elevated position, looking over a flat surface, they can see up to three miles." When they nodded their understanding, Seth gave the nod to Jane to continue with the interview.

While his vote of confidence felt great, the signal to actively engage in the interview took her off guard. As she'd learned to do at a young age, however, Jane let her instincts guide her.

"I know you've been through the academy training, and are better able than most to quickly access a situation. You've given us some great details, but is there anything besides the man's size that stands out? You mentioned his deep grunts, did it sound like he was in pain?"

"He was dressed in all black, and had his hood up so I never saw his face. His hands were in his pockets, but his grunting was more guttural, and when I think of it, it almost sounded like he was in a panic."

"I know it was foggy and hard to see, but did you notice anyone else on the beach, and did he look up when you hollered out to him?"

"He definitely heard me because he looked up, then gained his footing and ran off. I did not see anyone else on the beach."

The group seemed to take a pause to fill their coffee cups with the oil-like substance in their pot, so Jane reached into her bag for a bottle of water with the hope that fresh coffee was nearby before she continued. "How long after he looked up did he run off. Do you think he saw you?"

Patrick's elbows were on the table and still, but his knees making contact with the underside of it made it clear that he was anything but relaxed.

"It was just a second or two, and no, I don't think it would've been possible to see me because of the fog and the mist."

Patrick shot up from his seat and marched around the table, as if he was trying to formulate words that would have the desired effect, but without the anticipated reaction, and said, "You saw him, so he could have seen you. We're not going to take any chances. You will stay here in town with me until we get a handle on this guy."

It was Maureen's turn to shoot up from her seat, but she didn't parade around; she stood head-to-head with her brother.

"I will do no such thing, I have a job and we're coming into our busy season. I will not leave it because there's a razor thin chance this guy saw me. If it makes you feel any better, I'll keep my weapon with me rather than locked up in my truck or the cabin, but I'm going back to my job and to my cabin in the woods."

Kate was very familiar with the protective nature of brothers and tried to diffuse the charged situation with a little reasoning she hoped would suit them both.

"I get it, Maureen, I really do, but try to understand it from this side of things. We need Patrick to help us catch this guy before he kills again. Trust me, I have six brothers and know how you feel, but I also know that if he's worried about you, he won't be able to give his full attention to the case." The red, angry cheeks on her face seemed to fade, so Kate continued, "If we can come up with a solution that makes both of you happy, would you be willing to consider it?"

All the heads at the table rotated from Patrick back to Maureen, and when they both nodded their agreement, George, the sheriff from Mears, spoke up.

"I could let you have Jake, my undersheriff for a few days. You both know him, and he knows the State Park as good as anybody." Patrick and his sister seemed to be locked in a staring contest as they contemplated George's office.

"Jake is a solid cop," Patrick said, "and a good guy. I'd be willing to try that, but I'm telling you right now: the first sign of trouble and you're out of there, and your morning workouts are back in the gym for now."

Maureen looked from Patrick to Kate, and after a moment, agreed to the arrangement. Patrick pulled his wallet out of his pocket, and handed a key card to one of the officers from Hart.

"I'm checked in to room 142 at The Dunes over on N. Comfort. Will you take my sister there, and then wait outside of her room until I get there?" Patrick asked, and then to Maureen, said, "I'll get with George, and Jake, and then pick you up and take you home after our briefing."

It was pretty obvious to Jane that Maureen wanted to argue, but knew it would be fruitless, so she just shrugged her shoulders and followed the officer out of the room.

"Okay," Seth announced, "everyone take ten. I'll get Abbey on the phone. I know she has an ID on our victim, but knowing our extraordinary technical analyst, I'll bet she has more, and we need someplace to get started."

Jane immediately got on her phone and googled the closest place to get coffee, and learned that Stella's Coffee Haus, at a mile and a half away, was just a bit too far to walk on a ten minute break, so she decided instead to scrub the pot in their conference room, and start from scratch.

Chapter 16

Day One – Monday - 9:30 AM

Ionia State Penitentiary

I was surprised to see my Janey on the news this morning, and knowing she's on a case back here in Michigan gives me much to think about. My first reaction to seeing the bitch reporter, Candace, was sheer outrage. When she started her verbal assault by hurling my name and possible involvement at Janey, though, my lips curved up into what I've been told is a smile that nightmares are made of, and my fury was replaced with unequaled brilliance.

To the untrained eye, Janey's reaction to Candace's constant goading about her connection to me and my connection to the crimes is professional and reserved. Hell, they probably give her credit for not going off on the bitch, but I know better. Janey's restraint isn't about her ability to separate herself from me. She's acting aloof, but every time Candace throws a question about my involvement, my daughter is battling with two inner demons. One is a fear that I *am* involved in every aspect of her life, and the other is a fear that she could be just like me, the very type of savage she's pledged her life to stopping. Of course, either of those thoughts will help my mission of breaking her down, so that I can build her back up into my image, so I've decided to allow Candace to continue her style of reporting.... for now.

Since I got out of isolation a month ago, I've written two letters to the three women and two men I believe are ripe for my brand of manipulation, and I'm certain that at least one of them will be ready to quit living vicariously through the leading man in their sad and pathetic life and take real action that will not only become their own world, but will honor mine. My daughter is surrounded by some of the most brilliant profilers and criminologists in the world so I'm sure they'll make the connection, and when they do, Janey will realize that she alone is responsible for the deaths of innocent women. Her indoctrination into my world ended when she was 15 so I'll still have a ways to go with her, but I have no doubt that before long my daughter will be basking in the same power I feel when I reign over another's death.

There were not a lot of details available on the woman that was found on the beach, but my psycho-sense is pinging because the FBI would never use its resources for a single murder. I'll keep my eye on the case but will also have Jacob dig around because there may be others. While it's too soon to attribute this death to my letters, it's definitely a thread I need to tug. Following Janey through Candace is like an unexpected gift on the day after Christmas.

When Jacob delivers his report to me on Sanchez and his sister I'm going to put him in contact with one of my contacts in Virginia. I want some light surveillance on my former sister-in-law. Judy Newell is the only living person I couldn't fool with my charm; in fact, I tried to avoid her because it always felt like she was looking straight through me. After I went to prison, when the conniving bitch was allowed to adopt my daughter, she was charged with clearing out and selling my house in Holly. I'm all but certain she found my personal manifesto on Janey's cultivation, I just don't know if she shared it, hid it away, or burned it. Having that information could provide me with leverage when I decide it's time to complete my daughter's transformation.

Chapter 17

Day one – Monday - 9:30 AM

MSP – Hart, MI

Just about the time Jane started smelling the freshly brewed brain juice, she heard Abbey and her expressive voice playfully admonishing Seth for taking so long to contact her, so she poured two cups of coffee and sat beside Seth.

"Well, good morning, Jane. How is the team's colt doing today?" After her first case with the team, Abbey declared that colt suited her much better than rookie, because like a yearling, Jane stood tall and strong.

"I'm great, Abbey. What color is your ring today?" Before Abbey had the chance to answer, Bill and the rest of the group filtered back to their seats, and with the freshest coffee ever to come out of the building, prepared for their briefing. Bill craned his neck so he could see her face in the small phone screen and greeted their analyst.

"We're not set up for Skype yet, so we'll have to make do with FaceTime," he told her. "What have you found out about our victim?" Jane took the notebook out of her bag and smiled when Kate brought fresh coffee to Patrick and sat beside him.

"Okay, my superheroes, your victim is 25 year old, Kristen Taylor. Her prints were on file because she got herself in a jam last year. Not big like holding up a gas station trouble, but just a little trouble."

"Abbey?" Seth prompted as a way to keep her on track, but Jane noticed that besides herself, Kate and even Patrick were grinning at what was clearly their analyst's method of coping with the harsh realities of the job.

"I know, stay on track," she said. "Kristen was taken in last year because the car she was riding in was pulled over. The driver was under the influence, and well, let's just say her head was not visible to the police when they pulled up. When she came up for air, she got a little belligerent with them, so they arrested her with the driver."

The local officers dipped their heads and chuckled, and then the Hart officer, Steve Rayburn, told them why. "We remember that case. The patrolman that made the stop was a rookie and blushed all sorts of shades when the guys ribbed him about what he interrupted. Seems to me she has a really rich daddy who made it all go away."

Bill leaned forward in his chair, and said, "What else have you found? We're coming into this case about 24 hours later than we like, so we really need to stay on track."

"Officer Rayburn gets the jeweled crown this morning, because mommy and daddy are quite well off, and they must also be supplementing her income because she lives in a swanky condo in Hart and drives a 2010 Lexus GT, which by the way, has not been located." Rayburn visibly relaxed, and Jane appreciated how Abbey's effervescent charm and her delightful, yet peculiar, way of phrasing a sentence cut through the tautness in his shoulders.

"I've already emailed you the vehicle information, her address, and her parents information. They live in Pentwater and the local police chief knows them, so he made the notification."

Patrick left the room, and the group heard him giving the desk sergeant the information on Kristen's car to issue the Be On The Lookout. "I extended the BOLO pretty wide, so there'll be a lot of law enforcement vehicles looking for it."

"That's great," Bill said, "we may be able to find some evidence in it, or at least her phone. What else can you tell us about Kristen?"

"Well, and you probably couldn't tell from the photos you saw, but as you'll note by the photo I've sent you, she was a beautiful woman.

Even in her driver's license picture, which no one likes themselves in, she was gorgeous, with long, really dark brown hair, big brown eyes, and was nearly 6 foot tall." Everyone took a second to reflect on how different she looked in life than what they had seen in the crime scene photos, and then Abbey continued, "Kristen's employment history looks like a whole lot of stripes on a Bengal Tiger: they start and end, then start up again in a different place. Her tax returns show the same thing, which gives credence to officer Rayburn's assessment of a daddy supplementing her extravagant lifestyle. She dropped out of college after one year."

Kate put her phone down, and asked, "Did you get any hits on ViCAP? With the Bible verse and the way she was displayed, it sure looks like this Unidentified Subject, or UNSUB, has done this before."

"Nothing on ViCAP, which as we all know, could just mean that a department hasn't inputted it yet." Abbey put her stylus between her teeth and huffed in frustration, then took it out, and with a smug glow of accomplishment, continued, "but all is not lost my crusaders for justice. I read the newspaper."

"I beg your pardon?" Seth asked, "would you please enlighten us?" He had just a hint of frustration in his voice, but the rest of the group smiled at Abbey's sing-song voice and unique idioms.

"Sorry boss, but I figured a crime like this would make the news, even if it were just a local paper, so I did a statewide search using Bible phrase and torture as parameters, and I got one hit. I'm sending the article to your emails now," she continued, "but I'll give you the Cliffs Notes. A sweet college kid, Jolene Wilson, was found posed at Muskegon State Park at the end of April with a Bible verse perched up behind her." When their phones all dinged with a new email, the group took their focus off Abbey, to take a look at it.

The short article didn't take long to read, and when the heads came back up, Seth asked, "It says here the file was sent to a detective in Traverse City. Can we reach him?"

"Once again you underestimate me, Gray Fox. The detective's name is Mike Fuller, and he's kind of like a contract detective for all of Northern Michigan, but I've left a message for him at their precinct that we have a similar case, and I gave him Bill's cell number to call back." With that said, Abbey put the end of the stylus in her mouth, and mimicking a drag on a cigarette, said, "You're welcome."

The group chuckled, and began talking amongst themselves. Abbey went on to tell Seth that she had requested a record of charges on Kristen's credit card, and her cellphone records, and then abruptly said, "Abbey Louise, out."

Bill drew everyone's attention back to the table, and told Kate and Jane that they would have the use of a Ford Taurus seized in a drug raid while they were in town.

"Until we hear from the detective, about all we can do is talk to the parents," Seth said. "The college ID picture of young Jolene in the paper shows a young lady with dark brown hair and eyes. Seems like our guy may have a type, but it's too soon to tell."

Bill stood up then and asked the locals to print everything they had and to get the case board set up. "I'd like all four of us to talk to the parents" he said to the team, "because you two are great rapport builders and we're going to need it. Once we're finished there, you can meet with the Medical Examiner."

Patrick tossed Kate the keys to the Taurus, and said, "I'm going to take Maureen home. Jake is going to meet us there, and we'll hook up later. I think the news crew has left, but keep your eyes on your mirrors. We do not need them following you."

While the group began to adjourn to their respective duties, Jane's thoughts went back in time to another person with a type. She'd forgotten until Seth pointed out the victim type that after her father's arrest, while she waited alone in a room at the Holly PD for her aunt and child advocate to arrive, she heard the FBI agents and police officers talking about Wilkins' victims. "Seems he had a type. They've all had dark brown hair and eyes, just like his dead wife."

What else have I forgotten she thought, and why are the memories slamming into me now?

"You ready rookie," Kate asked, "we're going out the back."

Chapter 18

Day One-Monday-10:30 AM

Residence of Larry & Jacqueline Taylor-Pentwater

Kate took the wheel of the silver Taurus and Jane grinned while she found the lever and scooted the seat up nearly as far as it would go; she sat quietly as Kate adjusted her mirrors and raised the steering wheel so it was not resting on her lap. She waited until Kate turned the key before taking her shot.

"If Patrick ever drives this car, you might want to warn him to move the seat back before he tries to get in. His ability to father children could definitely be affected if he tries to squeeze himself into that tiny space."

Kate laughed, but then turned to Jane and suggested they talk about the case, and what they wanted to accomplish when they interviewed Kristen's parents.

"Okay, I agree, but first I want to talk to you about the meeting the other night. Don't worry I'm not going to get all sappy, I just want you to know how damn proud I am of you. I know that couldn't have been easy, but I have a feeling your story will resonate with a lot of people, because by sharing it you stopped being a victim. Now you will not only be an advocate for other women who've been assaulted, but an advocate for yourself. I can already see the difference in how you relate to Patrick. I'm just wondering when you'll trust him enough to share it with him?"

"Geezus, rookie. I thought you weren't going to get all deep with me. I appreciate that you're proud of me; hell, I'm proud of myself, and relieved that it's finally out in the open. I don't feel like a victim anymore because I took the power and control it had over me, away. And I have to be honest, I think being a victim hampered my bad ass persona a little." They both laughed at that, and Kate continued, "As far as Patrick goes, being with him feels right, and before I make the choice to take our relationship to the next level, I will share it."

Jane was satisfied with that response, and happy that the door to the topic was at least open now. "This is like over-the-top opulence," Jane said as they went through the gates of the Apache Hills Subdivision. "I wonder if their door will be answered by a butler with an English accent."

Kate pulled into their driveway and turned the engine off. "That's enough of that kind of talk, Jane. They may be wealthy beyond measure, but today they're just parents who've lost their only child in a violent death, and we're here to get to know the girl so we can help them get the justice for her they deserve."

Jane turned to her partner, ashamed of herself for using sarcasm as a way to cover up how badly she felt intruding on these parents only an hour after learning that their child had been murdered. "You're right, and I'm so sorry. Thank you for putting me and my biting wit in check."

Bill and Seth met the women as they got out of the car, and they stepped onto the porch. The eight-paneled, cherry wood doors opened automatically, as if the couple standing inside the opulent foyer was awaiting their arrival. Bill verified they were Mr. and Mrs. Taylor only as a pre-introduction formality, because their swollen eyes and the raw skin underneath the red swollen nose of Mrs. Taylor, made it clear they were meeting a couple whose lives had been completely upended.

When the couple stood aside the team stepped into the house, and as the team leader Bill spoke first: "Mr. & Mrs. Taylor, we are so sorry for your loss. I am Bill Jacobs, and this is my team. We're with the FBI's violent crime unit, and are here to help find the person who hurt your daughter. Is there someplace we can sit and talk?"

As they were led through a family room, Jane noted that the walls seemed to tell a story through the family portraits. Their only daughter was clearly showcased in what was a chronological story of childhood dance recitals, to a stunning young woman in ski gear standing on top of a mountain.

Jane felt as if the solid stone fireplace was the heart of this family when she realized that it was the main focal point of both the great room, and the kitchen. She remembered her own childhood home, and was saddened when she realized there was no warmth, or happy ambiance to it. She hoped her face did not reveal the grimace she felt when she flashed back to her father's hard, cold stare when she asked him why there were no pictures of her mother or of them in the house. She forced herself back to the reason they were there when she realized that he never even hung her rudimentary drawings from school on the refrigerator like her friends' moms always did.

Mrs. Taylor invited them to take a seat at the kitchen table, and then joined them with a sterling silver coffee server. Jane took the initiative and poured everyone a cup of coffee from the carafe.

"Thank you," Jane said, "and again, please accept our condolences. Do you feel up to answering a few questions? The sooner we learn about Kristen, the quicker we'll be able to hunt down the person responsible for her death." Mrs. Taylor took a tissue from the box she'd been carrying around since their arrival, and nodded that she was ready.

"Had Kristen mentioned anyone she was having a problem with lately?" Kate asked, "Or has her behavior changed recently?"

Mrs. Taylor's body language seemed to shift from the limp posture of a broken and grieving mother to a tightly wound woman resisting the urge to lash out. The lines in her temples defied the Botox injections when she glared at her husband, and her angry eyes turned to mere slits.

"Everyone loved my daughter," Mr. Taylor said. "I can't think of anyone who would do that to her." It was clear to Jane that she wasn't the only one on the team who noticed the drastic change in Kristen's mom, so they all turned toward her, and waited for her response.

Jacqueline Taylor slammed her hands on the table, stood up, and confronted her husband.

"Of course she's changed! Why don't you tell them the truth? This is all your fault. You've coddled her since the day she was born." Jane compassionately placed her hand on Mom's, and after her breathing evened out, she sat back down.

"Mrs. Taylor, the only one at fault in your daughter's death, is the person who murdered her," Jane said quietly. "Were you aware of anyone who'd want to hurt your family? If you can't think of anyone who had a beef with Kristen, how about you, or your husband?"

"Her lifestyle has changed lately," Mrs. Taylor admitted. "She's been drinking more, and hopping from man to man. It was only a matter of time until that lifestyle caused a tragic end. The truth is, we're not surprised that it all caught up to her."

Seth, in the quiet voice he reserved for sensitive interviews, asked them both to talk a little more about her lifestyle, and knowing the answer to his question, but wanting their response, he asked, "Did she have any friends from college, or her job that seemed a little off to you?"

In a voice stronger than she'd had since they arrived, Mrs. Taylor answered Seth's question. "He let her quit college, and she's never had a real job," and pointing at her husband, added, "and he supported those stupid choices. She said she needed time to find herself. What the hell does that even mean? He even rewarded her with a condo and a brand new Lexus."

Kristen's dad seemed to find his voice, and responded, but he was talking to his wife, not the agents. "I bought her the damn condo because when she was living here, you were always on her ass about something, and I couldn't handle the arguing anymore. And she has worked a lot of different jobs, but just hasn't found the perfect fit yet." Almost immediately Mr. Taylor realized he'd spoken of his daughter in the present tense: "She hadn't found her niche yet, I mean, and I don't know any of her friends. She gave them all up soon after she left high school."

Jane handed him a tissue from the box, and gave them both a minute to collect themselves, although she sensed that they'd gotten everything they would be able to get from the grieving parents, at least for now. The quiet around the kitchen table was interrupted by Bill's ringing phone, so he checked the caller ID, and then excused himself to the other room to answer it.

Kate took a hand from each parent, and said, "You are facing the worst thing that anyone could ever face in their life, and you need to stand in support of one another. It doesn't matter what choices Kristen has made recently, she did not deserve this. We're going to find the only person responsible: the monster who did it. Nothing either of you said, or did, caused the death of your daughter." Jane watched in quiet admiration at Kate's genuine compassion because it helped her relate to the family on a level that went far beyond the training they'd had at the Academy.

Bill walked back into the room, and by the mission-oriented gait and the look on his face, the team sensed it was time to wrap things up. "Did your daughter leave a laptop computer here," he asked, "and would you give us permission to go through her condo?"

"Yes, of course, anything you need. I'll get you the key, but she didn't leave anything here when she left. But I do have a question: how badly did my daughter suffer before she died? Was she raped?"

Seth stepped up to the parents and gently took one of Mrs. Taylor's hands into his, "The medical examiner will confirm this, but there was no indication that she'd been sexually assaulted, and her death was very quick. I will have the ME call you when she's ready, and you can make arrangements on where you want Kristen sent, or possibly even go in and see her."

When they got to their cars, Bill told them about the phone call he took.

"That was Mike Fuller, the detective from Traverse City. He won't be able to get down here until tomorrow, but he told me about the girl in Muskegon. He's also found two others that resemble ours, so if it is the same unsub, it brings his total to four. Our case just took on a whole new sense of urgency. No one sleeps until we have something on this guy. You two go to Kristen's condo, and then talk to the ME. Seth and I will go back to the command center and update the case board with what Fuller sends over."

Chapter 19

Day One-Monday-10:30 AM

Shack at the edge of Manistee National Forest Custer, MI

Just the act of unlocking the cabinet in my barn and removing my bullwhip was like an aphrodisiac, and as I locked it, along with a new Tyvek suit in my truck's toolbox, I was glad Junior was still busy in the chicken coop. He does not have a taste for what I do inside the shack so I shield him from it. However, my appetite for it lately seems insatiable.

Almost by rote, my truck turned onto US31, and my mind entered the trance-like zone it always did before an encounter with a new captive. My muse wasn't even affected when neighbors and townspeople recognized my truck and waved. When I returned the friendly gesture, they had no idea that the smile on my face had nothing to do with them, and everything to do with where I was headed.

The track back to the shack was more of a logging trail through the woods than a road, so the risk of someone stumbling on it by accident was slim to none. Even with the bright sun outside the inside of the shack would be in total darkness. That sensory deprivation adds to their terror when they're trapped and alone, but a part of my thrill comes when I turn on the flashlight and see the look of abject horror in their eyes.

I waited to turn on the light until I had the heavy door behind me shut, and the interior slide lock fully engaged. I like to play a game with myself in those few seconds from darkness to light, by guessing if the squeaks and whimpers I hear are from the rats or the woman trying to scurry away from the threat. One of the first things I noticed about the woman cowering in the corner was the dye job I did in haste last night. It certainly wouldn't pass a litmus test for being even a half-assed job, but the color was dark enough to satisfy my need.

"The rats and mice have a better chance of staying away from me than you do. Now come out of the corner, and I'll free your arms." The Tyvek suit and arm length plastic gloves made me look like a prop out of central casting, but it was intimidating. The sensory loss they experience in captivity seems to alter their sense of self preservation, and they usually shuffle out that first time, on my command. Alicia did not disappoint, and when I cut her hands free, instead of trying to flee, she attempted to cover her nakedness.

"Ok, now walk over to that chair, then turn around and straddle it so the front of your body is touching the back of the chair, I can't stand to see your face."

The bitch suddenly became noncompliant, so I grabbed a fistful of her hair and shoved her into it. The horror she felt was apparent because her entire body seized up in a cascade of rolling convulsions, and broken words trembled pleas from her tongue. My hands nearly slipped off her sweaty wrists when I jammed her arms through the slats on the back of the chair, and bound them together with the duct tape I kept in my construction bucket. Alicia Singleton was now essentially fastened to the wooden chair with her bare back wide open and ripe for her punishment, and I entered an entirely new zone.

My bullwhip was coiled at the bottom of the bucket like a snake, waiting for me to take it by the handle and provide the force it needed to lunge at its prey. I had appointments this afternoon and couldn't spend as much time with her as I'd like, but by the time I left, she'd know why she was here, and that there'd be more punishment to come.

"In the interest of fair play," I told her as I uncoiled my whip, "you're going to want to prepare yourself for a sound as loud as a sonic boom."

I aimed the handle of the whip away from her and threw practically all my body weight into the cracking of it. Being able to break the sound barrier with the force of a single snap gave me an almost godlike feeling of power, and although the physical exertion needed to achieve that perfection caused a sheen of sweat on my forehead, I was in the zone. As I re-wound the whip, I smiled at the trembling backside of the sinner in the chair. My ears, and I'm sure hers were still ringing, so I raised my voice. A punishment without reason seems very unfair, and I wanted her to know why she was chosen.

"You were chosen because of your bad and sinful choices. Forsaking your husband is the same as forsaking your father, and a penance needs to be paid, Jane."

When I cracked the whip this time, the thong connected with her quivering back, and she screamed out in pain. I wasn't ready to end things yet, so I added more lashes, and to create an almost artwork of injury, I stepped in close for some, and stood back for others. The skin breaking open, while music to my ears, caused sobbing so deep that she nearly hyperventilated, and since I did not want her choking to death on her own snot, I did not tape her mouth shut.

I had to leave for my appointment, but took comfort knowing that I'd have more sessions with her, and smiled when I wound up the whip, and took my knife out of the bucket. As I cut through the tape to free her from the chair, she began to shake her head violently, and in a quavering voice, pathetically uttered, "I am not Jane."

What started as just a haunting cackle morphed into a loud roar, when, in her petrified state, I could almost watch the light of hope in her brown, saucer-sized eyes diminish when she realized that she was going to die in this dirt hovel.

"I'm leaving now, and you should feel lucky that this segment of your punishment was a short one. I will return for more retribution that will make your skin pop open like a champagne cork." I took my protective overalls off, but left my gloves on, and as I opened the door, recited a verse from *Proverbs 19:18* that I altered to fit the situation, *"Whoever curses her father, or her spouse shall be put to death."* Still laughing when I closed the door, I said, "and you're all Jane."

Chapter 20

Day One – Monday - 11:00 AM

Home of Kristen Taylor – Hart, MI

Jane heeded her own advice when Kate handed off the car keys for her to drive, and moved the seat back before she tried to get into it.

"What do you think of the Taylors?" Kate asked. "Are your super senses alerting you to anything off about them?"

Jane turned to her partner and said, "No, nothing at all. They are genuinely devastated, and can't understand why anyone would want to hurt their daughter. Blaming each other is normal because they're trying to make sense out of it all and are just grasping for a reason." Both of the agents went quiet because they knew that the only person it made sense to was the psychopath who killed her. Even the men and women who study and hunt them have a hard time making sense of it all, which is hard to accept. Sometimes just removing them from the gene pool has to be enough.

Kate pointed to the driveway on the left, and as Jane pulled into it, she said, "This part of the investigation is the hardest part because we don't have enough information to build a victim profile, not to mention a profile of the unsub." Jane considered Kate's words, and recognized it as a good training moment, and added her thoughts.

"Then let's find something in this condo that will help us get to know Kristen, because Abbey is working on tracking her movements, and once we're done with the ME we'll have some information that we'll be able to use to start a profile on the unsub. Who knows what the detective from Traverse City may be able to add."

When they stepped into Kristen's condo, the agents put their disposable gloves on, and with eyes trained in observation, assessed the unit as a whole. Once they had a sense of the overall space, they split up for a room-to-room search. Their hope was that they'd find a laptop, or, as antiquated as they'd become, an address book, with the hope of learning who she communicated with on a regular basis. In their experience, they knew that a friend was going to know much more about a person than the parents.

After perusing her nightstand drawers, the closet shelf and ensuite bathroom, Kate told Jane that nothing personal was in the master bedroom. "She clearly has a taste for designer clothing, and a shoe collection that holds even mine to shame, but no laptop, no journals, nothing that might lead us to someone we could interview."

"Nothing in the kitchen, either," Jane said. "Let's check out the spare bedroom."

The extra bedroom, like the rest of the home, was very well appointed with a queen-sized bed that had a large, upholstered headboard that blended perfectly with walls that seemed to be the best combination of seafoam and fern green. The warm appearance seemed to say: Welcome! Make yourself at home. The quilt on the bed, however, was only visible in patches, because atop of it was what appeared to be a menagerie of product samples.

"Her parents said that in her personal journey to find herself, she tried selling a lot of different things," Jane said. "I think we've found all her samples." Together the two sifted through the samples and learned that at some point in the last year, she'd been a consultant for a high-end brand of skin care and make up products, that she'd partnered with a company who produced all natural vitamins marketed for their enhancement properties to fitness centers, and judging by the abundance of reusable food containers with color coordinated lids, her attempt at selling Tupperware was a dismal failure.

"I wonder how much it cost her parents to buy all these samples," Jane said, and then noticed large bags on the floor, propped up against the bed. "The labels on those bags tout them as being farm fresh, all natural pet food, available only in Veterinarian's offices."

Kate looked at the bags and told Jane to check the nightstand, "maybe we'll be able to find a list of her contacts for some of this stuff."

Jane started to answer that she'd already looked, when they noticed a blinking light on the old school answering machine on top of it. "Looks like she has a message," Jane said, "with any luck, we'll get the name of a friend we can talk to."

Going through a victim's home feels intrusive, but as an investigative tool, getting to know them on a personal level can be a tremendous help. When they pressed the retrieve button and heard Kristen's cheerful greeting on the machine, it stopped them cold because it was hard to relate it to the grisly pictures of the lifeless woman from the crime scene photos they'd seen.

"And just like that, a darkness has replaced light." Jane said, and tuned back to the machine again after the beeps.

"Hi Kristen," the equally cheerful voice said, "this is Riley Ann, and I was just wondering how you were doing with the pet food. Let me know if you need anything, or if you want me to visit any of the Veterinary offices with you."

"This message came in yesterday morning, after she was already dead. We need to track down this Riley Ann. Maybe she knew Kristen on a personal level and can give us some details into her life," Kate said, and then added, "I just got a text from the ME, she's ready for us. Let's go see if she found anything that'll help."

Chapter 21

Day One-Monday - 2:00 PM

Mecosta County Medical Examiner's Office-Hart, MI

Jane started the Taurus and waited while Kate finished up a phone call in the driveway. Her minutes alone lately all seemed to take her back in time. In her mind, and in her sessions with Dr. Isles, she referred to her life as before, during, and after. Her memories from the day the FBI stormed her house were mostly just a journey of connecting the dots, because the more she learned about psychopathic serial killers, the better she felt at not having known what a monster he was. She thought she had come to terms with the horror of learning what her own father had done, and of being reunited with and learning to trust the aunt she thought had abandoned her. What was troubling her most was the flashbacks she'd been having from the years before Tad was arrested, when she thought she was living a normal life as a happy girl.

As Kate joined her in the car, Jane consciously closed the lid on the box that held those thoughts because she had a demon to catch. She didn't need Kate to tell her that her partner had been on the phone with Patrick because her eyes sparkled like diamonds, and her cheeks had a rosy glow.

"I told Patrick we'd meet him at the command center when we finished with Dr. Laura. There's a Subway up on the right. Do you want to grab a sandwich and eat it in the car?"

"No wonder you're such a good interviewer, you are better than anyone I know at deflecting a conversation. Don't think I don't notice your dreamy eyes and flushed skin whenever you are around Patrick, but I'm starving, so we'll table that conversation until after we eat."

As Jane turned into the drive-up lane, Kate shook her head and chuckled, "Dreamy, really?"

They both managed to finish their subs without dripping sauce on themselves, and when they walked into the Medical Examiner's office, they were met by a receptionist who told them Dr. Laura was waiting for them in the autopsy suite. The two agents stopped for their sterile gowns, gloves, and booties, and were met in the hallway by a very tall, very handsome gentlemen with an appealing British accent and a thick head of dark blonde hair.

"Good afternoon ladies," he said, "My name is Roy Adamson, and I am interning with Dr. Laura. Kindly follow me and I'll take you back."

When they fell into step behind him, Kate nudged Jane with her elbow, and signaled that she needed to keep her eyes up. When they entered the autopsy suite, they were met by a beautiful woman with skin the color of cocoa. Her closely cropped hair and soft features put off a feminine appeal. Jane felt that Kate was probably sizing her up because of Patrick's reference to her at the morning meeting.

"Hello," she said, "obviously we can't shake hands right now, but I'm Dr. Laura Tibbits, the chief Medical Examiner for Mecosta County, and you've met Roy. While he doesn't use the title, he did obtain a medical degree from the Brighton Sussex Medical School, in the UK, and has come here to intern with me because he'd like to go into forensic pathology and some of the best colleges for that are here in the US."

Jane and Kate introduced themselves, and walked with her into the icy cold autopsy suite where Roy had already retrieved Kristen from the storage drawer, and wheeled her into the middle of the room. Viewing the body of someone whose life was ripped away from them was always a solemn experience. It took Jane a minute to process the feelings before she was ready to hear the clinical details involved in the violent death. As if the doctor understood, she and Roy bowed their heads and waited until the agents were ready.

"As you can see," Dr. Laura said as she pulled down the sheet, "the killer did virtually no damage to the front of her."

The recently sutured, Y-shaped cut on her torso was done low enough that if her parents wanted, they'd be able to see their daughter, and even have an open casket. As if reading her mind, Roy stood at Kristen's left shoulder and helped Dr. Laura turn her on to her stomach, which is when the doctor's calm and professional manner seemed to crack.

"Her back, however, shows this killer to be a real sadistic son of a bitch." Jane and Kate both gasped at the carnage that had been made of the poor woman's back. It looked like an open field of deep, angry red slashes with skin splayed open like a boasting Peacock's feathers, but instead of brilliant blues and purples, they saw deep gashes that exposed shredded muscle and tendons.

Jane and Kate simultaneously reacted, "Oh my God," and then Kate asked, "Seth from our team thought she'd been whipped. Is that what made her back look like a slaughter house?"

"Yes, all of this carnage was done with a bullwhip. If you'll look at these wounds," she said and pointed out the lacerated skin, "they were made by the thong of the whip, which is at the end, just above the fringe, and are made when the perpetrator is standing close, but the wide open wounds where her muscles and tendons are exposed, are from the popper, which is closer to the handle."

The group tuned into Roy's genteel sounding voice when he added, "Whoever did this has had a great deal of practice, and likely some instruction. To achieve the actual popping open of the skin, the whipmaster must be standing a bit of a ways from the target and this young beauty has a great deal of that type of injury."

"Is the cause of death, exsanguination then?" Kate asked.

Dr. Laura directed them to the back of Kristen's neck, and said,

"Actually, blood loss is not the cause of death." Then lifting the hair up off her neck, she pointed to an inflamed gouge at the base of her skull, and said, "This is. She more than likely passed out from the pain of the whipping, and would have eventually died from those injuries, but your unsub severed her spinal cord and brain stem when he plunged a knife into her skull. She would've been completely incapacitated until she died, which would have been within minutes of the stabbing."

Dr. Laura paused for the agents to absorb the information and rolled Kristen over, then she covered her with a white sheet. When the agents seemed as if they'd mentally returned, she went on.

"Severing the brain stem and killing someone with a knife in this way is not as easy as it would seem," and taking a 3D, lifelike rendering of the human skull off a shelf, continued her explanation with a visual aid. "The bones of the spinal cord are encased with vertebrae that make up the spinal column, and between them are intervertebral discs, which are kind of spongy and cushion the joints. In order to achieve this wound, you'd have to cut through the disc in order to get to the spinal cord."

"Do you think this sadistic bastard has had some medical training?" Jane asked.

"Not necessarily," Dr. Laura replied, "he could have taken anatomy classes online, had some practice, or hell, even watched a video of it on the internet, but I'll leave that to you and your team to figure out." The different paths the investigation just took were foremost on their minds, and as they walked out of the suite, Kate asked the doctor if she was able to find any prints or DNA on her body.

"No prints, but I did take a swab of what I think was sweat off of Kristen's shoulder blade. It could be her own, but it was in a strange place. I'll send it to the lab for a DNA profile, and if it isn't hers, maybe we'll get lucky, and the person will be in the system."

"That'd be a great find," Kate exclaimed, "I'd like to send it to our lab for processing if you don't mind because it'll get put through a lot quicker."

The doctor smiled, and said, "We'll use the FBI resources anytime we can." She then turned to her intern and said, "Roy, will you please get that as well as everything else we have, and what crime scene was able to gather, and give it to the agents?"

Jane noticed that like her, Kate also grinned when the intern respectfully ducked his head and backed out of the room to get what they needed. As the three women were removing their PPE, the ME told them that Kristen had been dead for less than two hours when she was found because rigor mortis was just starting in the facial muscles and shoulders.

"It would have been nearly impossible to get a body in full rigor up, or even back down, that spiral staircase. There's a reason they're called 'stiffs,'" she told them, "I estimate her time of death to be between 3:00 and 5:00 AM. I realize you don't have a lot of information on how long she'd been missing yet, but if it helps you narrow it down she had absolutely nothing in her stomach."

Roy brought the evidence out to the lobby as they were leaving. "Thank you both," Kate said. "You have my cell phone number, so if you find anything else, please give me a call. I'll tell Jeff at the police post to keep an eye out for your full report."

The sun had warmed the inside of their car and it felt good to the ladies after being inside the cold morgue.

"We need to get back to the MSP command center," Kate said. "We have an awful lot to add to the case board. Hopefully we can start making some connections."

Both women were quietly processing all they'd just seen, and Jane was trying to come to terms with the level of terror and pain that the beautiful young woman must have endured. From the mice and rats nibbling at her ankles, to what she imagined the resounding boom the whip made just before it struck her bare skin, Jane imagined Kristen begging for the sweet release of death. Before she shook off the chilling visual of it all, she thought of how well Seth handled the question from Kristen's parents, and how he managed to evade any details of what she went through before the quick death. Her resolve to cage society's worst brand of evil began after her father's arrest, and with every evil monster she'd encountered since, her steadfastness in the quest has become heightened to a steely determination.

"About a mile and a half from the police station is a coffee house called Stella's," she said. "Let's stop and grab some decent coffee for the briefing."

Chapter 22

Day One- Monday - 3:00 PM

Petersburg, VA

To take her mind off the apprehension she felt after watching Candace hound Jane in Michigan, Judy went to the River Street Market in town. She loved the uniqueness that each vendor offered, whether it was handmade jewelry and soaps, or locally grown produce and fresh baked goods, Judy loved the diversity that each of the local merchants offered. By the time she was in line to pay for the custom blended tea that she and Isabelle enjoyed, she had almost convinced herself that Candace being at the site of Jane's new case did not mean that Tad was involved.

Judy spotted an open seat at a picnic table in the sun, and decided to take the traveler cup of tea she'd bought and enjoy the day a little longer. Her favorite season had always been the spring because after what she viewed as her period of hibernation during the dark days of winter, seeing the new buds of growth on the trees and feeling the warmth of the sunlight that made it happen seemed to free her from the cocoon she'd been curled up in. She felt an unspoken agreement of respect with her tablemates because each person, whether they drank from their bottle of artisan water, or their venti cups of coffee or tea, greeted one another with just a smile and did not try to engage in unwanted conversation. Judy was grateful for the solitude because it allowed her mind to smooth out the tangle of paths her thoughts had taken.

She could not help but wonder why, after so many years, she couldn't stop thinking about the detailed journal Tad kept on his plans to turn his daughter into a killer. It was written in outline form, and Judy calculated that when he was arrested, he'd been just months away from his final act of moving Jane out of her home, isolating her from everyone and everything she'd ever known. He did not reference the term gaslighting, but his prowess in the psychological control and manipulation of his victims was a textbook definition of it. Tad knew, and journaled about how his own daughter would develop a psychological bond with him that went deeper than any father-daughter bond ever could, and that she'd be an eager partner in his killing world. The scientific label for it was Stockholm Syndrome, and Judy was beyond thankful that he'd been arrested and removed from her life before that happened.

The preciseness of his written plan, while always alarming, was suddenly very frightening to Judy, because in light of his recent recurrence in her life she realized that his determination hadn't faltered. She also knew he had enough power and control, even from his prison cell, to at the very least insinuate himself into his daughter's psyche. Judy's job, as it had been for the last 13 years, would be to counter those attempts, and to protect the woman who was like a daughter to her. She needed a plan and knew that the time had come for her to share the lurid details of the book she found; she just had to decide if she should take it directly to Jane, or to her team. Lately she'd noticed an occasional blank look on her niece's face, and while it didn't last long, it had Judy wondering if perhaps Jane was recalling some memories from those early days. As she placed her empty cup in the bin for recyclables and headed toward her car, Judy decided to table her decisions and to just enjoy the rest of the day because at her core she knew that Jane had grown into a bad ass in her own rite. The power that Tad Wilkins thought he'd have over her would not be the easily won battle it would have been when she was 16 years old.

With her bag of fresh croissants and raspberry jam in one hand, and her bag of fresh tea in the other, Judy pushed the anxiety of her sinking premonitions that this new case was going to take a toll on Jane into her mental vault and closed it off. Still enjoying the spring warm up, she set her bags on top of the car to retrieve her keys, but as she was digging through her purse, she shuddered because the tiny hairs on the nape of her neck seemed to stand on end. Instinctively she looked to her left and her right when her shoulders arched up and her chin dipped into her chest, because despite the chill in her spine she felt the heat of a stare, as if she was being watched. Seeing no one, Judy shook off the bad vibe and got into her car, but spent the 20-minute drive in silent conversation with herself because as hard as she tried to ignore them, the memories of what she'd read of Tad's plan to turn Jane into a killer, could not be abated.

Chapter 23

Day One – Monday - 5:00 PM

MSP Command Center

When Jane and Kate walked into the conference room with a tray of coffee from Stella's, they were greeted almost gleefully. Jane deduced she was not the only one with an affinity for coffee, but a disdain for the brown liquid with an oily film on the top that this group pretended was coffee. As the task force descended like vultures, Jane noticed that not only was their case board well underway, but a computer had been set up so they could Skype with Abbey rather than all trying to squeeze around Seth's iPhone.

"It looks like we've got a lot of catching up to do," Jane said to Kate as they took their seats.

"It sure does, and we've got a lot to add as well. Glad you got coffee . We're going to be here awhile."

Once everyone was seated, Seth stood up and addressed them all. "Okay everyone, we have a lot to go over, so let's get started."

Bill walked over to the whiteboard and explained that Detective Fuller would be in town later the next day, but that he'd sent over what he had on the young lady found in Muskegon. "Her name was Jolene Wilson, an 18-year-old college kid from Bowling Green, Ohio." Using his pencil, Bill pointed to her picture and continued, "As you can see, she had long brunette colored hair, deep brown eyes, and was very beautiful." Bill went on to explain that in Fuller's notes, her friends told him she was an early admission, scholarship student at the University of Michigan, and that she took her education so seriously they had to plead with her to loosen up a little and come camping with them.

"Her boyfriend," he went on, "was the one who found her. As you can see by the photos, her arms were duct taped to the sign pole at the end of the Muskegon Luge track at The State Park. This sign was nailed to a post and stuck in the ground behind her.

It is for discipline that you have to endure. God is treating you as sons. For what son is there whom his father does not discipline? Hebrews 12:7 – ESV

Seth went to the front of the room and told the group that Jolene was found on April 30th and judging from the pictures, and Fuller's written report, she was also whipped on the back.

"He's bringing a couple of files from earlier victims, and although they were whipped, there were no Bible verses, so we can't attribute them to our unsub-yet." On the way back to his seat, Seth turned it over to Kate and Jane for their updates.

Jane started by telling the group how well appointed Kristen's condo was, and while it was very warm and welcoming, it lacked any personal touches. "She had some lovely artwork on the walls, but no pictures of friends, family, or even adventures she may have gone on." It went without saying among the group that it's hard to build a profile on a person for whom they knew very little, so Jane continued, "I've emailed you a picture of product samples she had in her spare room, and are hopeful we'll be able to connect some of them to customers in town. We're assuming all her contacts are on the cell phone we haven't found, because we found nothing in her home."

Still looking at the report on his phone, Patrick said, "it says here that she had a message on her machine from a Riley Ann asking about the pet food. Does anyone by chance have any idea who she is? If nothing else, it's someone to talk to."

Steve Rayburn, the officer from Hart who'd been so arrogant earlier, spoke up. "I know of her, most everyone does. She has a farm maybe 10 or 15 miles north of here. She keeps a few head of cattle, and a couple of pigs that she either sells at auction, or to some of the meat markets in town to be butchered. She also delivers eggs and fresh produce to most of the markets, and in the summer to the Farmers markets."

"Can you get a hold of her and ask her to come in, or at least let us talk to her on the phone?" his boss, Jeff, asked. "Find out what, if anything, she knows about Kristen?"

Steve ran his hands through his beard as if considering the question and said, "I don't even know her last name, or where exactly she lives. To tell you the truth, I don't think anyone does. I ain't never seen her socializing. I'll go to some of the shops and ask them if they know how to reach her, but I think her route takes her damn near as far as the Upper Peninsula, so there's no telling when she'll be around."

The group gathered around Seth as he initiated a Skype call with Abbey. After the shrill beeping tone of the two computers connecting, Abbey's pleasant voice greeted them all.

"There you all are, and it's high time I might add that you upgraded from the tiny phone screen. I like to see people's faces when I dazzle them with my brilliance."

"Hello Abbey," Seth said. "The gang's all here, so astonish us with what you've learned about Kristen." Jane loved watching the facial cues of people meeting with their technical analyst for the first time. From her violet streaked hair, and diamond studded horn rimmed glasses, to the eclectic, often mis-matched outfits, Abbey in no way fit the mold of a typical computer guru, or an FBI agent.

Abbey set down the unicorn bobble-head she'd been playing with, and turned toward one of her computer monitors. "I have run her credit card purchases for the last 30 days, and holy shopaholic, she goes through money faster than you can say charge it." Predictably, the tension inherent in a task force trying to stop a serial killer eased a bit with how Abbey's voice and dialect animated her information.

"She buys most of her clothing at Woodland Mall, near Grand Rapids. Personally I'm a thrift store aficionado, but that mall is definitely high end. Kate, since I know how you treasure your footwear, there is a DSW shoe warehouse nearby."

"What else have you found Abbey?" Seth asked, "we really need to stay on track."

"Sorry boss, I am glad I'm not superstitious because her last charge was on Friday the 13th at 1:30AM when she cashed out her bar tab at Kristi's Pour House, there in Hart. I haven't been able to get the warrant for her cell phone records yet, but I did do a thing."

"A thing?" Bill asked, "Abbey, I've told you before that when you do a thing, you do not have to tell me. In fact, I'd rather you didn't. But what did you learn when you did your thing?"

"Like her credit card, there has been no activity on it since the 13th. The last tower it pinged off was the one closest to the bar she was at, and by 2:00 AM, it went silent. But the thing I did that is spectacular in its plan was set it up so that if it pings back on, I will be notified immediately and will be able to tell you where it is."

As Abbey turned her chair around and woke up a different computer screen, Jane stepped up to the case board and added the dates and locations their analyst had found, and when she heard the subsequent tings alerting everyone of an incoming email, she had a thought.

"Abbey, the message from Riley Ann came in on a landline, can you get those records, too?"

"I just texted you that number," Kate said, "and if you have a problem getting access without a warrant, give her parents a call. I wouldn't be surprised if that phone is in their name and I'm sure they'll help you get your hands on those records."

"I'm on it like a fly on a fruit salad, but I have just sent over the police reports Seth asked me to find on the other two possibles detective Fuller found. The reports include the icky crime scene photos, but there isn't much info on the ladies; in fact, they've never been identified. There were no hacked Bible verses at the scenes."

"That's good work, Abbey, thank you." Seth told her. "Stay nearby for a little while because we're going to get into the medical examiner's findings and may need you again."

"Abbey Louise, standing by, but out for now," She said before the screen went dark.

"Ok, Kate and Jane," Seth said, "will you fill us in on the findings from Dr. Laura?"

"We have a lot," Kate said, "and to quote Abbey, it's really icky."

Kate began by reviewing the information in the report the doctor had sent to Jeff, adding what information both she and her assistant Roy told them about the wounds on her back.

"The torture was done with a bullwhip, and was inflicted over a few days because there was some healing in some of the wounds. Note that on some of the deeper wounds there is a lot of muscle and tendon exposed because when the perpetrator stands far enough away, the popper section of the whip strikes the victim and makes their skin pop like a champagne cork."

"Bullwhips are certainly diabolical tools of torture," Seth said as he reviewed the written report, "and to be this good at it, this guy has either had a lot of practice, or instruction."

Jane empathized with the LEO's, because not too many law enforcement officers, even in big cities, ever had to face this type of barbaric torture so up close and personal. She continued with information that was not in the report.

"She had no ligature marks, and the adhesive residue was only on her wrists. The soles of her feet were stained with ground in dirt, and on her ankles were tiny pustules, which are almost like abscessed blisters. Dr. Laura said they were probably from mice or rats nibbling on them." Jane, with her deep-rooted fear of any rodent, cringed more at that piece of information than she did with the horrific images of Kristen's back.

"She also had a lot of the damp, moldy dirt underneath her nails," Kate added. "The ME took clippings for analysis. I sent those, as well as the sweat sample she found, to our lab. Hopefully we'll get a hit on the DNA from the sweat."

Bill pointed out that their crime lab at Quantico was so advanced that it was possible they'd even be able to narrow down where that particular type of dirt was most prevalent. Jane wasn't sure if the mannerisms of the locals meant they were relieved, or impressed, but she did know that Bill was right when he said they'd eventually come around.

As Jane went to refill her coffee cup with motor oil, Seth stood up and spoke to the group.

"We've managed to add quite a bit of information to our case board today, but without some intersecting lines connecting it all, we're no further ahead. I'm going to call Abbey. Hopefully she can get us some information on the blade that killed her." As he opened the laptop to connect them to their analyst, Kate took her notes from Dr. Laura and sat beside Seth.

"Hello, Abbey, thanks for hanging in there for us." Seth said. "I'm going to turn you over to Kate. She has a few details on the type of knife used and we're hoping you can help us track it down."

"Good evening distinguished guardians, I love it when I can use my mad skills for the greater good."

Kate's spontaneous laugh helped clear the snapshot of the horrific images they'd just looked at, and while the reprieve was brief, it was cathartic.

"Thank you, Abbey. Our victim died by a stab to the base of the skull, but to cause her death, the placement had to be very precise. I'd like to describe it to you with the hope that you can help us determine what the best choice in blades would be."

Abbey's voice sounded almost enthusiastic when she replied, "I am already poised over my keyboard. Do you want to time me, or should I just dazzle you with my speed?"

Consulting her notes, Kate explained, "In order to sever the spinal cord at the brain stem, our unsub would've had to fit the blade between the spongy stuff that protects it, and the vertebrae. The knife would've been held flat against the base of her skull with the sharp edges toward the spine." Kate paused to give Abbey a chance to catch up, and then continued, "The blade point would be angled toward the front center, and then yanked firmly down, towards the spine."

The visual of a knife being plunged into someone's skull and then wrenching it down with enough force to sever a brain stem was enough to make even the most seasoned LEO wince, but Abbey seemed to take it in stride, and turned her camera around so they could see what she'd found.

"Some people are just not humanlike, are they? But the blade you've described sounds like a dagger, shown here, and are known to be used for fighting. They're good for thrusting or stabbing in close quarters, have a very sharp point, and a double-edged blade. They are short enough to conceal, but long enough to do great bodily harm, or yes, cause death."

Jane studied the picture of the knife and told the group that Dr. Laura felt that the ragged edges on the skin, and the damage to Kristen's bones was consistent with a dagger, and if they could find the weapon, she would be able to forensically match it to the wound patterns.

"Abbey," Seth said, "is there any chance of tracking down where it might have been purchased?"

"Ahead of you there, boss. From Amazon to Walmart, and every store in between, you can buy one of a dozen models of daggers. Add the knife and gun shows, and the search becomes as productive as hiring a unicorn to find the pot of gold at the end of the rainbow."

Bill stepped up to the screen and thanked Abbey for her help before signing off.

"First of all," Bill told them, "nothing we discuss leaves this room, and your press liaison must be told that the presence of the Bible verses should never be revealed. It's our hold back, and will help us evaluate any suspects and recognize copycats. It's also a big part of the profile we're starting to build on our unsub."

The group all acknowledged they understood the directive, and Bill continued, "I've been in contact with Judy Newell, a psychologist on contract with The Bureau, who specializes in criminology to work up the profile for us. She's more than qualified, and our BAU team is away on another case. I'll send her the information tomorrow."

The locals all stood up and turned toward Bill as if waiting for their next assignment.

"First thing tomorrow I'd like Steve to hit the local markets and try to track down this Riley Ann. Aside from her parents, she's the only one who may be able to fill in some blanks on Kristen. Jeff, you and Patrick should visit some of the local businesses with Kristen's picture and the products she was selling, and go to Kristi's Pour House, too. We'll try to build a timeline of her last days, and I think as locals, you'll get farther. George, you can do the same in your town. Once you're done in Mears, get in touch with Jeff. If we don't have enough to run down, we may extend the search parameters."

Seth stepped up to the case board and pointed out, "Given the fact that she was held and tortured for approximately 36 hours before she was killed, means she was kept someplace remote enough to conceal what he was doing, which would be easy to do in this area."

"Until we can review the reports on the victims Fuller found, it's hard to build any kind of a profile," he added, "but the fact that all the damage, including the kill, has been done from the back, tells me that this guy gets off on the torture and not the kill, and that he more than likely hates women."

Kate agreed with Seth, and said to the assembled group, "For that reason I think we could, at least preliminarily, categorize this unsub as a torture sadist."

Bill built on Kate's assessment, "I agree, and even though at this stage we can only connect two victims, the wounds on their backs seemed to grow and get deeper between Jolene in Muskegon, and Kristen, which is alarming because it shows that with each victim his rage grows, but so does his pleasure."

Jane loved watching her team share their thoughts and theories, and more, she felt comfortable enough to contribute a thought of her own.

"I'd like to dig into our killer's signature. Those Bible verses, albeit hacked, must be significant to him. I'm thinking of visiting the local churches, to see if they can shed some light on their meaning in a more spiritual way than we're able to see. They may even know of a member who may be disheartened, or has left the flock recently."

"That's a great idea, Jane," Bill responded. "You and Kate start with those in the morning; Seth and I are going to come back here and prepare what we do have for Judy. Fuller from Traverse City texted and said he'd be here late morning, or very early afternoon, so we'll plan a briefing then."

"It's getting late, and we need to eat," Seth said, "but first thing in the morning I'm going to ask Abbey to get as much information on Ketamine as she can. Dr. Laura pointed out a couple of spots on Kristen that looked like she'd been injected with something, most likely to subdue her, but the liver metabolizes Ketamine quickly and nothing was found on her tox screen. She also mentioned that the mark looked like a larger than normal needle gauge was used, so we'll have to explore that as well."

Bill thanked everyone for their input, and then asked for recommendations on where they could eat.

"If you want a lot of food, quick and without much fuss, I'd recommend the Pink Elephant," Jeff said. "It's on State Street, you can't miss it because it has a big, pink elephant sign out front. Their breakfasts are wildly popular, and offered anytime."

Jane's mind tuned out the chatting locals and the smile on Kate's face as she huddled with Patrick, and tried to make sense of why she had a sudden craving for blueberry pancakes and sausage. And since she'd had a veggie wrap for lunch, decided that she could, if she chose to, justify having them for her late dinner.

"You ready rookie? I'm starving."

Chapter 24

Day One – Monday - 7:00 PM

Shack at the edge of Manistee National Forest –Custer, MI

Knowing what I had planned for my evening brought a smile to my face as I headed north toward my happy zone. When I brought Junior to the barn and gave him the card with the verbiage I needed on the sign, he questioned why the wooden post it was nailed to was so long. I needed it longer for a couple of reasons, but have learned over the years to keep my explanations simple and brief. When I explained my mission, and why I had to take the women, his face was blank, and I knew he didn't understand. When I told him the women were just like my mother, and needed to pay a penance because they'd forsaken their husbands, which in God's eyes was the same as forsaking their father, he seemed to understand the mission. I still shielded him from the part of the punishment that fulfilled me the most because I don't think it would settle well in his gentle soul. As it was, his simple mind never made the connection between the fiery trauma on the backs of the women he helped to obtain, to the lifeless bodies he helped dispose of.

When I parked my truck in front of the shack, I smiled because it seemed I'd arrived by auto pilot. From my tackle box in the front seat, I removed a syringe of my Special K because often times, on the second go around, the sluts are a little less compliant and need to be subdued. Adrenaline and fear can provide them with superhuman strength, and I couldn't afford for them to claw at the only skin still exposed: my face. When their bodies were examined, the only thing I wanted them to find under their fingernails is the damp and moldy dirt from the walls they gouged attempting to trench their way out of their prison.

The last ray of outside light illuminated the shack when I pushed the door open and I sensed immediately something was amiss, but kept my routine of turning on my flashlight and sliding the lock back into place before I investigated. Instead of being huddled in the corner and ready to pounce as they usually were on my second visit, Alicia was curled up in a ball on the wooden chair. One of my first thoughts when I saw her chin almost buried in her chest wasn't that she was dead, but that the under layers of her long hair as it flopped over her head, were still blonde. When I grabbed a hunk of it with my gloved hand and pulled her head up, her eyes popped open in terror. Her weak attempt at a scream sounded more like the hoarse sound of an evil presence being expelled from a soul during an exorcism.

I was relieved she wasn't dead, but she clearly had no fight left and I couldn't help being a little disappointed when there was no resistance as I turned her around, so her naked back was toward me. I was taken a little aback by the extent of the carnage that was left on her back from our earlier meeting though. I thought I'd held back like I usually do on the first go around, but the depth of the crimson lacerations told a different story and I realized that while she may not be dead, she was damn close.

Knowing she was not strong enough to even struggle against the lashes, I dropped the syringe into my construction bucket, and fully aware that I had to limit the pummeling to just a few lashes, removed my bullwhip. The pleasure was not as rewarding without the agonized screams or the thrashing, so I put the whip away, and grabbed my dagger. As I was stepping into my paper jumpsuit I admitted to myself that this final act was more of a means to an end and didn't affect me one way or another. Her breaths were short and shallow when I parted her hair off the back of her neck and pinpointed the exact spot I needed in order to achieve my desired result.

That task completed, I left Alicia in the chair and went outside. It was too early to leave her at her final resting place, so I unlocked the tool chest in the bed of my truck and went back inside the hut. As I hoisted her over my shoulder like a fireman might do as part of a rescue, I carried her out and dumped her inside her temporary coffin. I had to place her on her side, and when I bent her legs at the knees to make her fit, I knew I'd pay hell and probably have to crack her knees to get her out after her body stiffened up. Oh well, I thought as I tossed my protective jumpsuit and plastic gloves into the shack and locked it up: just another occupational hazard.

As I made my way toward home I contemplated who I'd choose to be the next female to repent her sinful ways.

Chapter 25

Day one – Monday - 7:00 PM

The Pink Elephant Diner – Hart, MI

Jane was warmed by the camaraderie within her team, and as they all talked about their summer plans and made friendly wagers on how likely it was that they'd be called out on a case and miss most of them, the sense of belonging she'd felt earlier became more solid. Even Patrick got in on the action and wanted to know the over-under before he decided on his wager. They were still laughing about it when they walked into the diner and a friendly young man, who introduced himself as Jackson, handed them their menus. As they passed through the restaurant Jackson cautioned them about a slight slope between the rooms as he led them to their table at the back of the building.

"Oh my God," Kate exclaimed. "It smells like fresh coffee and warm syrup, and did you guys see that bacon cheeseburger?"

"This place is popular not only for their amazing breakfast," Patrick told them, "but also because everything they serve is made fresh. That's no frozen beef patty, it's the real deal. I try to get in here to eat whenever I'm up visiting my sister."

Jane already knew what she was having, so as the rest of the group perused the menu she allowed her mind to pull in a memory that had been hovering just out of reach since someone mentioned blueberry pancakes and sausage. The last time she'd eaten them she was 14 and Tad made them for her, but she sensed it wasn't a pleasant memory, so she dug deep to see more and then almost wished she hadn't.

I remember being thirsty after I'd gone to bed, she thought, so I went downstairs for a glass of juice, but when I got to the bottom stair I noticed my father's office door was open. Somehow, I sensed that he would not like me watching him, but instead of retreating, I flattened my back against the landing wall and peeked around the corner. He had an open duffel bag on his desk and was stuffing it with what looked like giant sized, white footie pajamas, and then he reached into the closet and pulled out the freakiest looking doll I'd ever seen. Its hair was a mass of curls in construction cone orange, and the painted on, neon green eyes made it look like a paranormal apparition. The freckles painted across the doll's cheeks and nose literally took my breath away, so I silently backed up the stairs and into my room.

I turned off the light and climbed under my covers when I heard him moving around downstairs. Several hours later I woke up to headlights shining in my bedroom window, so I pulled back a tiny corner of my drape and watched as Tad stuffed his duffel bag into a black garbage bag. As he walked to his open trunk, he glanced up toward my window. I quickly went down on my knees, below the window ledge, and crawled back to my bed. I wasn't sure then if he'd seen me, but as I relive the next morning now, I'm certain that he did.

When I woke up to the smell of warm syrup and fresh sausage, I almost convinced myself that the freaky doll and footie pajamas were just products of what my dad called my overactive imagination. Hindsight being omnipotent, I realize now that I made my father's job of mind control easy because when I told him about what I'd seen, he used the voice he used when he wasn't happy with me to tell me I was being ridiculous. He reminded me that I'd always had crazy dreams, and if I really thought he was playing with freaky clown dolls in the middle of the night, that I should've knocked on his bedroom door and just asked him. Then his bright blue eyes sparkled like diamonds, and he flashed his bleached white smile at me, and told me to eat my blueberry pancakes and get ready for school. I never thought about, or saw that crazy orange hair again, until just now in my mind. What else have I blocked out, and why are they flooding my thoughts now?

When Kate raised her voice to get her attention, Jane knew she'd probably called her name more than once.

"Are you ready?" she asked, "you've been talking about pancakes since we left the station. Is that what you're going to order?"

Jane laughed, but thought about it a second and said, "No, I think I'm going to have a crispy chicken salad."

As the waitress walked away with their orders, Jane called her back and commented on the richly delicious smell of the fresh brewed coffee, and asked if they could get a carafe of it for their table.

"Of course, I'll bring it right out. I'll fill a pitcher of ice water, too, in case your glasses go dry." When the waitress, whose name tag read Sandy, seemed to linger before leaving to call in their orders, Jane figured she knew the FBI was in town, and wanted to ask them about the case. When Sandy brought the coffee back, she pulled a chair from another table, and sat behind, and kind of between the two woman agents. She got both Kate and Jane's attention, and immediately apologized for the intrusion. Jane could almost feel the poor woman's distress, so she kindly asked what they could do for her.

"I'm worried about my daughter," she said, "and I heard about the murder over at the State Park. I'm afraid someone has my girl."

Sandy's face had turned red, and her breaths seemed fast and labored, so Jane put her hands on her shaking knee and said, "Please take a deep breath and explain why you're worried. How old is your daughter?"

"I'm sorry, I'm really shook up and when I saw the FBI come in, I asked for you to be put in my section. My Alicia is 25 and has never missed our weekly breakfast date - until today."

"Maybe she got tied up, did you try to call her?" Kate asked.

"Yes, of course I have, and her phone goes straight to voice mail. I tried calling her husband, too, and he hasn't seen her either, but said she probably just took off for a spa trip or something. I'm telling you: Alicia would not leave town and blow off our breakfast without calling me. And she never turns her phone off, ever."

"Have you called any of her friends?" Jane asked, "Is it possible she's with one of them and just lost track of the day?"

"Her friends are all from the beauty shop where she works. She was the only one with appointments yesterday, but I did call her best friend and she hadn't heard from her either. I even tried to file a report, but the police told me that since she's an adult, it was too soon to consider her missing. I just know my daughter, and she would never up and leave without contacting me, she just wouldn't."

Jane and Kate exchanged glances, and told Sandy they'd discuss it with their team and the State Police Commander and see if perhaps an exception to the missing person protocol could be arranged. When the waitress went to collect their orders from the kitchen they filled the men in on what they'd just heard, and like them, they had some concerns that their unsub may already have his next victim.

"I know it's late, but if you two aren't opposed," Seth said, "I think it's worth getting more information from the mom, but as a missing person report only. Don't tell her you're looking for possible connections to a killer."

Jane took Sandy's address when she brought back the food, and they agreed to meet at her apartment at 8:30 and would file a missing person's report.

"I'm off shift at 8:00, and that'll give me time to pick my dog up from doggie day care."

The table got quiet as everyone devoured their food, and when they did speak it was to give high praises to the cooks at The Pink Elephant. As Jane reached into her bag for her wallet, she heard Patrick invite Kate to breakfast with him and his sister at the State Park the next morning.

"We have much to do tomorrow, so if it's ok, we'll go early."

"Sounds great," Kate replied with a smile, "I'll meet you in the parking lot at 5:30."

Jane didn't even rib Kate about how early she'd have to get up in order to primp for her early morning date, but instead, when they got into the car, she looked at her and said, "I have a bad feeling about this, but before we talk to Sandy I have a question for you, and I'll need an honest answer."

Chapter 26

Day One – Monday - 7:00 PM

Ionia State Penitentiary

It seems as though the irons I have in the fire are starting to heat up. Jacob seems to have embraced his new role as one of my stewards and has performed to my expectation. I don't know if it's greed or fear that drives him, but every directive I've given has been executed as ordered, in the timeframe given.

The report on Judy's surveillance is about as I expected it to be. She hasn't made any moves to indicate she's aware of my continued plan to turn Janey, although my overseer in Virginia believed she sensed an unseen presence. I'm not surprised at that because aside from me, Judy is the most intuitive person I've ever run across. She even warned her sister to break ties with me, told her I was a man without a soul. She was spot on accurate with that assessment, but all it really did was force me to up my game. I'd spent a lifetime building the façade I lived behind, and having a perfect wife was an integral part of that. Fortunately, I was steps ahead of Judy and was able to make Hannah believe it was in her best interest to pull away from her big sister.

When my wife refused lifesaving treatment for her brain cancer, I was livid: for the first time in my life I was faced with something even my chameleon-like charm could not change or control. I didn't know how to deal with feeling powerless and knew I needed an outlet that would make me regain that control over others. When I choked the life out of my first prostitute, I knew I'd found my destiny and have been looking forward ever since. As a matter of fact, the last words I spoke to my wife were, thank you. During those last weeks, Judy, who I've come to consider as my kryptonite, moved in to help with the newborn Janey, and I needed to avoid her. Being the brilliant psycho nut that I am, I took a lot of business trips. I wasn't really lying, because to me, my business now was ending lives, and while I was still learning, I was damn good at my job.

My end game is near, and I know that soon Janey will be ready to take the reins of the family business I've spent building, but it's imperative that I stay ahead of Judy. She alone has the influence and power to fight, and possibly even win, the battle for my daughter's soul, and I cannot let that happen. Knowing what she did with my journal documenting Janey's transformation is critical. When Jacob comes back tomorrow with another update on the east Michigan murders, I think I'll arrange for a listening device to be planted in Judy's home because the only way to beat kryptonite is to get out ahead of it.

Chapter 27

Day One – Monday

Chippewa Creek Apartments – 8:30 PM

Jane and Kate watched Sandy walk her little dog to a grassy area at the end of the building, presumably to do her business before she took her inside for the night. Jane had spent the ride over telling Kate about the flashback she had in the restaurant. When she was finished telling it, and before Kate even had a chance to process it, Jane asked her the question that had been hovering over her like a storm cloud since her nightmare trip down memory lane began.

"Did you know all these things?" Her tone was almost accusatory when she added, "Does my aunt know about it all, and why hasn't anyone mentioned anything to me? Certainly I have a right to know what went down when I was a kid."

"Woah, slow your roll, Jane. Of course, I had no idea of crap that went down before the bastard was arrested, and highly doubt Judy did either."

The passion behind Kate's response was genuine enough that Jane not only believed her, but calmed her down enough to say what was really bothering her. "I cannot believe I fell for his bullshit and actually blocked it from my mind. Had I spoken up, it may have saved lives."

"Okay, there is all sorts of wrong in that last statement, and we'll get to them all, but for now, listen to my words." Jane was relieved she had shared her recent mind trips because Kate's direct, often blunt, voice of reason would help with her perspective.

"There was nothing normal or right with your childhood. You were raised by a serial killer who was a master manipulator and an expert at gaslighting you. I don't know why you suppressed those memories, but I know you, and know enough to theorize that they're coming back now because you are ready to handle them. I also know that every odd was against you becoming a functional adult, much less a bad ass seeker-of-justice who will always stand for the underdog, and the victims of heinous crimes. That's who you are at your core, and are probably the most formidable opponent Tad Wilkins ever faced, regardless of the flashbacks you're having. You won, Jane – that miserable son of a bitch will never be able to control you."

Jane processed her mentor's words, and as she watched Sandy go inside her building, decided that after this case, she would talk with her aunt and Dr. Isles.

"Thanks, Kate. It looks like Miss Daniels is back in her apartment. Let's get this done and head back to the hotel." With an exaggerated wink, she added, "You have a very early morning."

As they took their seats around the kitchen table, Sandy thanked them for coming so late, and then apologized for the excited mini-golden doodle vying for their attention by dancing around them on her two hind legs. Tears welled up in her eyes when she picked up the 30 pound bundle of red curls, and said, "Alicia was worried about me being here alone, and thought Annie would be good company."

Jane's face went blank when Sandy nuzzled the dog's head with her nose. Kate noticed, but kept the conversation flowing. "Tell us a little more about Alicia. As much as you know, anyway, about her daily routines, her friends, job, and her marriage."

Jane tuned back into the present, and readied herself to take notes of their conversation.

Sandy went to the refrigerator and returned with bottles of water for them all, and took a drink before she started. "It's always just been the two of us and we're very close. My friends have told me they envy the relationship I have with my adult daughter." Seemingly unmindful of her actions, Jane picked Annie up and settled her on her lap as the conversation continued.

"When she was 19, she was swept off her feet by an older man with promises of an easy life. I can't really blame her; she watched me bust my butt all her life just so I could afford this place. She wanted more, and I wanted more for her. I just couldn't convince her there were no short cuts."

Jane empathized with the frightened mom, but needed to keep the flow of information steady, so she asked her, "Has Alicia's behavior changed recently? Has she mentioned any problems in her marriage, or with anyone from work?" When Jane noticed Sandy's rapid eye movement, she sensed the woman was uncomfortable, so she continued. "Sandy, we're not here to judge anyone. We want to find your daughter, and the more information about her and her life that we have, the easier it'll be."

"My daughter is 25 now, and while she hasn't said anything to me, I'm afraid she's realized that she gave up her youth, and is trying to get it back. If I'm being honest with myself, I've suspected that maybe her home life isn't as happy as her social media pages would indicate. I've never said it out loud, but it has crossed my mind that she may be having an affair."

As Jane was catching up with her notes, Kate kept the discussion flowing.

"What is her husband like? Do you suspect foul play between them?"

Sandy's surprise at the question was evident by the wide open, deer caught in the headlights stare of her eyes, and it took her a minute to formulate her response.

"Foul play? I don't understand what you mean by that, and while I'm not Edward's biggest fan, I don't think he'd hurt my daughter."

"We are not automatically jumping to foul play, so please don't read anything into that question." Jane told her, "It's our job to ask the questions is all. Will you write down his name and contact information, the beauty salon she works at, and any other friends of hers you can think of? We'll start talking to people in the morning if you haven't heard from her yet."

Kate concluded by asking her for a picture of Alicia and giving her a card with her contact information on it. "Please call us if you think of anything else, or if you hear from her."

Sandy handed them the list they'd requested and told them her pictures were in the living room and she'd get it on the way out. Jane set the dog down on the floor and as they walked out of the kitchen, quietly told Kate, "I had another flashback in there and it was as horrifying as the other one. I'll tell you about it in the car."

At the front door, Sandy handed them a picture of a beautiful young woman with long blonde hair.

"Thank you, she's quite beautiful. Is her hair color the same, or has she changed it recently?" Jane asked her.

Sandy was emphatic with her reply, "Oh, no, her hair was her crowning glory, and she would never change it. Thanks again for coming so late. I hope I hear from you soon, I'm sick with worry."

Chapter 28

Day Two – Tuesday - 5:30AM

Silver Lake State Park

When Kate met Patrick at his car, she smiled because like her, he'd grabbed each of them a roadie cup of coffee.

"Great minds think alike," Patrick said as he poured out the two he carried. "There's only two cupholders in my squad car." Kate tipped her head back and laughed, and as she put her seatbelt on was reminded of how comfortable she was with him. She started the conversation by telling him about the report they took from Sandy Daniels.

"On first look, it could be argued that her daughter just took off for a spa weekend or something, but for some reason, our instincts don't agree. Sandy's relationship with her daughter seemed very close, and I believe her insistence that Alicia wouldn't do that without calling her. The fact that her cell phone is turned off is another red flag. We'll present it all to the team this morning and see what they think. So, what's for breakfast?"

Patrick laughed and told her he had no idea, but that his sister was an excellent cook, and if he had to guess, he'd say it would be a traditional, full Irish breakfast.

"Shut up," Kate joked. "I haven't had a full Irish scrambler since last Christmas. My Pa goes all out, with beans, fried tomatoes, homemade hash, the whole bit."

"Well I'm not sure she'll have all of that, but it will be good. And she's promised to invite the man she's been seeing so I can meet him."

It was still dark when Patrick turned into the back entrance of the

State Park, but the stars that blanketed the sky, coupled with the light from the full moon, illuminated the tree lined path enough for Kate to notice how different the trees looked since she was in Michigan in October. The vibrant reds and yellows of the leaves as they floated off the trees in the fall were just as beautiful as the spring green, because to Kate it signified that all lifeforms are about cycles. For the first time in many years, she felt like she had shed the old and was beginning a whole new life cycle. As they continued past a spattering of tents and travel trailers at an idling speed, she cracked her window just enough to breath in the fresh smell of springtime and late-night campfires. Some embers still glowed in the firepits, and as she pictured the smores, hot dogs, and marshmallows that were roasted, she had fond memories of summer vacations with her family.

As Patrick veered off the main path and onto a narrower artery, he explained that the ranger's cabin was separate from the public's camping area.

"You almost have to know it's here, or you'd miss it," he told her, "and it's the only way in or out. Just ahead you'll notice a small opening with a sheriff's car parked in it. It'll be manned 24/7 until we catch this creep."

"It is beautiful back here," Kate told him, and as a small log cabin with a wooden deck almost as large as the building itself came into view, she added, "Now, be easy on the new guy, okay? Don't go all macho and overprotective because it'll embarrass her."

Patrick didn't have time to respond because as they pulled in front of the cabin and turned off their headlights, Maureen bound through the front door and crossed the porch before they'd had a chance to step out of the car. After she'd wrapped her arms around her brother's neck in a bear hug, Maureen turned to Kate and hugged her, too. When she returned the embrace, she thought about her own family and how everyone joked that if you left the house, even to take the garbage out, you had to not only hug everyone goodbye, but you had to hug again when you came back in.

"It's so good to see you again, Kate. I didn't have a chance to tell you when I met you at the police station, but I've heard so much about you from my brother. It's great to put a face with the name I've been hearing for the last six months." That comment warmed Kate's heart, but it seemed to grow in size when she smiled at Patrick, because even through the dark of night she could see the blush that started as his collar and worked its way up his face.

They followed Maureen onto the porch, and before she opened the door, she said, "Kate, you remember my friend Laura, and her assistant, Roy?" Kate stepped all the way inside and greeted them.

"Of course I remember. Nice to see you again Dr., and Roy, how are you?"

"Please drop the Dr.," Laura told them. "It's way too formal for a breakfast with friends."

Dressed in pleated dress slacks and a polo golf shirt, Roy seemed more relaxed than he was in his lab coat at the morgue as he held out his hand and introduced himself to Patrick. Kate jumped in and helped Laura and Maureen set the table, but tried to keep one eye, and an ear, on how the men's conversation was progressing. She was also an only sister, so she felt a kinship with Maureen, and if things seemed to be heading in an uncomfortable direction, she felt it was almost an obligation to sisterhood to divert the conversation. Their postures were both relaxed though, and when they began laughing, Kate was sure Maureen would be happy with the morning's outcome.

"Ok, breakfast is ready," Maureen announced. "Have a seat and dig in."

Kate sat beside Patrick and agreed with the compliments about how delicious everything looked, but she also savored the aroma of the sizzling sausage, fresh coffee, and perfectly basted eggs. That fragrant combination felt familiar, and was as comforting to her as being wrapped in a favorite blanket. Kate felt like she was sitting at a much smaller version of her family's breakfast table, and while she was as engaged in the fun conversation as everyone else, she still kept her eye on Patrick and his sister. The back and forth banter between them reminded Kate of the close bond she shared with her brothers. That familiar feel also added to the warm feeling she had that she was exactly where she was supposed to be.

The conversation was halted when the sharp tone of three different phones started to ring. Laura, Patrick, and Kate simultaneously excused themselves from the table, while Maureen and Roy looked on.

"If I were a chap that was prone to betting, I'd say that I'm not going to make my tee time," Roy said as the others returned to the table.

Kate dropped her social persona and spoke as an FBI agent, "I'm sorry but we have to leave. A dead woman was just found in Ludington."

"Roy," Laura commanded, "when we get in the car, call for a crime scene unit. We'll stop by the morgue and get the transport van."

On their way out the door, Kate gave Maureen a hug and thanked her for a wonderful morning. Patrick did the same, and then told Laura, "Once we get out of the park, I'll turn my lights and siren on. Follow me to Hart. We'll meet you at the scene once you get the van."

Chapter 29

Day two – Tuesday - 6:30 AM

Ludington Sculpture Trail – Waterfront Park

After Jane hung up with Kate, she put her long dark hair into a ponytail and raced out to her Taurus in time to see Bill and Seth race out of the lot in their own SUV. The only thing they'd been told by The Ludington PD, was that a woman was duct taped to a post fashioned out of what looked like splintered wood from an old pallet that had been planted into the ground. The victim was spotted by the maintenance crew as they prepared to mow the lawn at the park, and was conspicuously posed to appear as part of a sculpture along the Mason County Sculpture Trail. Jane turned at the sign for the Waterfront Park-Historic Sculptures, and followed the road toward stop #405, 'Hooked on Hamlin.' She knew she'd arrived when she spotted the florescent yellow crime scene tape, and the flashing lights of the multiple law enforcement agencies that had responded.

Jane parked beside Bill, put a fresh notebook in her messenger bag and stepped out of the car, but waited to proceed to the scene because Kate and Patrick peeled in right behind her. Patrick walked ahead to tell Bill that the ME and a crime scene unit were on their way, and Kate hung back with Jane.

"Before we step up to the horrible reality that brought us here, how was your breakfast?"

"It was really nice; that is, until you called," Kate chided, "but you will never guess who Maureen's new boyfriend is. She is dating the handsome lab assistant with the sexy accent, Roy, who, by the

Jane's Punishment

way, was nothing like the socially awkward man we met."

"Holy crap. I want to hear more about that, but right now, let's go see what's waiting for us on the other side of that tape. The maintenance man who found her said she was a brunette, so I'm feeling hopeful that it's not Alicia."

After showing their credentials and signing into the crime scene, Jane and Kate put on the booties and gloves, and ducked underneath the tape. Jane opened the camera app on her phone and started snapping pictures. Somehow, viewing it through the lens seemed to soften the blow of the macabre scene as it was presented. The bronze sculpture she zoomed in on was of a man and a boy, each sitting on a tree stump with fishing rods in their hands. It was framed by tall foliage that looked almost like the cattails she saw in the rivers near her hometown, but as she moved her camera to the third sculpted tree stump, her breath caught in her throat, and she almost dropped her phone. By design it was supposed to be empty, but instead it was occupied by a woman who was duct taped around her waist and her neck to a wooden stake that had been pounded into the ground behind the stump.

Jane stepped back to give Seth a better vantage point. He noted that the layers of tape around her neck kept her head upright, and that there were no visible wounds to her face. "That, combined with the Bible verse leaves no question that this is our unsub."

Attached to the top of the handmade stake was another piece of wood that held the spray-painted verse:

Let marriage be held in honor among all, and let the marriage bed be undefiled, for God will judge the sexually immoral and adulterous. Hebrews 13:4 ESV

Jane snapped a picture of the bible verse, then moved away to allow room for Dr. Laura and Roy to view the victim. When she moved the hair off of her face, Jane and Kate both went wide-eyed because the young woman's face, even with the blank stare of the dead, was without a doubt, the same young woman whose picture they'd seen last night.

Laura made a small incision in her upper right abdomen, and inserted a thermometer into the tissue of her liver to determine her core body temperature. As Roy worked on a calculation that factored in the outdoor temperature, the Dr. examined the rigidity of her limbs. Stiffening of the limbs start at about two hours after death, and reaches its peak at about 12 hours.

"She's in full rigor mortis," she said, "and combined with her core body temperature, I'm estimating she died between 7:00 and 8:00 last night, or about ten hours ago. Of course I'll have to confirm all of that after I get her back to the lab."

Roy parted her hair with his gloved hands and added, "She's a natural blonde to be sure. Her hair has been dyed brown. Recently, and quite poorly if I might add."

Laura gestured for the handlers in the van to bring the stretcher. "I'm ready to move her, but we're going to leave her attached to the post and take the whole thing. I'm less likely to lose anything of forensic value if I cut her free at the lab."

The crime scene techs had already processed the ground around her, so Bill and Seth wiggled the post free from the ground. Because her limbs were bent at the knees as the rigor worked its way down, the morgue assistants, along with Laura and Roy, lifted her off the stump and carefully placed her on her side on the stretcher. "Hold on, just a second," the doctor told them as she leaned down for a close-up visual inspection of the victim's cold and waxy skin. "She was on her right side when she died, you can see where the blood pooled, but whatever she was on has a distinct pattern that embedded itself on her side."

The team stepped up for a closer look, and Seth asked if she could tell what the pattern was. "I can't with the naked eye, but when I get her back to the morgue, I will use a magnifier. That might help determine it."

Kate signaled for the men to join her and Jane on the perimeter of the scene, and explained that the victim was Alicia Daniels, the daughter of the waitress, Sandy, who they interviewed just the night before.

Jane reached into her bag and passed around the picture they'd gotten from the girl's mom. Seth took the photo to the Hart police chief, Jeff Sterling, and they all watched as he hung his head in acknowledgment that it was Alicia. When Seth returned to the group he told them that Jeff knew Sandy and would go make the notification.

"Let's head back to the post," Bill told them. "We'll regroup with what you learned last night. Seth and I will stop for coffee and bagels."

Jane tried to be subtle with her fist pump of excitement that coffee was close, but as Kate got into the passenger side of the Taurus, she joked with her partner that fist pumping at a death scene was in poor taste. "We have about 20 minutes. Why don't you tell me about your latest flashback?" Kate requested.

"Do you remember me telling you about the puppy I brought home when I was a kid?"

"I do," Kate replied. "Your dad got mad and told you she'd run away or something."

After a shudder and shake of her head, Jane answered. "It didn't run away. That monster strangled her to death. I was out riding my bike one afternoon, and as I passed by an alley, I noticed my dad standing by a dumpster. Even back then I must've had decent instincts because I knew to be quiet. Anyway, he was holding that sweet puppy by the throat and shaking it."

"Oh my God," Kate said as she rested her hand on Jane's knee.

Jane took a deep breath and went on, "Last night at Sandy's, I saw it so clearly and it was so awful I don't even want to say what that poor thing looked like. Makes me want to puke. But as scary as that was, the look of sheer joy on Tad's face was horrifying and I remember thinking that he had two distinctly different smiles, and that recently I'd seen the evil looking one a lot."

Kate was exasperated, and at a loss for any kind of comforting words, so she asked, "How did he convince you that you hadn't seen that?"

Jane smiled at her mentor, comforted that she knew her so well, and replied, "I freaked out, and bolted out of the alley but my foot slipped off the pedal of my bike and I must've made a noise. I rode home as fast as I could, parked my bike and ran to my room. He came up a little while after that and when he saw that I'd been crying asked what was wrong, so I told him what I'd seen."

Jane took a second, and then in an angry tone, said, "I am, or was, so stupid! I believed him when he told me that he had been home all afternoon, and that my bike never left the garage. He said he looked in on me an hour before and I was sound asleep. Then he wiped the tear-soaked hair off my cheek and said I probably dreamt that because I was so sad about my puppy running away."

"Listen to me, rookie. Your sperm donor is a very smart maniac and knew exactly what he was doing. Forgive yourself for being a 14-year-old kid who had no one but him in your life. He made sure of that. You grew into who you are despite all of his mind games – you beat him, Jane. I know the memories coming back at you are hard to handle, but like you told me: once you face them, you will no longer be a victim to that son of a bitch. Now put your bad ass hat on, we're almost back and we have a serial killer to stop."

Jane knew Kate was right. She also knew Kate trusted her enough to know that her ability to do her job would not be compromised by her dark memories. Jane forgot about the Brazilian blend that waited for her inside when they pulled into the parking lot of the post, and saw what waited for them in the parking lot.

Chapter 30

Day Two – Tuesday - 7:30 AM

MSP – Hart, MI

As Jane pulled in, her focus was on the wall of news vans and the reporters that stood beside them who were doing their best to block the path into the building. Muscle memory must have taken over, because before she and Kate had a chance to digest it or make a plan, the Ford Taurus was parked and the engine off.

"What the hell, Jane," Kate exclaimed. "Not only is the local station here, but all of the national networks, and even the news-only stations are represented."

"A small, beachside town with a serial killer on the loose is bound to hit the national wires. I just wish we'd had more time. And look who is standing out amongst the horde: my shadow nemesis, Candace. I just wish I knew what her obsession with me and Tad is all about."

"She thinks it's her path to greatness, and as much as I think she's a bitch, she must do her research because she seems to have information that, while available through public records, no one else seems to have spent the time on. Right now, just ignore her and the others, keep your head down, and your voice quiet. They can't get inside the building."

Like a couple of charging bulls with their heads bowed, they marched through the mob toward the entrance. Jane thought she'd be unable to answer a question even if she wanted to because every reporter, with every news outlet in what she figured was the free world, seemed to drown each other's words out in a competition on who could shout the loudest. As they stepped toward the door, though, the unmistakable screech of Candace's voice broke through the cacophonous din of the crowd.

"Is it true another woman was found murdered this morning? Is there a serial killer loose? Should the people of Hart be concerned? The public has a right to know. Is Tad Wilkins involved in these killings, too?"

Jane hesitated with the last question, but Kate took her elbow and opened the door. Bill and Seth were just inside the door and told them that Patrick and the rest of the group was waiting for them in their command center.

"Oh, and the Mayor of Hart is in there as well," Seth said. When he noticed the look of uncertainty on Jane's face, quickly followed up with, "Your coffee is also waiting in there."

Jane relaxed and followed them into the room because she knew Bill was as skilled in the politics part of his job, as he was in doing the actual job. Jane and Kate headed toward their seats at the table, and their coffee, and watched as Bill greeted everyone and introduced himself to the Mayor. It didn't take long before the quiet conversation between the two men got loud and borderline confrontational.

"I know your team has been here less than 24 hours," the Mayor said, "but Memorial Day weekend, which is the kickoff to summer, is only two weeks away, and now the damn story has gone national. If this case doesn't get cleared, it's going to hurt tourism, which will hurt commerce, which will hurt the people of my town who depend on the summer season."

Bill's response was not audible to the group at the table, but Jane could sense by his calm demeanor, and their affirmative head nods, that the two men were coming to a meeting of the minds. Bill walked back to the table, and after having a drink of his cold coffee, filled them in.

"I've agreed to make a statement to the press. The Mayor is worried about a panic, not to mention the loss of tourism, and hopes we can comfort them with all the resources we have on the case. Jeff, will you go out and tell them that we'll be out to make a statement within the half hour?"

Jane remembered how relieved she was that she wasn't called upon to speak at the press conference they held after Lloyd Tally was arrested, but it wasn't because there were no questions directed at her. The veteran members of her team warned her against allowing Candace to get under her skin with her comments and questions about Tad. There would be no questions taken from the press today, but Jane had grown in the last six months and felt confident that if she had to, she'd be able to handle even Candace's nonsense.

Jane felt almost excited as they walked single file through the station, in the order Bill wanted them to stand outside. He wanted himself, Jeff, Patrick, and the Mayor to be in the front, but wanted George from Mears, and Steve from Hart, to be just as visible in the back.

"The communities involved need to see that the local cops they've known for years are just as involved as the Feds." Seth explained.

They were barely situated on the front entryway when the questions started to fly.

"Is there a serial killer on the loose? Why is the FBI here? How many women has he killed?" Jane was impressed with how Bill let them scream themselves out before he stepped up to the microphone.

"Good morning, I am Supervisory Special Agent Bill Jacobs from the FBI, and I'm here with my team to help your local police forces apprehend a killer. I am prepared to make a statement this morning, but will not take questions because it's too early in the investigation to comment on." Jane could tell by the huffs and head shakes from the press pool that they weren't happy, but they did quiet down as if to say they'd play by the rules…this time.

"Two days ago, Kristen Taylor from Hart, was found murdered near the Silver Lake State Park, and just this morning another young woman was found murdered near Waterfront Park, in Ludington. We're not releasing her name until her family has been notified." Jane was impressed with how he was delivering just enough sound bites to keep the hounds off his back, at least for a while.

"We are investigating a possible third victim, Jolene Wilson, who was murdered at the end of April and found near the Muskegon State Park. It takes three killings to be considered a serial, so we're waiting until we can conclusively determine she was killed by the same perpetrator to officially label it." That comment started another round of shouted questions, but again, Bill's silent stance hushed them so he could conclude.

"We are following every lead, working around the clock, and using every resource we have available to close this case, but at this point in the investigation there isn't much more we can give you. This department's press liaison will provide daily updates, but the families of these young women deserve to see justice for their loved one, and that's a job we do better than anyone. I will ask you to allow these devastated families to grieve in private. Now, Jeff Sterling, the chief of this State Police Post is going to provide a few safety tips for the residents."

As was planned, Bill stepped to the side and Jeff took the microphone and advised women to travel in pairs and to be aware of their surroundings.

"We do not want you living in fear, or putting your lives on hold. Just pay attention to the world around you, and if you see or hear anything that doesn't seem right, please give us a call."

The press conference clearly ended with Jeff, but before they had the chance to retreat back inside, the shouting started anew. Jane felt like it was becoming easier to ignore the mingling of a dozen or more people hurling questions when the unmistakable wail of Candace overpowered all the rest.

"Jane, Jane Newell," she hollered. "Is the Beach Town Killer sending you messages from your father? Is he behind these, too? Are you going to ask for his help?"

Seth started toward the microphone, but Jane held him back.

"I've got this," she told him. Then, to Kate she said, "This is the chance you said I'd get and I'm not passing it up."

With a deep breath, Jane stepped in front of Bill and the locals, and took the microphone.

Chapter 31

Day Two – Tuesday - 7:30 AM

PENTWATER, MI

Seeing Jane Newell step up to the microphone, all cocky and sure of herself pissed me off so bad that it almost took away the pleasure I got watching the cops and Janey's boss fall all over themselves at that sham of a press conference. Even though I had to veer away from my plan with Alicia, I still managed to stay off their radar. It's funny to me that the brightest minds in criminal apprehension have no clues; hell, they'll probably never connect the two hookers I did first, and I wasn't even careful with them.

I turned the television off and got into the shower before that neglectful bitch started talking trash about her father because my mission is in his honor, and I am not going to subject myself to listening to her lies. Besides, I need a clear head to plan my next move. Having to change things up and think on the fly with Alicia, while risky, added a new thrill, and I want more of that. The feeling I got when I met with customers yesterday, knowing she was curled up in the bed of my truck, was intoxicating. Those fools had no clue that a dead woman was within their reach, or that the very killer that has the whole town on edge, eats in their diners, drinks in their bars, and is one of their own.

I often wonder if he knows that his letters have not fallen on deaf ears, and that I'm able to read what he doesn't say, as well as what he does. I feel as though we're kindred spirits, but without letting him know how much I understand him, it feels almost hollow because I have no idea if he's even aware of what I'm doing for him. I wish I could find a way to let him know that the burden of his anger is now shared, and that it is an honor to fulfil our mission.

I stepped into the shower looking for ways to add more risk, and to elicit more of a thrill with my next fallen woman. The best high I've ever felt was when my artful deception enabled me to normally conduct business with a dead woman in my toolbox. And when an epiphany as bright as the northern lights virtually slammed into me, I knew what my next move would be. It would be my finale, at least with this phase of my mission, and would create fireworks so bright they'd be seen from miles away.

Chapter 32

Day Two – Tuesday - 8:00 AM

MSP Command Post

After she got a nod of approval from Bill, Jane tapped the microphone as if to test it, and took that brief second to carefully plan her words. She needed to make herself clear, but also knew she needed to be very careful because reporters, especially Candace, would do their best to convince their viewers of what she meant to say, and divert their attention from what she actually said.

"Good morning. I am agent Jane Newell, and as a part of the team tasked with stopping this killer, I have a few words." A few of them started to bark out questions, but Jane held her own and continued. "The first thing I want to say is that this perpetrator is a killer who preys on innocent people. He does not deserve a name, and by providing him with one, you're making things personal – for him. We've found that once the press gives a moniker to someone like this, they feel validated in what they're doing."

When Jane paused for a breath, a reporter from a national network asked, "Is it true that Tad Wilkins, known as The Mother Killer, is your father?"

Jane was prepared for the question, but before she answered, she looked to her team for the go-ahead signal, and when she answered she looked not at the young man who'd presented it, but directly into Candace's eyes.

"Yes, he is my father, and is serving multiple life sentences for the murder of 15 young mothers. I am not in contact with him now, nor do I have any intention of ever contacting him. I'm aware that some of you have been led to believe that he had a hand in the murders of three Holly women last year, but I assure you, there has been absolutely no evidence linking him to those murders. They were copycats and nothing more. Some of you have even tried to connect him to the killings in this town."

And then narrowing her stare to more of a glare toward Candace, she continued. "The man is in a maximum security prison, so it's ludicrous to think that he'd be able to insert himself into these killings. The mere hint of it only adds to the narcissistic power games he enjoyed so much before he was caught. Don't give him that kind of pleasure because he doesn't deserve it."

Jane put the microphone back in place, and amidst a barrage of questions from the pack, turned and walked back into the building with the rest of her team. Jane remained quiet while they all got their coffee and sat down because she wanted to assess their mannerisms and gain a little insight into how they felt about her words. She realized that under normal circumstances she would never presume to be the face or the voice of the team, but felt just as strongly that she was perhaps the only one who could dispel the rumors swirling around about her father. When her eyes connected with Kate's she saw what she thought was a look of pride and respect, but it was Bill who spoke first.

"You handled them well, Jane, although I doubt it'll change much with Candace; but your statement was compelling, and I'm sure it reached those that matter – the general public."

"You stayed calm even when Candace tried to get under your skin," Seth told her. "You stated the facts as they're meant to be heard, and let everyone know you are nothing like your father. In my book, it could not have been better timed, or gone any better than it did." After Jane thanked both the men for their encouraging words, Kate chimed in.

"What do you think guys, do we have our new voice for the press?"

Once the chuckling died down, Bill said, "Okay, does everyone have coffee and their notes? Our case just got bigger, and we have a lot to cover this morning."

Seth started it off by telling them that he'd already contacted Abbey to run down as much as she could on Alicia, and then turned the meeting over to Kate so she and Jane could fill them in on their interview with her mom.

"She gave us a list of her friends, and she works as a nail technician at Studio 49, over on State Street," Kate told them, and then added, "Her husband is much older, and a successful veterinarian."

Jane held her notebook up, and added, "It was pretty clear that mom isn't crazy about him, although when we asked, she would not elaborate. She also said that while she wasn't convinced that her daughter's marriage was very happy, she did not think he would harm her."

Seth, who seemingly loved a confrontational interview, said, "Jeff is notifying the girl's mom, but when we're through here I think Bill and I will take the good doctor. I have Abbey on the line, let's see if she has anything new for us."

Abbey practically sang her good mornings, and then, as if she knew she had to stay on track, got right to it. "I haven't had a lot of time, but I can tell you that Alicia's cell phone stopped sending signals at around 2:30, Monday morning. The last ping was north of Ludington, somewhere on Monroe Road. The last charge I can see on her card was at a gas station, on Monday afternoon. I sent you all the name and address of the place."

Before he responded to Abbey, Bill asked Steve to check out the gas station, "show both women's pictures, and see if by chance they have any surveillance cameras." And then to Abbey, said, "That was quick. Thanks Abbey," Bill said. "What have you learned, that we don't already know about Ketamine?"

"Aside from your beautiful faces, what I love most about my job is that I seem to learn something new every day. Strangely enough, Ketamine is growing in popularity, and is not just for the Veterinarians anymore, but it is still not easy to get, nor have the bad guys learned to make it themselves - yet." When Abbey paused to take a drink of her foam topped latte, Jane silently blessed the fairies that must've floated in to make fresh coffee in the recently cleaned pot, and by the time she sat back down, Abbey had continued to enchant the group with her melodious tone.

"I noticed the doctor reported that the pinhole on her shoulder looked bigger than the puncture she usually sees with a Ketamine shot, so I checked into the different needle gauges. What was weirdly interesting to me is that the smaller the number, the larger the needle will be. Who knew, right? Anyway, the typical gauge sizes for humans are 18, 20, and 22, but with the thicker hide of an animal, a 16-gauge is preferred."

Seth thanked Abbey, and left her with instructions to dig more into Alicia, but also to check into all the Veterinarians within a 45-mile radius of Hart. "See if any of them have anything criminal; go back about 20 years, keeping an eye out for issues at school like bullying, or if the school's social worker was ever called in. This unsub was more than likely abused as a child, and the tortured becomes the torturer."

Kate picked up the topic after Seth disconnected the line. "Dying Alicia's hair makes it clear he needs her to be a brunette, which takes us to the next logical step that he is killing a surrogate."

Seemingly more open to playing nice with others than he was when the team arrived, Steve asked, "So what's his next move?"

"By all indications," Seth answered, "he kept Kristen for nearly three days, but Alicia for less than 48 hours. That could mean he's devolving, which is when they usually make the mistakes that catch them, or he's feeling let down after each kill because she's only a surrogate to who he really wants, and he'll be going after his real target sooner rather than later."

Jane watched the eyes of everyone go wide when Bill told them that the only way this type of killer would stop killing is by getting caught, or getting dead.

"Killing with these rituals fills a need in this unsub," Kate said, "but reality cannot live up to the fantasy, so like a drug addict, they're chasing a high with every kill, and will continue to do so until they're caught."

Even though she'd met him only a handful of times, Jane's admiration for Patrick grew when she noticed him watching Kate because it was almost as if she could see the pride and respect on his face. Bill was explaining to the group that Fuller from Traverse City would be there sometime today, but to help speed things along he was having the autopsy reports of the other three possibles sent to Dr. Laura, and to Judy Newell.

"I've sent her what we have so far," he said, "and she'll work on the profile once she gets the rest of the reports. Steve, you need to have a conversation with Riley Ann, and while you're making your stops through the town, see what else you can learn about Kristen. The rest of the locals should show Alicia and Kristen's photo around and try to recreate their last days."

Jane volunteered that she and Kate would go to the beauty shop and talk to Alicia's friends, and then stop in and see the ME before they returned for the afternoon briefing. "They were only loosely affiliated with two different churches, so instead of chasing around to all the ones in town, we're just going to visit with those. It's a very thin thread, but we have to give it a pull."

"Patrick, I'd like you to go with the locals, but before everyone leaves I'd like to have Kate and Seth take just a minute to tell you what we've come up with so far."

Kate stood up and began, "bear in mind that this is still a very fluid investigation, with a lot of missing information, but we think it's possible that there are two unsubs involved because logistically, the disposal sites would be almost impossible to reach and to stage by only one person. Having said that, it's very rare for a serial killer to work with a partner."

Seth added that when a partnership does happen, one would stand out as very dominant, and more than likely be the one to inflict the torture. "We're also considering the likelihood that this unsub is local to the area and does not stand out. These are very small, very tight knit communities, and an outsider would be noticed."

The locals, not surprisingly all came to the defense of their towns. "We know these people, and they aren't murderers," Steve said.

Seth was calm when he answered, and Jane knew he'd anticipated the counterclaims.

"We don't have the full profile yet, but remember, this is all just a starting point, so while you're making your rounds in town this morning, keep an eye and an ear out for someone who may fit. These guys will blend right in, and you can bet they've already chosen their next victim. It's on us to get ahead of them, or else we're going to have a whole lot of bodies."

Chapter 33

Day Two – Tuesday - 10:00 AM

Ionia State Penitentiary

Through my contacts, both inside and outside of these prison walls, I've managed to keep up with Janey's life, and for the most part stayed out of it because I knew my plan for her required time, patience, and planning. When her path took her to the FBI I had to adapt, but was still confident I could complete her transformation. After seeing her speak at the press conference this morning, though, I may have to change my path because Janey is not the same girl I left. Judy's influence seems to have made her less malleable which could make the remodeling process of my daughter a little more challenging. I blame Judy for delaying the inevitable conversion, but there could be a way to get my retribution, and win back my daughter's soul with one brilliant plan.

Another thing that became clear in the press conference is that the countdown on Candace's days are up. She hasn't taken Janey's mental state to the edge, much less push her over it, so it's time for her to go and I know just how to make it happen. The last time I spoke with Jacob, he reported that his mole in law enforcement told him that Bible verses were found with each of the dead women, which makes me certain that one of my loyalists are acting in my honor. My intention when I put them in with the letters I wrote was twofold: not only would it be a clear indicator to me that the killings were for me, but they would be a brilliant forensic countermeasure for Janey and her team. I laugh to myself just knowing how the FBI must be

Jane's Punishment

dedicating time and resources to them. Jacob is due to come today, and I think it's time I let my followers know just how heartsick I am that my reuniting efforts with the daughter I lost have been thwarted by forces beyond my control.

Alas my love, even from the confines of my walls, my name is besmirched, and my daughter denies me. I seek in my heart to forgive her as she has been indoctrinated and influenced by the words of another. Those vicious words, spoken by a sinful and vile woman, are much louder than my own because they are carried over the air waves. Janey can, and does, ignore my voice, but she cannot get away from hers. Perhaps I should wave the white flag and just submit to living out my days alone and without the love of my beautiful angel. I want you to know, though, that at night, when the iron bars that surround me clang shut, and my world is plunged into total darkness, I am comforted by the light that is you. That light is what gives me the fortitude to face another day. Until next time.... yours in Faith, Tad.

Jeremiah 17:9 - The heart is deceitful above all things and beyond cure. Who can understand it?

Now that I've made the choice to quiet Candace's loud and obnoxious voice, and taken the action to make it happen, I will focus my thoughts on how to finish what I started when Janey was a little girl. I knew when she was young that she would make a perfect partner because she was not only intellectually gifted, but she possessed the athleticism necessary to build the physical strength and stamina required for the job. The plan I'd so meticulously journaled was about to lead me to the final phases. I was her whole world, so molding her brain, or as the dictionary would define it, gaslighting her, to believe my truths, was happening according to my timetable. My final step, her isolation from everything she knew, was scheduled to begin that summer, but the damn FBI ruined that plan, which makes finding, or at least knowing what happened to my book of Janey, imperative.

Chapter 34

Day Two – Tuesday - 10:00 AM

Office of Dr. Edward Singleton, DVM

Bill and Seth were quiet in the car because notifying a man that not only had he just been made a widower, but that her death came at the hands of a serial killer, took a lot of mental preparedness. A delicate balance of compassion and suspicion had to be found because about 55% of all murders were committed by the spouse, so their job was to quickly determine if they were comforting a grieving spouse, or questioning a murderer.

Bill looked over to Seth as they stepped out of the car, and said, "I know you're thinking about the feeling Kate and Jane got from Alicia's mom, but you need to set it aside and form your own impression. This is more than likely going to be the worst day in this young man's life, and we have to be sensitive to that."

"You're right, and I will. While I hate making the death notification, being able to assess a person's initial response is a great investigative tool. I won't allow any preconceived impressions to interfere."

Instead of being greeted by the sound of a dog's nails trying to gain purchase on a tile floor, or traumatized cats huddled in their crates, the only indication they were in the right place was the smell of the ammonia they used to mask the various animal odors.

"Good morning," Bill said to the young woman behind the reception counter. "We need to see Dr. Singleton, please."

"Do you have an appointment? He's booked all day."

Seth waited until they'd opened their billfolds, and when the FBI insignia was showing, he said, "I think he'll make the time for us. Will you get him, please?"

The receptionist put the glasses that hung from her neck by a decorative chain on the end of her nose, and stepped up to get a better look, then pivoted and walked through the door behind her. The woman who returned did not present herself like the gate keeper who'd left, but instead, cast her eyes to the floor and sheepishly backed her way out of the reception area and into a room that appeared to be the sales area for pet supplies.

Stepping through the open door right behind her was a tall man with surfer blonde hair cut in a stylish, longer-on-top type of fade. The tailored dress shirt and silk necktie he wore seemed to be a conspicuous effort on his part to take attention off of his basic white lab coat.

Seth figured the doctor considered the monogram on the upper right side of the coat was all the introduction he required, because without so much as an attempt to introduce himself, he started railing against his mother-in-law.

"Do you mean to tell me that crazy Sandy called the FBI about my wife? It's only been a day." Seth was glad Bill was allowing him to continue because without even realizing it, he was revealing to the agents a lot about himself, and his marriage.

"Alicia is like a petulant child" he continued, "who occasionally gets a bug in her bonnet and takes off, spends a bunch of my money, and then comes home as if nothing happened. I'm sorry you wasted your time, but my wife is just out living the high life somewhere, on my dime, and will be home soon because she doesn't want to give up the good life I've given her."

When it seemed he'd exhausted his tirade, Bill quietly asked if they could go into his office and talk. The doctor plunged his hands into his pockets and led them through the door and into his office.

Once he was seated behind his ornate executive desk, Seth looked at him squarely and spoke. "We are very sorry to inform you that your wife was found deceased early this morning in Ludington." They'd given many notifications, and seen many different reactions to them, so they weren't too surprised when he reacted in disbelief and anger.

"Wait, what?" he bellowed. "Are you trying to make me believe my wife is dead? Seriously, I'm going to need to see your credentials again because I wouldn't put it past those women to stage this as some sick sort of lesson."

Bill and Seth handed him their billfolds for a closer inspection, and when it was clear he knew they were legitimate, Seth got verbal acknowledgement that it was his wife and her mom he was accusing of setting him up, then asked, "What kind of a lesson do you think they'd want to teach you?"

"There is no reason, but they're like a couple of stealth barn cats silently stalking their prey."

"So, Ed, tell me why you consider yourself their prey?" Seth knew it was inappropriate to use his name in such a familiar way, but wanted to judge his reaction to it because it would be helpful in his psychological profile. He was not surprised by the tone of his response.

"I am not Ed, nor am I ever called just Doc, so please respect my degree and refer to me as Dr. Singleton. And why are you wasting my time with these questions? I'd like to process my wife's death, and make arrangements for her burial."

Bill picked up on Seth's frustration, so he continued the interview. "I assure you, Dr., the questions are routine, and we won't take up a lot of your time. Please bear with us because the sooner we get the answers, the quicker we'll be able to track down the person who murdered your wife."

Seth was more interested in eye movement, facial tics, and body language than he was in the man's verbal response, because regardless of their initial reaction, one of the first questions a loved one always asked was how they died, and Dr. Singleton never even asked.

The widower dropped his face into the palms of his hands, and then swiveled his desk chair backwards and looked out his window.

When he turned back around, he seemed to have gathered himself and asked them if Alicia was the body they'd found in Ludington that morning.

"Dammit, I'm going to have to call Sandy."

"The chief over at the State Police Post knows her, so he's already broken the news," Seth told him. "We just have a few more questions, and then we'll give you the pathologist's name and number over at the morgue so you can tell her where you want Alicia to go."

Dr. Singleton was indignant when he lashed out at the fact that his mother-in-law knew before him that she had been murdered. "Did you interrogate her, too?"

"Sir," Bill answered respectfully, "we aren't trying to interrogate you as much as we're trying to get a sense of who your wife was, who she may have been quarreling with, or who might have a reason to kill her."

"And Miss Daniels was interviewed last night by two of our agents because she wanted to officially report her missing," Seth told him, and then asked, "We know Alicia was a nail technician and will be talking to her co-workers, but who else did she socialize with?"

"Oh, she had that little job because she liked to play beauty parlor. I think it cost me more than she ever made off of it, and the only other one in her life was her mom. I did hear whispers in the diner that she had a boyfriend, but didn't believe it. She loved her life with me and would never have done anything to jeopardize it."

Seth was growing tired of trying to weave empathy into his questioning, and pointedly asked, "How was your marriage?"

"What do you mean by that? I just told you she loved her life. You don't actually consider me a suspect in this, do you?"

"The sooner we rule you out, the quicker we can look at others," Seth told him. "Do you mind telling us where you were last night from say 6:00 until 11:00 PM?"

"I was at home. Alone. Waiting for my wife."

Bill was sure they'd get nothing further from Dr. Edward Singleton, at least for today, so he leaned across the desk with the picture of Kristen Taylor, and asked if he knew her.

"No, I don't know her." He rattled off, then stood up as if to signal that for his part, the interview was over.

The agents stood, and while shaking his hand offered their condolences on his loss once again. "We can show ourselves out," Seth told him as they walked out and closed his office door behind them.

Experience had taught them to keep their impressions to themselves until they were in the car, but Seth motioned to Bill that he'd like to stop in the product sales room and take a look. The gatekeeper followed them, which gave them the opportunity to ask her if the off-brand, all-natural dog food they sold was available at a grocery store.

"No it is not," she told them. "Dr. Singleton buys that directly from the rep."

The men exchanged knowing glances because the dog food they'd referenced was the same as the product sample that Kristen had in her spare room. When they got into their car, Seth turned to Bill and said, "Sometimes I wish I could arrest someone for being an arrogant, entitled narcissist just for the fun of it, but the fact is, that man is hiding something."

Chapter 35

Day Two – Tuesday - 11:30 AM

MSP

Jane and Kate, after gathering as much information as they could for their afternoon briefing, headed toward the Pink Elephant. They'd called in a carry-out order so the gang back at the police post could enjoy a working lunch. Jane knew that Kate was more than likely processing what they'd learned, but her thoughts were on a phone conversation she'd had with her aunt. Judy was not surprised when Jane opened up about the dark moments from her past that she'd been flashing on. Much like Kate did, Judy assured her that she was strong enough to handle them, and that when she got home, they'd sort through it all. As usual, confiding in Judy gave her a confidence boost, but there was something more to it today, almost like she also had something she needed to share.

As Jane turned toward the Pink Elephant sign, Kate shared her hope that someone would recognize the waffle-like pattern that was embedded in Alicia's skin. "Roy took a digital image of it for us to take to our briefing."

"Speaking of Roy," Jane said, "is he really not the socially awkward guy we see at the morgue? The only sign I saw that he wasn't a robot, was the pale blue golf shirt he wore under his lab jacket. What's up with the horse logo anyway?"

As they stepped out of the restaurant and put the bags in the backseat, Kate told Jane she thought it was a golf logo or something.

"Well, pony boy won't be playing any golf today. Let's go see what everyone found because we really need something to shake loose. Fuller from Traverse City is due soon; hopefully he'll be able to add something."

While the ladies were the last to arrive for the briefing, they were certainly the most popular because everyone's days had begun as early and abruptly as theirs, so no one had time to eat breakfast.

Jane took a bite of her salad, then set down her fork and began, "We started at the beauty salon, and they were all devastated. They told us that Alicia was a private person who never talked about herself, but until a few months ago, she seemed distracted, even a little depressed. Then one day she started cancelling a lot of her afternoon and evening appointments, but her attitude changed, and she seemed much happier. One of the stylists overheard her say the Viking Arms Inn as if she were confirming something."

Jane paused to take another forkful of her salad, so Kate continued, "The churches led us nowhere. Neither of them were active, and they had no knowledge of anyone feeling shunned or let down at all by their faith."

Patrick stood up and said Kate called him because he and Jeff were already in Ludington, so they stopped at the Inn with her picture.

"It was clear they recognized her, but cited confidentiality and protecting the privacy of their guests. Jeff happened to know the manager, so he told him that whoever she was with Sunday night was more than likely the last person to see her alive, and was possibly the one who murdered her, but unless we could speak to him, we wouldn't know." When Seth took a bite of his bacon cheeseburger, Jeff continued the reporting.

"He was really shaken when he learned she'd been murdered, so he admitted that Alicia was there a couple times a week. It took a little strong arming, but he told me who she'd been meeting. His name is Dan Harris. We graduated high school together. His parents own Larson & Son, a hardware store in town. He worked there during school, and after college he took over running the place. He's a good guy, but I do have my guys checking into him."

Seth updated the case board as Kate continued: "The ME confirmed that the cause of death was exactly the same as Kristen's, and that she'd also been whipped on the back, but unlike Kristen, there was no healing yet on her wounds." The group all conceded that the reason for that was because she hadn't been held, or beaten, for as long as their first victim.

"The lacerations she did have seemed more brutal, and definitely deeper than the earlier wounds left on Kristen, though, which adds weight to this guy being a torture sadist," Kate said, and then went on to report that Alicia also had ground-in dirt on her feet and under her nails.

Jane pulled the enhanced picture of the embedded pattern along Alicia's right side, and passed it around the room. "It almost looks like tiny waffles, or squares." She said as she tacked the picture to the board hoping someone might recognize what it might be.

"Steve," Seth asked, "were you able to catch up with that Riley Ann lady?"

"Doc Hollman, a Vet in town told me how to get ahold of her. I guess she's also a Vet tech that he contracts with. When I talked to her on the phone, she said Kristen was a part of what she called her downline, and was trying to sell all-natural pet food to the local vets, but she didn't know her personally." He paused while the FBI agents studied the board, and then went on, "The gas station attendant did not recognize either of the ladies, but he did give me a copy of the surveillance they have on the pumps."

"That's good," Seth replied. "We'll watch it when we're through, but as I look at the board, I'm seeing too many veterinarian connections to ignore. I want to get Alicia's husband in here for a more formal interview. That jack wang lied about knowing Kristen, and I knew he was hiding something. I intend to find out what it was. We also need another conversation with this Riley Ann, find out if she stocks Ketamine, and if so, who else may have access to it."

Jane considered the information gathered so far, and believed that some progress had been made, they just needed a few more pieces before the puzzle could be fully assembled.

"I sent the files over to Judy," Bill told them, "and she's gotten the autopsy results on Jolene from Muskegon, and the other two victims Fuller found that could be connected. She'll have our profile soon, but in the meantime, I'm going to have Abbey do a deep dive into Alicia's husband, and her lover. Even if he's cleared for the murder, Alicia may have opened up to him about why she was unhappy in her marriage."

"I'll send one of my patrolmen over to get Singleton and Harris in here," Jeff said as he walked out into the squad room.

Kate took the thumb drive Steve brought back and put it into the laptop. "If nothing else, this may help us with our timeline."

The group of agents, and the locals all gathered around to watch the surveillance. They knew her last appointment at the salon was at noon on Sunday, so they fast forwarded the images to 2:00 PM, and began looking for her Audi SUV. The camera picked up the pumps, and the parking directly in front of the store, and about seven minutes into it, Jane jumped out of her seat and pointed at the screen.

"Right there, pump two, that looks like her car." Kate slowed down the feed, and the group watched in slow motion as Alicia put her credit card into the reader on the pump. As they waited for her to finish pumping her gas, Jane looked around at what she could see of the building, and other gas pumps.

"Look there," she said, and pointed to a large truck that was parked in front of the store, "does that metal toolbox in the bed have a square pattern to it?" Kate adjusted the angles, so they were able to see it more clearly.

"Damn right it does," Patrick said, "I knew that pattern looked familiar, but a lot of contractors have them in their trucks. Could be a coincidence, but just in case, can we get a plate number, or a shot of the driver?"

After some more manipulation of the views, Kate told them that she could not get a clear shot of the driver, or the plate, and put the recording back in motion in time to see Alicia's car pull away.

"A coincidence is looking less likely," Patrick said, "because the truck is pulling out right behind her." Seth pointed out that while the truck may well belong to their unsub, the timing did not fit because they knew Alicia made it to the Viking Arms Inn.

"It may have been surveilling her though," Bill mentioned. "Can we get a screen shot of the truck? If we put it on the news, it may spark some leads. Let's all take ten to finish our lunch, and then we'll regroup with what we have."

"Showing it on the news is not a bad idea," Jeff said, "I've seen that truck, I just can't place it."

"I've seen it, too," Steve said, "you might be on to something with this guy being local."

Chapter 36

Day Two – Tuesday – 12:30 PM

Petersburg, VA

Judy had been huddled in her office, reading over the case files and autopsy reports from Jane's new case in northern Michigan for a couple of hours when Isabelle brought her a cup of hot tea.

"Thanks, Isabelle. I have my notes in order; now I just have to assimilate it all so I can present a profile that makes sense because there are a lot of contradictions to everything we know about a serial killer."

Judy opened her word processing program, and began the task of transcribing her notes into report form. The inconsistencies in this killer's behavior were layered, which would undoubtedly make it harder for the team to identify and stop the person responsible. Usually when she had to work around her deep and foreboding intuition she would queue her classical music and get lost in Mozart's Concerto 40, but she needed her headphones for her notes, so that was not possible today.

Ever since she realized that Candace was reporting on another of Jane's cases, her thoughts kept circling the drain around the deep well of Tad Wilkins and his determination to ruin her niece's life. Jane's defiance against allowing his dark shadow to follow her around was clear at the press conference and made Judy believe that she could shake it as well. She'd taken back control of her mind-space once before and was determined to do it again, despite the fact that she couldn't shake the feeling that someone was watching her. Before she started the profiling process, Judy had hoped that the facts of the cases would clear her uneasy feelings, but the more traits she added to her report, the more dread she felt.

Judy agreed with Dr. Laura Tibbits that the victims from November and January were committed by the same perpetrator. It was the victimology that had Judy concerned for her niece's safety and what made her decide to call Bill to deliver her profile ahead of the typed, official version. If she was correct and Jane was in danger it was time to provide her team with the information she'd kept buried for so long.

Judy pulled Bill's card out of her drawer and dialed the personal cell number he'd written on the back.

"Hello, Bill. Is this a good time to talk?"

"Yes, it's actually a perfect time, the team is taking a coffee break. How's the profile coming?"

"That's why I called," Judy responded. "I want to talk through some concerns. Is Seth with you, by chance?"

Judy could hear the apprehension in his voice, but wanted to include Seth in the conversation.

"He's right here. I'll put you on speaker." Judy heard a door close and after some shuffling, Seth told her he was with them. "First of all, Dr. Laura has confirmed that the first two victims were killed by the same unsub as the other three, and I agree with your earlier assessment that we're looking for a torture sadist. The ME reports and photos show how much the level of brutality has increased with each kill, but the unsub's MO has changed."

"The information on the police reports for the first two was pretty sparse," Seth said, "so anything you can tell us will help a lot."

"They were both prostitutes," Judy told them, "and seemed to be chosen at random. They were whipped, but the attack seemed more frenzied. For example, the last three had two distinctive wound patterns inflicted with different areas of the bullwhip, but the first two women had fewer lacerations and they were all inflicted from close up." Judy took a sip of her tea and continued, "And whereas the knife wounds on the last three were almost expertly placed to achieve an almost instant death, the first two victims had much more trauma by the dagger at the base of their skulls. Cause of death was the same, a severed brain stem, it just took more tries to get to it, but Dr. Laura assures me that she can forensically prove they were all done by the same dagger."

"He definitely evolved in four months," Seth said, "almost like he gained a new focus, a new reason, and he obviously used the time to learn because his torture was intensified, and the actual kill was quicker."

"Clearly it's the torture that drives him," Bill said, "and the kill is just secondary to it, although the way he poses them at his disposal sites, and the fact that they've all been brunette, is also an important part of his ritual. What is your theory, Judy?"

"As you know, finding the stressor that triggered the serial to start killing is a key component of the profile and for identifying him. I think in this case, our unsub had two stressors: one that made him lash out in November and January, and then another one in April which almost makes him seem like a mission killer." Judy took a deep breath and consulted her notes, then went on, "This is where I need you to bear with me because it's entirely possible I'm being influenced by my instincts."

Judy went on to tell the men how she felt about Candace showing up everywhere Jane was, always taunting her with questions about Tad and his involvement, and how she practically accused her of getting information from him to help solve her cases.

"During the last case, Tally admitted that Tad wanted to ruin Jane's career by getting inside her head, but I happen to know that his plan for her is much worse, which I'll explain in a minute. For now, back to the stressors." Judy didn't have to continue because Seth finished the thought for her.

"Wilkins went into isolation at the end of October, and came out in April."

As if he'd just found a piece of the puzzle that fit, Bill added, "And since all the women were brunette, or had her hair dyed to be, the surrogate could be Jane. Is that what you're thinking, Judy?"

"Yes, I believe that whoever is doing the killing now is a Wilkins sympathizer, or is even in love with him. When he went into isolation he lost all the contacts he had to get correspondence in and out of the prison undetected, which made the killer lash out angrily, but when he got out in April, was probably able to start the correspondence up again."

"That makes a crazy kind of sense, Judy. You said you had more?" Bill asked.

As hard as it was, Judy told them about the journal she'd kept secret for years. "It is a literal manifesto of his plan to make Jane his killing partner. He even journaled his time frame and boasted how he was able to make her believe every single thing he told her. He was just months away from her final phase. He planned to isolate her in that house Tally lived in."

"Holy shit," Seth said. "Excuse the language. I understand you shielding Jane from it all these years, but why bring it to our attention now?"

Judy told them everything, including how she felt like she was being watched, but mostly because with Tad seemingly on the periphery of everything Jane did she realized that his determination to turn her into a killer had not waned.

"I think Jane is starting to recall some lost memories, which indicates she's ready to deal with them." Judy told them. "I was going to show her the book when she gets back, but I believe there is a sense of urgency for her team to know what they could be up against. She is not the malleable kid he left, so the battle for her soul is not a foregone conclusion, but it's her physical safety I'm worried about now."

Seth told Judy that Jane was one of the toughest women he'd ever come across, and he knew she also knew that. "Why the sense of urgency now?" he asked.

"Because the profile points to Jane being the surrogate. Who knows what he's communicated to his loyalists. If they're committing these murders for him, what's to say they won't chop the head off the proverbial snake? What really pushed me in this direction were Bible verses he had in his journal; like those at the crime scenes, they seemed almost meaningless. We all know that after a while, surrogates don't satisfy a killer and they go after the real thing."

Judy, like the two men, sat quietly and considered all they'd learned.

"Okay," Bill said, "I'll talk to Kate, and try to keep Jane in house, but you both know she won't take it well. For the good of the case, though, she needs to be made aware of the full profile, and the fact that she could be in danger." Seth and Judy both agreed, but then Judy added, "I want to talk to Wilkins, and before you argue against it, hear me out. I am probably the only one on the planet that he is intimidated by. He knows that I've seen through him since day one. He even journaled about how he avoided me before, and just after, my sister died. If anyone can get information from that monster, it's me. Can you arrange a visit for me?"

Another inconsistency Judy saw, but did not share because only one in ten serial killers were female, but the lack of any sexual component to the attacks, and the fact that it was almost as if the killer couldn't face the women, troubled her. The brutality of the torture did not indicate a female either, so Judy kept that theory to herself.

Chapter 39

Day Two – Tuesday – 1:00 PM

PENTWATER, MI

I feel exhausted because my day so far has been like a pair of bookends. My early morning started with the rush of placing Alicia so thoughtfully on display, but then crashed hard at the rage I felt from the press conference, only to soar again in the shower when I decided on a bold and brilliant finale. Junior has finished with the truck, and is now working at getting the summer vegetables planted, so I decided to make us a couple sandwiches and then go and lay down for a much deserved nap.

I cut Junior's sandwich into fours like he prefers and set a tropical punch juice box beside it, then sat down to enjoy my tuna and ice cold Coke. Only one bite into it, the side door that connects to the garage burst open and my enormous cousin with his lumbering gait bound through it and seemed to be stumbling as much with his words as he was with his feet.

Holding a plain white envelope in his hand, he stammered, "I, um, you have, um, I mean that man with the long black car brought you another letter."

I always seem to be caught off guard when the letters, hand delivered by a man I've never seen, arrive. When they do show up, I'm almost ashamed to admit how delighted I am. It's almost activating to be singled out by such a wonderful, albeit misunderstood, man. My fatigue forgotten, I took the envelope out of Junior's hands and headed to my room.

"I um, you, um, I mean, you forgot your sandwich." Junior said.

"You can have it," I said, and headed toward the shelf in my closet to retrieve the box that held my prized communications from Tad. I sat down on my bed, and as I always did when the letters came, became transfixed on the way he wrote my name on the front. I pictured him artfully crafting each letter with an old-fashioned quill pen and inkwell. Rationally I knew this would be impossible to manage in a prison cell, but visualizing it kept the anticipation of his words alive just a little longer.

With the paring knife I kept in the box, I carefully slit the top of the envelope open, and almost reverently took hold of the letter. Embracing the excitement of what was to come, I held on to the note for just a minute longer before I held it in front of my eyes. I sat silently and read through the letter a few times before I put it back into the envelope and took the box back to my closet.

Since Tad's letters started back up in April and I realized my true mission was for him, I'd felt almost a cerebral connection to him, as if I understood his desires without the need for his words. In a way, he is like my father was with nothing but love in his heart for his only child, yet told by society that his love is tainted, contaminated almost. My mother was jealous of how much love he gave me, but she understood a child's place and never got angry with him. I have scars on my back to prove that I endured, because honoring the father supersedes all else.

After reading Tad's letter, I need to alter the plan I'd made earlier, and it will add the extra bang I've been craving. I know he blames the break from his daughter on the sinful woman spreading the vicious words about him, so she needs to pay first. I'm certain that was his message in this letter, and when I'm finished there will be no doubt in his mind about everything I've done for him.

Chapter 40

Day Two – Tuesday – 2:00 PM

MSP Command Post, Hart, MI

As the group reassembled, Jane cleaned up the conference room, then washed the coffee pot out and started a fresh pot. The brew wasn't the greatest, but at least the deep scrub she'd given it made the consistency more like coffee than motor oil. She headed back to her seat when she noticed Bill, followed by Seth and Kate, walking toward the room. Her heartbeat sped up with anticipation when she noticed the heavy, dark brown folder in Bill's hand because she knew he'd received the profile from her Aunt Judy.

Bill waited until everyone got settled around the table before he began telling them about the profile, that Judy agreed with them about two people being involved, and that they were in fact killing surrogates.

"This is a hard one to profile," Seth told them, "because until we have them locked up in a box, we won't truly understand their personal dynamic, if we will even be able to understand it then."

Jane was taking notes on what they were being told, but did notice an eyeroll from Steve, the skeptic of their group. Kate must've noticed it, too, because when she added her insight she seemed to be looking right at him.

"The profile is not an exact science, but it is an invaluable investigative aid that helps narrow down personality and behavioral characteristics of the offender based on an analysis of the crimes committed. There is an extensive database of serial killer data that helps us build the profile, but as we said earlier, rarely do serial killers work with a partner so it's harder to pinpoint the dynamic."

The hard line of Steve's posture seemed to relax, so Jane tuned in to hear what Bill had to add.

"Finding and studying the first victim is key because it helps us determine the stressor, or what triggered this person to kill. In this case, we believe there were two stressors because between the second prostitute in January, and Jolene in April, the signature and the ritual changed." Jane looked around the table and knew that everyone, especially Patrick, seemed to be engrossed in what they were learning.

Seth went on to explain to the group that it was a forensic certainty that all five women were murdered by the same person, with the same weapon. When her bosses and her mentor all went quiet, and exchanged looks between them, Jane sensed something was coming, and her instincts told her she wasn't going to like it.

An almost imperceptible nod from Bill was the indication that he wanted Kate to proceed. "We've determined that it's quite likely the killer, or killers, are devotees of Tad Wilkins." Jane's mind felt dizzy, almost like her core had been knocked off its axis, but she also knew that even if she did possess the wherewithal to speak, her mind was incapable of forming a rational question.

Once the group's chattering disbelief quieted, Seth explained how they'd arrived at that information. "The first kills we believe were triggered by, and with, extreme rage, but in April, when Wilkins was able to smuggle correspondence back out of the prison, the kills became more planned, and mission oriented. The way the bodies are displayed, we believe the killings are almost a tribute, and it's probable that the dominate killer on this team is in love with him."

Jane was beginning to come out of her haze, and in spite of herself, was able to see the validity of the profile, but suddenly she felt as if a flash bulb went off in her head, and she knew where this was heading.

"I'm this killer's surrogate, aren't I?" she asked them. Finally on board and back on the job, Jane started to talk about Candace, wondering out loud if she could be privy to anything helpful, but they were interrupted by a commotion out in the hallway.

"My wife was just murdered, and you want to waste *my* time, bringing me here for more questions? Shouldn't you all be out looking for the guy who did it? This is preposterous, I demand to see your boss. I'll have your badge before the end of the day, Skippy!"

Jane was sure she caught Seth smiling when he asked Patrick to greet their guest as the MSP commander and to tell him that he'd be along shortly.

"This guy is anger activated," he told them, "He's also an entitled narcissist who doesn't even realize the information we get with his ramblings. I'd like to let him stew for a bit, plus I want to find out if Abbey has learned anything of interest on him."

As a way to keep her mind off her father and what kind of twisted game he could be playing this time, Jane set up the computer to bring their analyst into the room with them. After one shrill beep, Abbey's face appeared on the screen.

"Abbey Louise, font of all knowledge and here to serve," she said in her unique, lilting voice.

"Hello, Abbey," Seth said, "just checking in to see if you'd been able to find anything on Dr. Singleton or Dan Harris."

"Neither one of them have anything questionable in their past. Mr. Harris is the epitome of everything that is good, like the kind of guy you'd want your daughter to bring home. A lifelong resident of Hart, he won a seat on the city council by a landslide last year, so no red flags. Dr. Singleton's record is clean as well. He moved to Hart to open his own clinic right after college. He was born and raised in Dewitt, Michigan, and attended Veterinary college at Michigan State."

When Abbey paused for a sip from her thermal, unicorn cup, Jeff told the group that he'd spoken at length to Dan Harris, and that he was shattered when he heard about Alicia.

"They dated all through high school, but when he left for college, she took up with Edward and was swept off her feet with promises of a pampered life." Jeff went on to explain that they'd reconnected recently, and developed a relationship.

"She was very unhappy in her marriage, and was considering a divorce. She was going to talk to her mom about moving back home until she got back on her feet. It seems like a great motive if Singleton knew about it, but Dan wasn't sure if she'd told him yet. I did do my due diligence, though, and he was at work when both of the women were killed. He's clean."

Abbey set down her cup and turned back to the group, "I did find a credit card that Singleton kept in the name of his LLC, and there were regular charges to Ludington Beach House, which is a swanky hotel on the water in Ludington."

"Thanks, Abbey. Any luck on your search of veterinarians, or cases of juvenile offenders, or victims?"

"Not yet, sir, but I will continue my search, and widen the parameters. Abbey Louise, out for now, but standing ready."

"Seth and I will interview Singleton," Bill said. "Kate and Jane, I think Riley Ann just walked in. I'd like you two to talk to her. All of you can start working with Fuller once he gets here, which should be anytime."

The conversation with Riley only took a few minutes. She explained that she did use ketamine, and other drugs, on some of the animals she was called out to help.

"I've had to use it to calm a horse so I could get embedded nails out of their shoes, or on large cattle, even horses, if they're having a hard time during birthing." She also explained that she kept it locked in her barn, and while her cousin lived with her, he did not have access to it because she wore the key around her neck at all times.

After she left, Kate and Jane were satisfied with Riley's explanation and felt comfortable that no one else would be able to get their hands on her medications. Jane was quiet as they headed back to their conference room because she needed the time to process the fact that the demon she used to call Dad could be involved in another of her cases.

"How the hell is he doing this again," She asked Kate, "and why?"

"Well, the why of it is easy," Kate answered, "because he cannot handle the fact that you're no longer in his control. He's trying to make you lose your mind, and spot on this team. As far as the how, hopefully once we catch this new maniac, we'll get some of those answers."

Kate put her hands on Jane's shoulders, looked directly into her eyes, and emphatically said, "Pay attention to my words, rookie, I am proud of you. Instead of curling up in a ball and giving in to what had to be an impending panic attack when the bombshell about Tad was dropped, you got out of your head, and into the job. You made the surrogate connection, immediately came up with the idea to talk to Candace, and still had your head in the game when Abbey and the gang gave their reports."

Jane was quiet for a minute and digested Kate's words, then realized that she felt surprisingly calm about what she'd learned from the profile. She felt like she'd turned a corner and that her head space was finally free of Tad Wilkins.

"Thank you, Kate. I actually feel a little empowered with everything, like my goal of catching this new creep has gained momentum because when we do, maybe that reprobate doing life in Ionia will realize that my soul, and my life, is my own. I am going to call Judy, though, because I have a feeling she's keeping something back, and in order to do my job, I need it all."

Jane decided she'd had enough coffee for a while, and when she was getting a bottle of water out of the mini fridge she heard Kate's phone ting with an incoming text message, and then noticed Kate coming full steam ahead toward her.

"What's up, Kate?"

"Come on, we have to interrupt Bill and Seth. That was Laura. The results from the sweat sample are back. It did not match the victim, and there was no hit on the DNA in CODIS, but the sweat is from a female. Our killer is a woman."

Chapter 41

Day Two – 3:00 PM

The Dunes Express Inns & Suites – Hart, MI

I'm so happy I decided to meet with the FBI in person, and what a bonus it was that it was Jane I spoke with. They are clueless and the satisfaction I got from seeing and talking to her in person overshadowed, for a moment, my hatred for her. She is smugger and more self-absorbed than she appeared to be when she took center stage at the press conference, and that makes me even more excited to get her in my shack. She's going to be a guest for much longer than the others, though, and as much as I love to inflict physical pain, hers will be combined with a mental torture so extreme that she'll beg for the whip. I have to bide my time, though, and proceed with the timeline I set for myself after getting Tad's last letter. I'll have my opportunity, and the best part about getting Jane is that she'll know how badly she screwed up when she realizes she had me in her grasp, but let me go.

My first order of business, though, is Candace. I'd like to get her started today while I can still taste the bile I felt when I read how much of an influence she's had on Jane's decision to forsake her own father. That's the worst sin imaginable, and I need to make it right. Although I didn't need divine intervention to prove the righteousness of my mission, seeing Candace pull into The Dunes Inn where Jane's team is staying was a pretty clear indicator of my perfect opportunity. I pulled into the lot after her, and pumped my fist when it became clear she was going around to the back of the building where there are no cameras. My grab and go plan will have to be adjusted because

I don't have Junior's muscle, but I planned for it and have everything I need in my tacklebox right beside me.

A higher power presented itself again with an impending storm. The sky which turned daylight into dark will not only offer more cover, but the gloominess of it will add to Candace's sense of doom once she realizes what is happening. Generally speaking, a woman is not perceived as a threat, so when I approached with my dagger concealed up my sleeve and a capped syringe in my pocket, she offered a pleasant greeting which was the green light I needed to get close enough to strike.

With a bright smile on my face, and a deftness gained from practice, I slid the dagger out from my sleeve, and held it against her side with enough force to slice through her silk blouse. "We're going to walk to my truck, and if you make any attempt to draw attention to us or to run, I will gut you like a fish. Do you understand?"

Obviously petrified, Candace could only offer a nod to indicate that she'd comply. She has reported enough on my work that she began to hyperventilate when she saw the truck because she recognized it as a precursor to her own end. I opened the tailgate and ordered her to step up into the bed. She tried to twist her way out of my hold, but stopped resisting when my dagger pierced her skin and blood dripped down her side. With her pencil skirt and stiletto heels, her step up was less than graceful, but she made it.

At this point in an abduction, the fight or flight instinct usually kicks in, but I was ready for that and plunged the syringe into her neck before she had a chance. The effects were almost immediate and as her body went limp, I wrapped my arms around her and lowered her into the toolbox. Before I locked it I grabbed her purse, got into my cab, and was back on the road less than a minute after I'd arrived.

I always enjoy my trips to the hut, and this time was no exception. Knowing I didn't have much time to spend with her on this trip dimmed my light a little, but I took heart knowing that once I had her inside the dirt hovel she would be mine, and would serve at my pleasure, on my timeline. Her purse and phone were still in my truck, but as I removed the padlock from the door, decided I'd made the right decision to dump them, together with her clothes, in the swamp when I left. I had a cow to euthanize up in Mackinaw, but wanted to get a few whips in before I left.

After I propped open the door to my happy place, I turned on my tactical flashlight, set it down beside my bucket and stepped into the white paper overalls that would absorb any blood splatter. Once the stage was set, I almost skipped back to the truck to retrieve my newest captive. Before I opened the lid, I cut four pieces of duct tape for her wrists because while she'd still be groggy, I didn't want to risk her interrupting my ritual by grabbing at my hands, or face.

"I'm going to do you a favor and relieve you of those stupid slut shoes before we head into the lovely cabin that will be your new home." In her futile attempt to break free, Candace thrashed and jerked, but my firm grip on her forearms was enough to get her to her feet. Still under the effect of the drugs, her body was as limp and wobbly as a Raggedy Ann doll, but I was able to prod her along and into the shack.

Before I shoved her into the chair, I sliced off her skirt, her blouse, and her skimpy underclothes.

"Why do you wear such trampy underwear? For all the good they do you, you may as well go commando and wear nothing. Take a look around because once I leave, you'll be plunged into a darkness so stark you won't even be able to see your hands. Now sit your ass backwards in that chair over there and I'll let you know what you're in for."

Candace complied, like they all do the first time they're sent to the chair. "You seem very accustomed to straddling things," and after the sonic boom of the whip cracking in the air, I continued, "but I have a feeling you'll soon think differently about that mount you love so much."

The cunning and manipulative reporter before me managed to squawk, "Why are you doing this to me?"

That question pissed me off, so I cracked my whip again, this time making contact with the upper part of her back, and answered, "Because it's what you deserve for perpetuating a hatred between Jane and her loving father, Tad."

She tried to answer, but I took a few steps back, wound the whip above my head, and delivered a thrash with more force than the first one, to the lower part of her back. Her blood curdling screams were so loud they reverberated in my ears, and made my heart feel as if it was going to pump right out of my chest. Knowing I had to leave before I got carried away like I did with Alicia, I added a few more lashes before stepping out of my overalls and gathering her clothing.

Her screams had settled into just a steady whimper, and as I slid the bolt lock and opened the door, I pointed out that even though the walls, the floor, and even the ceiling were made of dirt, the place was airtight and escape would be impossible.

"If the color green had a smell, I'd imagine it would be that moldy, earthy odor you're smelling now. Kind of makes your eyes water, doesn't it? The mice and the rats love the damp darkness of my cabin, though, but don't get too comfortable because even though you can't see them, those rodents can see you as clear as day."

When I got back into my truck I smiled because I knew I'd made Tad proud, and with my plans for Janey, I knew I would also give him some richly deserved happiness before I was finished. As I made my way down the trail that would take me to the road, I heard a ting coming from Candace's purse, so I stopped the truck to find her phone. Once I read the text message I smiled again and decided I needed to call my customer in Mackinaw to tell him I'd be a little late, but first I needed to respond to the text.

Chapter 42

Day Two – 3:00 PM

MSP Command Center - Hart, MI

Jane and Kate watched through the glass of the interview room and waited until they could catch the eye of Bill or Seth. Barging into an ongoing interview is never ideal because the interaction between the agents and the suspect has a natural ebb and flow to it that is sometimes impossible to resume once that tempo has been interrupted. Jane's attention was drawn to the entrance when she heard the desk sergeant directing a man with a cropped beard that matched his jet-black hair to their command center. Her thoughts went to Nick because, like him, this man with the well-worn leather jacket, checked the tall, dark, and handsome box. In her quick mental assessment, Jane added a box for mysteriously sexy because his Wrangler Jeans and form fitting black tee-shirt lent him an almost weather-beaten vibe, whereas Nick, who was equally as sexy to Jane, wore button up shirts tucked neatly into his LL Bean Chinos and presented a more polished impression. Jane thought she had put her recent thoughts about Nick aside to work the case, so she was a little surprised, and also a bit ashamed, when she realized she'd probably been staring at the man who'd come to share his findings on three murders for just a little too long.

She gathered her head space, then nudged Kate and said, "I think that's Detective Fuller from Traverse City, I'll go talk with him."

Kate looked over at him, then laughed, and said, "Of course you will."

Jane stepped into the room as the handsome detective was stacking files up on one of the tables.

"Detective Fuller, I assume? I'm special agent Jane Newell. The other agents are interviewing a person of interest and will be along in just a few minutes. Do you want some coffee, or a bottle of water?"

"No thanks, I'm fine, and please call me Mike." The detective offered his hand for a shake, and said, "It's very nice to meet you, Jane." She wasn't sure if the flutter she felt was just a hungry stomach, or if it was caused from her impression that he seemed to look so deeply into her eyes she wanted to block her innermost thoughts for fear he'd read them. His lingering handshake felt both soft and firm, but jarred her mind back to the investigation.

"We've just had a new development," she said, and then explained how they had determined that their killer was a female. "Here comes the rest of the team now, so I'm sure our briefing will start with that."

"Mike, thanks for coming," Bill told him, and then introduced himself and the rest of the team. "I assume Jane filled you in that we're looking for a female, and in the interest of time we're going to get right to that before we study your files." The detective nodded, and Seth stood up.

"Real quick I'll tell you that Singleton had nothing to do with his wife's death. He's a bit of an ass, but does not fit the profile of even being our unsub's partner. He did admit to an affair, but when I pushed him about his wife wanting a divorce, he was surprised. His delightful narcissism wouldn't allow him to even consider that someone would not want to be with him. So, while I did enjoy having him in the cage and knocking him off his own pedestal, it's a dead end."

The smirk on Kate's face showed Jane that her mentor knew her team's individual nuances very well. "Science does not lie or make mistakes," she said, "so we are certain that the actual killing is done by a female. That in itself is uncommon, but add the especially sadistic nature of her torture, and it's a statistical rarity." Jane noticed that the local officers, and even her team, seemed to be as intrigued by Kate's stats as she was.

"The FBI didn't even recognize female serial killers until the 1990's, and only about 8% of all serial killers are female. There is research that states they're under-studied, and definitely underestimated, in their brutality and numbers. They've been referred to as the monsters no one sees coming, although that can also be said for most serial killers because they don't stand out in a crowd. They're our neighbors, school bus drivers, and clergy, and in most cases, the people who knew them are shocked once they're caught."

Kate sat down, and Seth continued, "We're pushed for time, but it's important to understand this because it helps us build a profile and stop them. Another study shows that 25 out of 30 female serial killers had something bad happen to them when they were young. For instance, Judy Buenoano, AKA The Black Widow, was executed in Florida in March of 1998 for killing her son, her husband, and attempting to kill her boyfriend. Her mother died when she was a young girl, so she and her brother were bounced around until their father remarried. When they went back to live with them she was not only abused by both, but was starved and forced to work as a slave. Her first stint in the prison system was when she was 14 for attacking her father, stepmother, and two stepbrothers."

It was hard for Jane to separate her compassionate feelings for the child from the disgust she felt at the murderer, but she also knew it was an occupational hazard, and without those human feelings she wouldn't be able to do her job.

"The significance of that stat plays a very big role in our search for this killer," Bill added. "We'll call Abbey in a few minutes with some new search parameters, but in the meantime Jane will fill us in on what we do know."

Always ready in case she was called upon was something Jane learned in school. Some of the kids would shrink down in their desks, but she was always prepared and those early lessons helped tremendously on the job because most often she had to think quickly on her feet.

Jane passed her phone around the table and told them, "We believe it's possible that this truck was surveilling Alicia before she went missing, and note the metal toolbox in the bed. That pattern could turn out to be a match to the indentations Alicia got post-mortem." Jane gave the group a minute to study the picture before she went on to tell them that they were having several copies printed out for the LEOs to take around town because, as they'd determined earlier on, local enforcement officers would receive a better reception than an unknown FBI agent.

"We think it's probable that someone can identify this truck, and the owner, so it could be the biggest lead we've had. We're also going to give it to the news outlets that are stalking us all."

Seth thanked Jane for the information and then told them he was going to get Abbey on the line with some broader parameters. Jane turned to Kate as she was setting up the laptop for the Skype call, and asked if it would be alright if she went into another office and called her Aunt Judy.

"Since I am more than likely this maniac's surrogate, I'd like to hear more about her profile. I'll also inform her that our killer is a woman." Kate agreed, and as Abbey, in what she called her cave of magic appeared on the screen, Jane grabbed her bag and left the room.

When the laptop dinged, the group watched as Abbey came into focus, and with the song-like cadence only she could deliver, said to Kate, "Good afternoon, and how is the team's pint-sized powerhouse today?"

The whole team smiled at the expressive greeting, and Kate answered, "Hey, Abbey, we really need you to work your magic on something."

"You came to the right place, magic is what I do. Give me the details."

Seth stepped up closer to the computer and explained that he needed her to expand the parameters she'd used in her earlier search. "We know our unsub is female, and from Maureen's recall, she's working with a very large man, which tracks accurate considering where and how she's displaying them. We also believe she's committing these murders as some sick type of homage to Tad Wilkins, and that Jane is more than likely the woman she's killing with each of the victims."

While the group watched Abbey's chin drop, Kate noticed a facial tic on Mike Fuller that almost looked like concern for her partner, but she didn't have a lot of time to analyze it.

"Since Wilkins is who she identifies with," Kate told her, "and all the victims have been around Jane's age, we're assuming the killer is close to, or a little younger than, Wilkins. So expand your search starting around 30 years ago, and take it all the way up to Mackinaw City. We can go across the bridge if nothing comes up."

Abbey seemed to take notes with a steely purpose, her feather topped pen being the only symbol of her unique personality. She offered no expressive dialect to interrupt their instruction, most likely in deference to the seriousness of her task, but Kate had to admit to herself that she missed how their analyst seemed to add levity to grim situations.

Seth took Kate's spot in front of the computer, and added, "You'll want to check into school reports to Child Protective Services because they're mandated by law to report any signs of abuse or neglect, and there is no question about it, this woman was abused as a child, most likely by her mother. Also include a younger male sibling or other relative. In partnerships such as this, with the female clearly being dominate, the partner is usually a subservient family member."

Jane walked back into the room as Kate finished up with Abbey, "You should check police reports and hospital records as well."

Jane stepped in front of the computer screen and greeted Abbey, and then said, "It is more than likely a dead end, because Wilkins has plausible deniability in everything underhanded he's involved in, but maybe check on his activity at the prison. Find out what we know about his new lawyer, Jacob Ray."

"Just don't get caught up in the Tad Wilkins hamster wheel again," Seth told her, "because even though we know what he's doing, I don't want to waste a lot of time trying to prove it. We have to catch a sadistic murderer before she takes her next victim."

Abbey finally spoke, "He has threatened our colt, a part of our family, so believe you me, I will go honey badger on this. Give me some time. If there's nothing else, Abbey Louise, out."

Jane took a seat across the table from Kate and Patrick, and wondered what was said while she was gone that had the entire group looking at her like they were holding something back. She caught the nods between Bill and Kate, and knew she was about to hear what they had discussed, and instinct told her she wasn't going to like it.

All eyes were on Jane as Kate made direct eye contact, and said, "In light of the fact that you are clearly the fill-in for this reprobate, we all believe that until we have her in our sights, or our custody, you should work from here where it's safer. With Patrick, the three of us are going to go over the files Mike brought down." And quickly, before she got the argument she knew she'd get, added, "and your Aunt Judy feels the same about your safety."

Predictably Jane was angry, but knew she had to choose her words very carefully and deliver her rebuttal in a clear and succinct tone, especially since she'd already made arrangements to leave the building – alone.

"I just got off the phone with Judy, and it's her opinion, and mine, that my father does not want me dead. He wants me alive so he can screw with my mind because he still thinks he can turn me into a killing partner. She told me about a journal she found after he was arrested, and just how much planning he put into manipulating and grooming me to partner up with him."

She took a drink from her water bottle and noticed that Kate's focus was on Mike because, like her, she was probably a little suspicious of his unusual focus on Jane. Before they could argue, Jane continued, "She has spent years profiling that man and believes that his psychopathy and narcissism will not allow him to admit defeat. He still thinks he's dealing with the 15-year-old girl that was so easy to gaslight, but he's not. I will never be a victim to that evil boor again."

The table got quiet, and Jane could tell that they were considering her words, which was what she'd hoped they would do when she told them that Judy, a respected criminologist, was in agreement. She was also faced with the dilemma of either coming clean about her text message to - and her response from - Candace, or if she should just disappear for the meet-up she'd scheduled. Level headedness prevailed when she remembered how much trouble her rogue actions got her into on the last case, so she presented her final argument.

"I think we need to get the picture of the truck on the airwaves as soon as possible, and Candace, as much as a pain in the butt as she's been, would be a good one to give an exclusive to." Jane held up her hand to signal to Kate that she wasn't finished, and went on.

"She must have sources or is a really good search engine because she seems to have information on Wilkins that no one else has uncovered. I know it seems like an obsession to her, but we may be able to use that to our benefit. I'd like to give her the photo, and whatever part of the profile you approve – exclusively - for a few hours, and in return she tells us what she knows or has learned about the possibility of his involvement in these cases."

When Bill and Seth huddled close, Jane was hopeful that the outcome would be in her favor, and she could tell that Kate felt the idea had merit as well.

"We need to do something to shake this case loose," Seth said, "and we do respect Judy's opinions, so in light of all that we'll sign on for your idea."

Jane was a little worried about telling them the rest but by this point was already all in, so she told them that she'd already texted Candace, and they'd arranged to meet at Stella's Coffee House "in a little less than 30 minutes, actually."

Kate abruptly stood up from the table, and said, "What the hell, rookie? What would you have done if we'd disagreed with your plan?"

Jane looked toward her boss and knew that he and Seth were also waiting for an answer, so she spoke the truth, "When I told you I learned my lesson on the last case, I meant it. If you had told me no, I would not have kept the appointment. How about if I go and meet with her, then come back and work on the Traverse City files with you? I'll stay put at that point if it'll make you all feel better."

Jane assumed her plan was a go, so she put a photo of the truck into her bag, checked her phone, pulled back her blazer enough to feel the firearm at her side, and prepared to leave the building.

Kate caught up to her on the way out of the room, and said, "Head on a swivel, rookie, like you always do. Be careful and bring my partner back in one piece. Text me when you're finished because I'll be watching the clock."

Jane smiled at Kate and as she walked out of the room, turned her head back, and said, "Don't worry, I got this. Remember, I'm a bad ass, right?"

Chapter 43

Day Two – 3:30 PM

Stella's Coffee House - Hart, MI

Jane jumped into the Taurus, thankful the coffee house was only a couple of minutes away because she wanted to get a cup of coffee before her meeting. When she went past it on Main Street, she noticed an outside counter that would be a perfect place to enjoy the liquid goodness of the arabica bean and to meet with the reporter. Another thing that attracted her attention was that the last place Kristin was seen alive, Kristi's Pour House, was separated only by a narrow alley from where she was going. There was an available parking spot in front of Stella's, but Jane decided to park behind the building and walk up. Crime Scene had processed the area for evidence of the abduction, but she wanted to walk it and maybe get a feel for something they may have missed.

The sunrise today was a test of one's faith because although it was late afternoon, the sun hadn't been seen. After seeing nothing new in the parking lot, Jane made her way through the shadowy darkness of the alley. She hoped the rain would hold off long enough for her to enjoy her coffee outside of the quaint little shop. After the mortifying shame and shock of her father's arrest in her driveway, Jane fled the small village of Holly where she'd grown up with a mental pain so deep she never wanted to return. The welcoming threshold into Stella's made Jane miss the small town vibe for the first time in 13 years. From the bell announcing her arrival, to the spicy-sweet, very enticing smell of cinnamon, Jane felt comfortable in her own skin for the first time in many years. While the clerk filled her coffee order, she decided that she'd come back in and buy some hot, fresh cinnamon rolls to take back as a treat to everyone at the post.

Jane set her cup of coffee on the bar out front of the shop, took her brown messenger back off her shoulder, and settled in to enjoy the minutes until Candace showed up. When her aunt told her about the book she'd kept hidden all these years, her first emotion was anger, but by the end of her phone conversation, Jane understood why Judy had handled it the way she did. It was clear enough now that everything Judy did, every decision she made in those early days, was because she wanted Jane to feel safe, secure, and loved. They also decided to read and then discuss the entire book once Jane got back. She felt relieved that her aunt would be by her side to help her with what would no doubt be an onslaught of emotion.

Finally cooled enough to drink, Jane took a sip of her coffee, but had to set it down quickly because her hands began to tremble as her eyes seemed to be watching a reel that she recognized as another flashback.

She and Judy were still in Michigan waiting for her petition to the court for a formal adoption and change of last name to be approved. Tad's case was still headline news and seemed to monopolize all of the television programming. To shield Jane from it all, Judy provided her with movies on DVD to watch when she had to be out because she didn't want an unknown, paid expert telling Jane how she should feel about the way her life had been upended. The mental picture that was playing out in real time seemed to cast a spell on Jane as she became absorbed in the memory.

In the early weeks of her devastating upheaval, believing what was said about her father was paralyzing, and since she still didn't trust her aunt she went through a period of denial. One day, when Judy had to leave her alone in the condo she'd rented, Jane turned on the news. When she saw that they were reporting live from the 50th District Court in Pontiac, awaiting the arrival of The Mother Killer, from Holly, Michigan, she picked up the phone and called for a cab. She needed to tell her father that she loved him and that she didn't believe the horrible things they were saying about him. Somehow, she had to get close enough to hold him and to tell him that she'd be waiting for him once the mistake was cleared up.

Traffic near the courthouse was at a gridlock, and not wanting to wait another minute, Jane told the driver to drop her off and wait because she wouldn't be long. She knew she stood a better chance of getting to her father on foot, so she took off at a sprint, ducking and dodging her way around all the people who hoped to get a look at a serial killer. It would be weeks before Jane figured out why the onsite reporters and gawkers alike seemed to step out of the way to clear a path: they recognized her and wanted a front row seat at what they were sure would be breaking news shown on news stations across the nation.

When she got as close as she could get, Jane looked around for the first time since she'd jumped out of the cab. The walkway into the courthouse was roped off on both sides and served as a neutral zone between the reporters and spectators, and the prisoner. However, the buffer did little to drown out the murmurs of the people spreading the word that the killer's daughter was there. Jane tried to ignore them, but when the intensity of the buzz picked up, she looked over her shoulder to see a van rolling to a stop at the curb. The white-panel van didn't need to be marked for Jane to realize she was looking at a fortified prisoner transport van, and that inside of it was her dad. The sound of her own heartbeat muffled the excited shouts around her when she saw her dad being led out of the van. The bullet proof vest he wore over the orange jumpsuit, and the shackles on his hands and his shuffling feet. did little to dissuade her from breaking free and ducking underneath the rope. In her mind's eye, all she saw were his crystal blue eyes and the way his teeth seemed to sparkle when he smiled, because once she saw that she knew everything would be fine.

Totally oblivious to the fact that she met with no resistance from the guards, Jane ran toward her father with her arms wide open in anticipation of the hug she knew would convey all of her love and support. She knew that once he felt her unconditional love, that his smile and his words would reassure her that he could not have committed the vile acts he was accused of, and that he'd be back home with her real soon.

Jane snapped herself out of her own flashback and took a drink of her now cold coffee. When she felt the moisture of the tears on her cheeks, though, she knew she had to go back and finish what her mind had started, regardless of how it ended.

Jane's feet came to a grinding halt when she came face to face with him because the smile she now saw in her mind was not of the loving father she so desperately needed to see. Instead, she relived the day of his arrest and how his liquid blue eyes turned to icy dark holes, and his smile, described by so many as warm and endearing, became a malicious jeer. On that day she realized that the mask of hatred she saw was not of the father she'd always known, but of a man very capable of the atrocities he was accused of, and collapsed into a heap of hysterics in her driveway. The stark reminder felt like a gut punch to Jane because in that brief moment of clarity, she knew she'd been an orphan since the day her mother died. Overcome with rage, Jane stepped up to her father, and ignoring the penetrating throb in her arms, pounded with all her might on his Kevlar protected chest.

Jane didn't know how long she'd been trapped in that dreadful flashback, but absent any type of visual, she could clearly hear the gravelly voice of her father when he told her, "Don't worry, Janey, our paths will cross again, and remember – you will always be mine." She remembered another voice from that day too, and somewhere in the far recesses of her memory it sounded familiar, but try as she might, she could not bring it to the forefront.

The next thing she did remember of that day was her Aunt Judy gently lifting her up off the sidewalk and escorting her away. Jane shook her head in an attempt to shake loose the images, so she'd be focused on her meeting with Candace. Her peripheral vision sensed someone coming from the left, so she turned her head toward the alley to see the woman they'd just interviewed, Riley, step toward her. Jane smiled and said hello, but then the whispery hair at the nape of her neck stood on end so she instinctively unsnapped the strap on her holstered side arm.

Chapter 44

Day Two – 3:30 PM

Stella's Coffee House - Hart, MI

I smiled when I went through the parking lot behind Kristi's Pour House, in part because I remembered the night I got Kristen. She was special to me because she was the first one I nabbed from my own stomping grounds and the days I spent with her were more than fulfilling, but I was also happy to see Jane's unoccupied Taurus in the lot because it meant I had the element of surprise on my side. Stealth and silence were critical components for the remainder of my operation, so I crept forward at barely an idling speed. When I felt I was at the perfect spot for concealment, yet close enough to reach quickly with an unwilling female, I stepped silently out of the truck. I'd even had the forethought a few miles back to stop and open the tailgate so both my hands would be free to coax Jane up into the bed where I'd be able to completely subdue her. Rationally, I knew I was making myself vulnerable to exposure, but the added risk was exactly the kind of thrill I longed for.

I was glad that I'd changed out of my work boots and into my rubber soled sneakers because my slow, deliberate footfalls through the alley were as silent as the prayer of thanks I sent to the universe for intercepting the text Jane sent to Candace. It seemed like the stars had aligned themselves perfectly today, and I smiled at the gifts of opportunity they presented to me. As I neared the end of the buildings, I flattened myself against the side of Stella's, and looked up and down Main Street, thankful again for the dark and gloomy day that kept most people at home. When I peeked around the corner of the building, I saw that Jane's hands were gripping a venti cup, but her eyes were fixed straight ahead. Clearly, she was absorbed in her own mind, and for the minute that I watched her, I never even saw her blink.

When she quickly, and seemingly without any outside stimulation turned toward me, I was momentarily taken aback, but I relaxed and praised the divine intervention of us meeting earlier when she smiled in recognition and said hello. I returned the smile and continued toward her, discreetly confirming that my dagger and syringe were in place and easily accessible. My run of good fortune continued because had I not been looking into her eyes at the precise moment I was, I would have missed how a screen of suspicion seemed to shroud the bright recognition they'd held just seconds before. It was the nonchalant movement of her blazer that made me forget the niceties, and leap to her side.

In the split second it took for me to pin her arms to her side, I realized that Janey may not go down as easily as the others had, and that my first move had to be getting the gun out of her holster.

"Thank you so much for unsnapping the retaining strap on your holster. It makes it much easier for me to relieve you of your firearm."

Jane was able to free her arms enough to ram her elbow into Riley's solar plexus. As close as she was, the blunt force trauma to her abdomen was enough to accomplish what the strike was designed to do. The breathing difficulty Riley encountered was caused by the momentary paralysis of her diaphragm, and gave Jane the opening she needed to strike again. This time she went for a blow to her mouth, but Riley recovered more quickly than Jane anticipated, so her jab missed its mark and only clipped her on the cheek. Jane realized immediately that instead of neutralizing her attacker, she'd stirred up a hornet's nest because Riley had her arm around her neck and a dagger to her throat in the blink of an eye.

"Okay, we're both going to smile and walk off this porch," Riley sneered, "and you should keep in mind that so far you only have a small slice in your neck, but this dagger is deadly sharp. If you even inhale too deeply, I will slice through your carotid artery, and you'll be dead before you exhale. Now move."

Jane moved along with Riley for no other reason than to give herself time to think through her situation. She was a sharpshooter, had been trained in martial arts, self-defense, and had been sharpening her street fighting skills using Krav Maga for half a year. One of the first lessons she learned from her dojo was how to quickly assess a threat so she'd be able to determine which technique best suited her situation. Her self-reproach for allowing her mind to get so lost in a flashback that a bad actor was able to get the jump on her would have to wait. Jane's immediate focus had to be on escape, and if there was any upside to having been stripped of her weapon, it was that Riley never retrieved it from where it fell when she fought back.

Chapter 45

Day Two – 3:30 PM

IONIA STATE PENITENTIARY

I received a lot of information from Jacob today and have to say that since he became my delegate, he's managed to gather a lot of intel. Although a decades old threat forced him into compliance, he's managed to operate quite well in his role of covert, off-the-books orders. Sometimes I wonder if he's playing out a childhood fantasy where he's James Bond and my clandestine assignments are matters of life and death. In a way he's right; they are a matter of life and death – but not to all of mankind, just to him. In any case, he's serving his purpose right now, and if he convinces me this is no game to him, I may keep him on and even give him a raise. I'll keep my eyes and the ears of my other assets on him, though, and if he diverts from the path I've put him on, then he'll be taken care of like so many of the other loose ends in my world. He was, however, able to answer the question I've asked myself since I moved in here, which was whether or not Judy Newell found the journal I'd kept on Janey's metamorphosis.

I still get pissed when I think of how close I was to completing the remodeling process of her brain. If I had known that I would lose my freedom in three weeks, I would've started the final stages of Janey's re-development sooner than at the end of her 8th grade year, when I painfully told her a brilliantly crafted lie about overhearing how her friends planned on ditching her because they thought she was weird. Her raw devastation was the perfect prologue to my own brand of empathy, which was to convince her that

I was the only person in the world she could count on and trust. I was confident that after a few more weeks of her moping, and my emotional support, that she would be more than happy to move to the beautiful home I'd bought in the country and finish her schooling at home. However, the truth, as it is inked in the book Judy has, is that my education plan for Janey would have nothing to do with textbooks or the internet, and everything to do with isolation and reprogramming. Her education at that point would be solely in my hands. I found it comically ironic that when my daughter finally saw the beautiful home, on the day she arrested the poser trying to copy my kills, she didn't know it was intended to be her luxury isolation ward.

The fact that Judy had found and saved the book gave me a lot to consider. My contact in Virginia reported to Jacob that he heard her on the phone telling someone about it. He couldn't hear the person on the other end of the conversation, but didn't think it was Jane because she spoke of her in the third person. What pleases me is that Judy mentioned Jane in the context of her being the surrogate to their killer, which will cause her unit chief to pull her out of the field. Admittedly, I haven't been on the outside raising my daughter for the last 13 years, but I've kept damn good track of her and know that her heart rules her head, which is going to make it nearly impossible for her to comply with her orders. When she realizes that she alone is responsible for the deaths of innocent women, and that she's powerless to help them find what she considers to be justice, she will feel defeated. Although it is now many years after I'd originally planned for this to happen, I will be able to swoop back in and make her believe that there is only one person on the planet that she can count on and trust, and that's me. After that, it'll only be a matter of time before she'll want to please her loving father.

I could, if I chose to do so, end Judy Newell and retrieve my book, but I'm going to hold off on that for now because it will be a good tool to use against her when my communication with Janey starts back up. After all, if Judy kept this a secret from her, what else might she be hiding?

Jacob's report on Sanchez was just as informative because he found out through his sister, Lacey, that he was going to be released soon. I chuckled when my lawyer replayed his conversation with Lacey because, apparently, she doesn't want to give up the financial windfall she gained with our alliance and actually thought she could roll with the big guys because she made veiled threats of blackmail. That will never happen, but I do respect her moxie. I instructed Jacob to be outside the prison walls when Sanchez walked out. After all, I am a man of my word, and I did promise the little weasel a job; I just never told him what that job would be. I found myself whistling on my way to dinner because forces were starting to sway my way.

Chapter 46

Day Two – 3:30

Alley in Hart, MI

She snickered when she left the station and Kate reminded her to keep her head on a swivel, because that movement was as ingrained in Jane as walking, but the memory of that day outside the courthouse hit her with such intensity, it was all encompassing. The hope of a passerby thwarting Riley's abduction was grim because the low hanging, dark clouds, had kept tourists and townspeople alike hunkered indoors and off Main Street. Jane also knew that Riley was a well-known part of the community, so no one would sense anything off when they saw her walking arm and arm with a friend, toward her truck. When they rounded the corner of the building into the alley, and Jane saw the toolbox in the truck with the open tailgate, she knew what Riley's plan was, but it also provided her with a plan of her own. The basic self-defense strategy of $\underline{S}$olar Plexus, $\underline{I}$nstep, $\underline{N}$ose, and $\underline{G}$roin, or S.I.N.G., the acronym she used to remember it by, wasn't fancy, but as her dojo had taught her, effectiveness didn't need to be fancy and overthinking a threatening situation could mean the difference between victory and failure.

Riley was as tall as Jane and had the strength, and calloused hands of a woman used to physical labor, which rang true because she knew that Riley took care of large farm animals and operated a small farm. Jane still wasn't putting up much of a struggle, but as they neared the back of the truck, Riley tightened her grip.

"You're going to step up into the bed of the truck," she whispered in her ear, "or else this trickle of blood dripping down your neck will gush like Niagara Falls. Do you understand that Janey?"

Jane did a good job of hiding the rage she felt at hearing the name that only Tad had ever used behind a frightened nod of compliance at the order. Lulled into a false sense of victory, Riley loosened her hold enough for Jane to raise her right leg up, and onto the tailgate. Instead, once her knee was chest level, Jane changed her leg's direction and slammed the heel of her boot into Riley's instep. Knowing she had only micro-seconds before her attacker recovered, Jane used the most powerful part of the hand and thrust the heel of her palm into the bottom of her nose. The palm strike, called shotei, was one of the first Karate moves she'd mastered, and when blood gushed like a faucet from Riley's nose, Jane took advantage of her momentum and rammed her knee into Riley's groin. She used Riley's disorientation to reach for the dagger that had been thrown to the ground after the surprise ambush, but in that nanosecond, Riley recovered enough to spit the pooling blood out of her mouth and utter, "You're going to pay for that bitch."

Since the dagger on the concrete was no real threat, Jane let it lie and assumed a fighting stance for another face off with Riley, who had so far proven herself to be a worthy opponent. Jane was a half a second too late, though, to notice the syringe in Riley's hand coming toward her neck.

Chapter 47

Day Two – 4:30 PM

MSP Command Center – Hart, MI

Kate and Patrick sat in the conference room with Mike from Traverse City and studied the files he had brought with him. The two earliest victims still hadn't been identified, and given their high risk lifestyle of prostitution, there wasn't much available to review. Fuller said he did make contact with a couple of motels known for their hourly rates, but of course no one knew anything about the women, so in the interest of time, their focus was primarily on the third victim, Jolene. They way she was posed at a popular tourist attraction, with a painted Bible verse and dark brown hair, added weight to Judy's profile that their killer found her mission and her muse between the two prostitutes and the young camper.

Most of the officers from the post used that lull to catch up on the reports that had fallen by the wayside since their towns became home to a serial killer. Bill and Seth were passing out the photos of the truck with the instruction to hold off on showing them around until Jane returned.

"She is going to offer the reporter, Candace, an hour lead time on running the photo in exchange for inside information on what Tad Wilkins may be up to," Seth told them. He then looked at the clock and asked Kate, "Have you heard from her yet?"

Her facial expressions, and balled up fists did little to hide the concern that had been festering for a while.

"No, and I've texted her a couple of times. Her meeting was

scheduled for 3:30, so she probably just doesn't want to be interrupted." Patrick took her hands into his from across the table and told her that he'd sent a patrol car past Stella's about 15 minutes after she left, and that Jane was standing at a little bar out front of the shop with a cup of coffee in her hands.

"I'm sure she's fine," he told the group, but I'll send another car around in a few minutes if we don't hear from her."

"Sounds like a solid plan," Bill told them just as the laptop at the head of the table blurted the notification that a Skype call was coming in, so he added, "That will be Abbey. Let's get the rest of the group in here and see what she's found for us."

Seth stepped up and accepted the call while the rest of the group assembled around the laptop. "Hello Abbey, please tell us you found something," Seth practically pleaded.

"Good afternoon, defenders of justice. I'm sorry to say that I did not find any crimes that matched. I even expanded the search to include all the states adjacent to Michigan, and couldn't match up even one of our parameters."

The wind the group seemed to have had in their sails was quickly knocked out of them as their optimism turned to discouragement with Abbey's report. "How many years did you go back, and did you check with schools and Child Protective Services?" Seth asked her.

"I went back over 30 years, and the reports for CPS and the schools are still running. That's an awful lot of records to filter through – but being the magician I am, I went another route, and think I may have someone."

Only half angry, Seth told her, "You could have led with that. What did you find?"

Before Abbey got started, Kate gave a nod to Patrick who was able to interpret that she wanted him to send another officer by the coffee house. Not hearing a word from Jane was totally out of character, and the bad vibes she was feeling seemed to turn the coffee she'd been drinking into straight-up stomach acid.

"Sorry boss, I have a linear thinking brain, but I'm bringing it home now. I figured that these small towns wouldn't have the resources to keep databases up to date, so I checked hospital records, and if I found anything hinky, would backtrack for a police report. Luckily the towns are small, and for the most part the emergency rooms deal with car accidents and heart attacks so there weren't too many, but I did find one that I think looks pretty good."

Abbey paused, and when the task force seemed to have their notebooks ready, she continued: "Turns out, a 15-year-old girl from Custer was brought to the ER at Spectrum Health Hospital in Ludington with scars and recent wounds on her back. She'd also been raped- repeatedly."

When Abbey paused to take a deep breath in preparation for the next part, Seth said, "That was a good find. Who brought her to the hospital?"

"Not her parents," Abbey responded. "The next part is why I continue to earn my guru distinction. I worked backwards from there and found reports from the school social worker, and yes, a police report, but the magic of it all was finding her name because everything was sealed due to her age, and don't ask, but yes, I did a thing. This poor young girl's name is Tia Anderson, and one of her classmates accidentally walked in on her when she was changing for gym, saw the rawness on her back, and ran screaming from the rest room directly to the school's nurse."

"Well, that was good thinking on that kid's part," Kate said. "How did they manage to convince her to show the nurse her wounds?"

"They followed protocol and called Child Protection Services immediately. Apparently, it wasn't the first time the school had reported suspicions of neglect, but anyway, due to the severity of the accusation, a social worker went immediately to the school, and brought the police with her. They called her parents, and transported her to the hospital within the hour."

Abbey was not only a wizard with computer searches, but she was also great at reading a room, so she paused long enough for the men and women in the room to digest and note the information.

"If you think all of that is bad, hang on because the creepy meter is about to go off the charts. Tia was still in the exam room when her parents showed up, and according to the officer's notes, the only emotion they showed was anger that an exam was being conducted without their approval. They had a younger boy with them that they identified as their "retarded" nephew, their words, not the cop's or mine, and his name was Billy Flynn, Jr. His parents died in a meth lab explosion, and they had custody of him."

Kate sensed that Patrick wanted to find and beat the parents senseless, just like her brothers would want, but he kept his demeanor calm and simply asked, "Where are they now, do you know?"

"You're getting ahead of me there, Big Irish, and I'll get to that, but the nurses came out of the exam room, and pulled the police and the social worker aside. Apparently, Tia was combative during the exam and claimed that her momma whipped her with a belt because her daddy showed his love for her more than he did for his wife, and that it went against the Bible and God to forsake her father, so she let him love her even if it meant getting beat by her momma."

"She certainly fits our profile," Kate said. "Whatever happened to her?"

"There are literally hundreds of pages of reports, which I'll send you, but the bottom line is that Tia and Billy were taken away and placed in a foster home in Custer. They went together because Tia refused to go anywhere without her cousin because he was special and needed her to look after him."

Kate took the pause to look up as Patrick took a phone call, and although she couldn't hear him, she did read in his body language that it was not a social call.

"In answer to the handsome Irishman's question, I'm still searching for them. The last thing I found was that when Tia aged out of the system, she left and took Billy with her. It seems as if she had the perfect combination of poverty and brains because she was awarded several college scholarships, but once they left the foster home, they went completely off the grid and I've found not even a bread crumb on either one of them – *yet*."

Kate stood up and walked toward Patrick when she heard Abbey tell them that both of the parents were now dead, but that she'd flip every rock, and would tunnel with the vigor of a ground hog until she found Tia and Billy's new den.

Patrick disconnected the call he was on, and got the team's attention.

"That was the patrol officer I sent to Stella's. Jane's brown bag, phone, and gun were underneath the bar outside of the shop, but she was nowhere to be seen. No one in the shop, or the stores nearby saw her leave. They've secured the scene and will stay on site until we arrive."

"I just tried to call Candace, too, and her phone goes directly to voicemail," Kate said. "I'm officially concerned something has happened. Jane would not have left without those things, at least not willingly."

"Kate's right," Bill said. "We need to get a crime scene unit to meet us there. Jeff, you can call them from the car, and tell the guys to hit the town with the picture of that truck. We need to roll. Now."

Kate's stomach felt like it was trying to digest a bowling ball when she told them she was going to stay back and call Judy.

"She needs to hear about this from me," she said, "not on the news that I'm sure will be camped out in front of Stella's before we even get there." Patrick wrapped Kate in a hug and whispered in her ear that they'd find her friend.

Chapter 48

Day Two – 4:30

Shack at the edge of The Manistee National Forest – Custer, MI

As she started to awaken, Jane knew something was off because of the grogginess she felt behind her eyes, but her sense of smell was at full alert. A sour odor so strong that it seemed as if she was inside an enclosed and rotting pasture stung her nostrils. As she forced the stench to the back of her throat, she shook her head and opened her eyes, then gasped when she realized she was in total darkness. It was when she tried to sit up that she realized her hands were bound at the wrists and her memory of the altercation with Riley in the alley broke through her hazy brain.

When her heart began to pound so hard she could feel it in her ears, and her breaths became rapid and shallow, she knew she was on the cusp of a panic attack and forced herself to focus on her training. Her first action needed to be a self-assessment for injury. Her neck had stopped bleeding and although her spare weapons were taken when her boots were removed, she was otherwise fully clothed and had full range of motion with her legs. Her bound wrists weren't the only challenge to her freedom, it was the complete and total lack of light. Jane knew if she wanted to avoid an ambush she would have to get herself into a cognitive zone so she'd sense, even if she couldn't see, Riley coming at her. She also knew she'd been drugged and needed to work off the lingering effects in order to make a plan; what's more, she needed to execute it when the opportunity presented itself.

Feeling revived after her mental assessment, Jane got on her feet to stretch before beginning a series of exercise reps she could do in place. Getting her heart rate up was crucial to eliminating the drugs from her system as quickly as possible, but her light stretching winded her much quicker than she expected. Jane worked to regulate her breathing and cautioned herself to adjust her movements accordingly because while her whereabouts were still unknown, the atmosphere felt almost airless.

When she realized the ground she stood on was like hardened soot, she started to connect the dots between the dirt on the feet and underneath the nails of the victims to where she was, and she remembered the bites on Kristen's ankles. She found it absurdly humorous that she could face an armed foe without hesitation, but when it came to a rodent, she would shamelessly clench her fists around her tucked in thumbs, curl her toes, and seek refuge on the tallest piece of furniture she could find. However, since her captivity made that impossible, she decided to just keep her feet in motion to detract them and started jogging in place. Keeping her balance without the use of her arms required focus, so she mentally channeled the voice that always grounded her. "Get your damn legs higher, rookie," she heard Kate say. "Don't wimp out on me now." Jane found her rhythm and was getting her knees up a little higher with each step when she heard what she thought was crying coming from in front of her.

Jane stopped running and called out, "Hello, is someone else in here?" Although she was stunned, she knew she wasn't alone when she heard what she envisioned was the quivering upper lip of someone trying to gain control of her gasping sobs.

"Yes," a woman answered weakly, and then a little stronger asked, "Is that you, Jane?"

Shocked at the unseen woman's familiarity, yet recognizing the voice, Jane replied. "Yes, I'm Jane, but who are you, and how do you know who I am?"

"It's me, Candace. Riley was bragging about the FBI bitch she'd bagged when she dropped you off, and told me it was you."

Why the hell Candace would be here was only one of the questions that assaulted her mind. Following a thought long enough to process it seemed impossible because it only stayed with her for about as long as a breaking wave stays on shore before it's whisked away. She felt like a cat chasing after the red dot on a laser pointer because every time she got close to pouncing on a thought, it darted away from her.

Being inundated with fragmented thoughts had become somewhat of a regularity for Jane since she'd started retrieving lost memories, and normally she was able to work through them with physical exertion. Her ability to do that in her present situation was somewhat limited, but she did manage some jumping squats. After a few reps of propelling her body up and off the dirt floor, when her thighs felt like they were on fire and sweat was pooling under her neck, she heard Kate's voice telling her to keep her back straight, and her knees bent in a full squat, because she was going to need her core strength to free both herself *and* Candace. And while she still hadn't formulated a plan, Kate's inner voice corralled her rambling thoughts into perspective because it was no longer just about saving herself. Another innocent woman's life depended on her training, so her mindset had to be on how to get the two of them to safety. For now, the flashback of her mental breakdown outside the courthouse so many years ago, and the questions she had when Candace's voice triggered another memory, would have to wait.

Jane carefully rotated herself to face where she thought Candace's voice was coming from, and called out, "Candace, do you think you can come closer by following my voice?"

Her sobs had abated some, but her stuttered voice when she answered was a clear indication that the woman was still frantic. Jane needed information from Candace so she could plan their escape, but knew she first had to ease the woman's distress, so in a quiet, almost monotone voice, she said, "Stretch your arms in front of you, and shuffle along with your feet. I can hear you, and my arms are out, too."

Jane stretched her arms forward, and with her feet separated to a shoulder width apart, and her knees bent slightly, her center of gravity was focused forward to offer her the best balance. Jane could hear Candace's feet shuffling across the dirt toward her, but since she couldn't see her she needed to be ready to absorb the impact of a hysterical woman so they wouldn't end up entangled on the dirt floor. When the short and shallow breaths brushed across her nose, Jane knew she was there, so she closed her hands around what turned out to be Candace's outstretched hands, and held tight to keep her upright when her knees buckled.

Keeping her voice as quiet as she could, with a confidence she wasn't sure she felt, Jane told her that she was safe and that she'd get her out of there. Finally, Candace's sobs tapered off to a quiet whimper, so Jane asked her to tell her everything she could remember about Riley's routine.

Candace's recall of the abduction didn't provide her with any information that would help them escape, so she pushed her to tell her what happened when she got to the shack.

"She dragged me from the truck because I was still too weak from whatever she drugged me with to walk, and then tossed me inside like I was a sack of potatoes." Jane tried to envision the surroundings when Candace replayed how Riley left the door open for light, then put white paper overalls over her own clothes, and with a knife from a construction bucket, cut all her clothes off.

Jane knew then that her own abduction was not planned and more than likely interrupted another part of Riley's day because she'd left her clothed, almost like she was in a rush to leave. Before Jane could appreciate how big of an error Riley made with her hasty move, Candace continued.

"She dragged me by the hair to a rickety wood chair, and made me straddle it. After she taped my hands between the back slats, she stepped away and seemed to go into a trance. I knew when the whip was coming because it was so loud, my ears would ring. She told me I was being punished because it was my fault that you'd cut your father out of your life, and that it's a sin to forsake your father. Why did she say that?"

Jane sat quietly for a minute to process the fact that Tad was behind another string of murders, and that she was his muse. Always there when she needed it, she heard Kate's voice tell her to put it away because he's a crazy bastard, and this was not the time to dwell on it. She squeezed Candace's hands a little to convey her compassion during the silence because she had more questions that needed to be answered in order to formulate a plan, and while it wouldn't be an easy win, Jane had been beating the odds her whole life.

She pushed her thoughts about Tad into her lockable brain space and said, "Riley is clearly as crazy as Tad Wilkins, so please don't let her get into your head. I'm going to need your focus and your help to get us out of here. Now, did Riley say when she'd be back?"

Candace was quiet for a minute, and then replied, "You've been here about a half hour or so, and she said she'd be back after she put a cow down in Mackinaw City, which is a couple of hours away."

"Okay, that's good," Jane replied. "Now I need you to focus and tell me everything you can remember about the layout of this place." Jane knew Candace was at the brink of losing it again because she not only heard her panting, but she also felt the hot breaths on her face. She knew firsthand that reliving a memory best left forgotten could be terrifying, but this information was critical if there was any hope for their escape so she had to push her out of her comfort level.

"You are a journalist, Candace, and it's ingrained in your brain to take in details. You know that, so block out everything except my voice, close your eyes, and watch it as it unfolded. You said you were huddled in the corner when she dumped me, how far away from the door was that?"

Knowing they had some time before Riley returned, Jane relaxed a little to allow Candace time to take her mind trip and absorb the details.

"I knew she was back," Candace said, "because I heard the truck door close, and that's when I backed away from the chair. I only took a few steps before I backed into the wall, so I squatted down, brought my knees up to my chest and held on to them."

"That's great Candace. Now I know we'll have a warning when she gets here. What happened next?"

Candace went on with the rest of the exchange like a reporter would as they prepared notes for their story, and it didn't seem like she missed a single detail. Jane felt like she could see the small rectangle room they were in by her description of how many steps Riley took before she dropped her, and knowing which way the door swung open helped Jane begin to plan for their escape. One of the single most important things Jane learned was that she'd have a few minutes of light when Candace first came in.

"You did a phenomenal job, and those details are going to make escaping from her possible. Hold on to the waistband of my pants, and let's see how many steps we are away from the door."

When Jane was younger, she and her friends used to go roller skating and one of their favorite games on the rink was when three or more of them would form a chain and dance their way around. Being the strongest, and most athletic, Jane was always the leader, and that's what she was thinking about when Candace clamped herself on and they made their way through the dark. After three and a half steps she touched the wall, and with the reporter still attached, she ran her hands along it. She didn't have to go far before she felt the distinct difference between the dirt wall and the wooden door, and when she ran her hand up and down the edge and did not feel any hinges, she knew she was on the correct side. She didn't want Candace to get panicky again, so she explained what she was doing as she flattened her chest against the wall with her arms spread away from the door, and inched her way like a worm until she hit the side wall.

Satisfied that they had the room they needed to lay in wait for Riley, she told Candace they would stay there, and that she was going to work out as much as she could, given their limited space.

"I have a plan, but you're going to have to do exactly what I tell you to do with no questions and no hesitation." Jane felt Candace's whole body move and knew she was nodding that she understood.

Chapter 49

Day Two – 5:00 PM

MSP Command Post

After her conversation with Judy, Kate sat alone in the conference room and focused her entire psyche on Jane. She always said that Kate was in her head, and right now, she hoped Jane was hearing her battle cry. There was no question that her bad ass trainee could handle most any physical altercation that came her way, and in reassuring Judy of that, it also helped her move to a calmer mental state. Jane needed everyone on the team to be at their best. There was no way that Kate would be anything less than exactly what Jane needed her to be.

Kate's thousand-yard stare was broken when Patrick's sister, Maureen, sat beside her with a turkey sandwich and a bottle of water.

"You need to eat something," she said, "and do it now because as you know, things often change suddenly and you may not have the time later."

Kate noticed when she took the sandwich that Maureen was dressed in her full uniform, with a side arm holstered at her hip. When she saw the questioning look on Kate's face, Maureen explained that she'd requested, and had been temporarily dispatched to the Hart PD, as additional support, should it become needed.

"I am fully trained, and capable in the field," she told Kate. "I needed to do this for my brother, my town, and my new friends from the FBI."

Kate smiled at the woman she felt like she had known her whole life, and asked if she'd heard anything from the team at Stella's. Maureen explained that they were just finishing up and would be back in a few minutes.

"Roy was out at the park with me when Laura called him. Your boss wanted her to come and help process the scene, so he left right away to meet her. I got on the phone with the chief after he left, then changed into my uniform and came right here."

Kate unwrapped her sandwich, but before she had a chance to bite into it, the conference room came to life with a flurry of commotion. It seemed to Kate as if their group had grown exponentially, and while she'd always heard how agents and police officers alike come together when one of their own is in danger, this was the first time she'd ever experienced it. She swallowed the lump in her throat at the show of solidarity when Patrick and Roy sat with her and Maureen as the rest of the group filed in.

"First off," Seth said from the front of the room, "we're lucky to have an extra body to help us find Jane and bring this case home. Maureen has had the same training as all of you, and the State of Michigan, and the Hart Police department have been gracious enough to dispatch her to our team for as long as we need her. Of course, Mike Fuller is still with us and will stay to see it through."

The room turned toward her as Seth sat down, and Bill stood up.

"Most of you were at the scene," he said, "so I'm not going take a lot of time. Jane's bag and gun, underneath an outside counter at the coffee shop, were visible from the street. Behind the counter were drops of blood that led around the corner of the building and into the alley."

Kate tried to mask the worried look on her face and keyed herself into Bill as he finished his updates.

"In the alley, there was a much bigger splatter of blood, almost like a fight ensued in that spot. Dr. Laura took samples of both areas to the lab. She can do a type match in only moments, and while it isn't strong enough evidence to take to court, it will tell her if it was Jane's blood or not."

The group's concentration was broken when the ME entered their conference room. Kate was literally perched on the end of her chair waiting for the report.

"The smaller drops we found that led us to the bigger pool of blood were Jane's, but the big area in the alley were not. Also worth mentioning is that Jane, and whomever else bled in that alley, did not lose enough to incapacitate them for long, and certainly not enough to kill them."

Although Kate had already regained the mental capacity she needed to work the case, learning that the biggest spot of blood was not her partner's cleared away any lingering doubt or fear because she knew Jane was alive, that she was smart and capable, and most of all, she knew her team was the best at what they did and that they'd bring her in.

Kate felt a surge of pride when she said, "Sounds like our girl kicked some ass of her own," and then asked if they'd found Jane's phone because her meeting was set up with Candace. "I'm interested in knowing if Candace is an unsub, or if she too had been duped."

Patrick held up an evidence bag with Jane's phone in it, and told her they were sending it to the crime lab, but on a quick visual inspection, they did see the text communication between the women. "It looks legit," he said, "but we'll have someone verify that it came from Candace's phone because hers doesn't even ring, just goes straight to voice mail as if it isn't even turned on."

Seth opened up the laptop on the table and told them that he was going to bring Abbey in and they would have her check for any cell tower pings on Candace's number. After the intermittent, high frequency screech of the call connecting, the group watched as Abbey came into focus.

Without any of the flowery dialect she usually greeted them with, Abbey simply said, "I'm so glad you're back. Tell me you found Jane."

"Not yet, Abbey, and we really need your help," Seth responded, and then asked if she'd had any luck finding Tia Anderson or her cousin, Billy.

"By design of the whole name-change process, those who make that change are typically hard, sometimes impossible to trace. In a name change, just like when someone goes into witness protection, everything about the person is erased. Even life histories can be re-written, but one thing that can never be changed is a date of birth, so it takes ingenuity and brilliance to ferret someone out."

"Can we move this along, Abbey?" Seth asked.

"Of course, sorry sir. It's important for you to know that normal channels are ineffective for this type of search, but as you all know, I am anything but a typical analyst and find normal channels boring, so I took a different path and dug through newspaper archives. Ladies and gentlemen, I think I've found your unsub, Tia Anderson."

Not even a rustle of paper could be heard in the room as Abbey explained how, with the exception of a government initiated name change, the subject is required by law to make an announcement in the newspapers of their intent to change, and that they had to reveal their birth names because they had to give creditors a chance to make a claim.

"So, my magic with a virtual shovel went to work. Everyone should tighten the laces on their boots because you've all heard of this lady. Tia Anderson changed her name to Riley Ann Wilson, and under that name got legal guardianship of her mentally challenged cousin, Billy Flynn, Jr."

The room suddenly began to buzz like an active beehive because as Seth told them all at the beginning, their killer was in fact one of them. The locals all knew her, but they never would have suspected she could be the sadistic cold blooded killer they were after.

After a brief word with Patrick, Maureen stood up from her chair and announced, "I did not connect it at the time, but now that I know who it is, the man on the beach fit all of Junior's mannerisms. I've known them both for a few years because they provide our eggs and vegetables during the summer, and deliver hay in the late fall." Maureen went on to tell them that Riley called her cousin Junior, and while he always helped with the deliveries, it was clear he was special. "He's a very sweet giant," she said, "and I find it hard to believe he'd have any part in what she's doing."

Steve and a couple of the other local police officers simultaneously shot up from their chairs, as if they'd all had an epiphany at the same time. Steve's voice was the loudest, when he said, "I knew I'd seen that damn truck someplace. Riley is in and out of town all the time with it."

When Bill stood up, the room seemed to come to order as he barked instructions to Jeff to get a warrant for Riley's house, any outbuildings on her property, and for her truck.

"Everyone needs their vests, and between all of you, the best two shooters should carry a long gun to flank the rear. The rest will go in with their side arms." Bill walked over to a long table and conferred with Jeff over an open map, and then told them all that they should get their gear and head out immediately. "We're going to stage at the Up North Farm Market off Monroe Road, about six miles from our target. It closes at 6:00, but Jeff is talking to them now about us going in. As soon as the warrant comes through, we'll roll from there. Radio silence from here on out; the media is going to hear about it soon enough."

The task force was comprised mostly of smaller town law enforcement agencies, but their effective coordination of preparing for the operation was impressive. Like a well-oiled machine, each person took care of his or her business without further instruction or prompting, and the room seemed to bustle with the activity of it all. While Maureen said goodbye to Roy and Laura, Kate noticed that Mike from Traverse City was also prepping his gear, and while she was grateful for the extra set of trained hands, there was still something about him that unsettled her a little. He'd been like a quiet overseer since he arrived, observing, but not really engaging. Although she couldn't really say that she had an uneasy feeling about his intentions, he just seemed a little off. As she stood up to leave, she noticed Bill coming her way and could tell he was on a mission.

"You're staying back this time, Kate," and before she could get the words of dissent out of her mouth, he continued, "I need you to meet Judy at the airport in Grand Rapids, and then go with her to the prison. She thinks it's possible that Wilkins knows something and she's the best qualified to find it. The problem is that he can refuse to see her, but he can't refuse to see law enforcement when it's about an ongoing case – and that person is you."

Kate couldn't argue that logic, and a part of her was happy to have the chance to meet the monster who'd caused so much heartache to her friend, so when Bill told her that their bureau jet already had Judy enroute and to grab the Taurus they'd brought back from Stella's and hit the road, she just nodded her head at him.

Chapter 50

Day two – 5:30 PM

I-96 – Gerald Ford Int Airport to Ionia State Penitentiary

Kate used the time on the trip to the airport to mentally process how quickly things in her life had changed in just four days. Her normal day often involved cross country flights, crime scene and medical examiner visits, new command centers at various police stations, and finally, a hotel bed, and she was used to that pace. What she really wanted to do on this road trip was to get comfortable with the personal growth and development she'd undergone. Her hope when she shared her story of assault was to forgive herself for the bad choices that precipitated the attack, but also to forgive herself for her lack of action after the fact. She recognized that she had feelings for Patrick, but also knew that in order to pursue any kind of meaningful relationship, she had to get her own mind in a good place. For many years she wore her deception like a second skin, and was thankful she was finally able to clear it away.

When Kate pulled into the cellphone lot to wait for Judy's plane, her happy thoughts of moving forward with Patrick jumped back to why she was here. In her 10 years of recovery, Jane being abducted had been the biggest test of her sobriety to date. While she waited in the lot, she called her sponsor who reminded her that her best friend and trainee had superior capabilities both mentally and physically, which helped, but when she bluntly pointed out that Jane needed a sober, clear-headed partner, it rang a bell for her, and she got her mind straight. Kate heard the buzz of a text message, so she left the lot and pulled up to the gate to collect Judy for their 40-minute ride to the prison.

Judy tossed her bag into the back seat of the Taurus, and when she buckled herself into the front seat, told Kate that she'd gotten an update from Bill and reviewed it on the plane.

"I'm sure they'll send us an update once they're finished at Riley's," Judy said, "and I also know I don't have to tell you to put it all away for now. Jane needs you, and, most important, we cannot allow Wilkins an emotional upper hand."

Kate asked for a little more context, so Judy explained that for this interview, their goal was to learn if he knew anything about Jane's abduction. If he sensed their unease, however, he'd treat their visit as a game.

"Psychopaths use silence as a weapon," she told her, "and there is no way to predict their behavior, but like fire, they need oxygen to burn. Quite honestly, I don't expect to get much more than a read on his reactions. There are no strategies to get a psychopath to confess because they'll always come up with a different angle, one they feel is quite believable, but you can't have a logical discussion with someone who makes up facts or data that only he knows about. However, I'm fairly certain I'll be able to read his body language and will at least know if he's holding something back."

The car's GPS interrupted their conversation with verbal notification that they were one mile from the exit to the prison. Though Kate was the reason they were not denied access to the prisoner, she knew Judy would be the primary, so she questioned her a little more about what their tactic was going to be. As they turned into the secured lot Judy explained that it was crucial to make Wilkins believe he was still the smartest person in the room, and while he'd be resistant to punishment, he would be highly motivated by reward.

"And he will see getting information on his daughter and causing me distress as a reward."

As Kate locked her weapon in the console vault of the car she explained to Judy that she would follow her lead, but hoped they weren't here for too long.

"I really want, no, I *need* to get back and join in the search for Jane. Riley is clearly unraveling. We need to find Jane before it's too late."

Chapter 51

Day Two – 6:00 PM

Ionia State Penitentiary

The warden informed me this afternoon that an FBI agent named Kate Jenkins was coming to talk to me, and that while I could have my attorney present, I could not refuse the visit because it was concerning an ongoing case. I was careful to appear contemplative before I told him that I did not need my attorney for the meeting because I really had nothing to offer them about anything. After he left and I thought about it, I became excited.

Meeting Janey's partner Kate was not as thrilling as it would be if it were my daughter, but it was damn close. I had no doubt that I could control the narrative with her, and that she would have no idea she was being played. She was just another female who thinks she's able to compete in the male dominated world of brawny men, whose biggest goal in life was to outdo all the other testosterone-fueled, self-proclaimed seekers of justice.

Needing a lawyer present for this meeting was a joke, and a waste of Jacob's time. He has important work to handle for me, and playing the misunderstood father who just wants to reunite with his daughter will be like child's play for me against this woman. I do not need a lawyer for that because I am a master chameleon, and having others see me as I want them to see me is well within my realm of expertise. Miss Kate does not stand a chance against my wiles, and I look forward to the meeting.

Chapter 52

Day Two – 6:00 PM

Residence of Riley Ann Wilson – Pentwater, MI

All of the police and Bureau cars formed a circle in the dirt parking area of their arranged staging area and waited in the center of it for instructions on how they would proceed once the warrant came through. With a rolled up piece of paper under his arm, Bill speed-walked through the group and asked them all to gather at a nearby picnic table because Abbey had gotten him a satellite printout of Riley's property, and he wanted to plan their approach.

As he unfurled the photo, he showed them how the only ingress onto the property was from the driveway, and that while there was almost two acres, the back was all vegetable garden, bordered by a six-foot privacy fence with no gate.

"The house is the first building we'll come to. Adjacent to that is a pole barn with the chicken coop behind that. We'll go in a caravan, without sirens." He went on to tell them that Jeff, along with Patrick and Maureen, would knock on the door and present the warrant. "They're local, so it may be met with less aggression than if we go in first, but Seth and I will be right behind them."

"We don't really expect to find Jane at this location," Seth added, "because it doesn't fit the profile, but our hope is that we'll find some evidence and will be able to take them both into custody and get them to tell us where she is. We sent an unmarked by the house and they reported there was no truck in the driveway, although it could be in the pole barn."

"George, take one of the staties and head for the barn," Bill ordered. "Steve and Mike, go around the side of the house to the door off the garage. I want the two sharpshooters to stay outside with the crime scene unit just in case they try to run." The group took turns studying the printout when Maureen raised her voice above the din.

"Please be mindful of Junior. He is a very large, and I assume very strong man, but he's of a simple mind and is going to be scared. He may or may not have an idea of what Riley has been doing, but please be vigilant that he doesn't become collateral damage."

As they acknowledged her concern, Jeff announced that the texted warrant had just come through, so the officers headed quickly toward their cars, seemingly on a mission and ready for the attacks on the women from their towns to be over. Seth took the lead in their SUV, thankful that he and Bill were out front because in his rearview mirror, all he could see was the cloud of dust their truck kicked up from the gravel road. He was impressed with the efficiency of the locals, both in their preparation and their organized, swift departure. He was sure that each and every one of them felt personally responsible for the town and what they felt were their people.

"So far I'm impressed with the locals," Seth told Bill. "I just hope they keep their cool and don't lose their composure and make a mistake in there."

"It is why I put the smaller jurisdictions with the larger, more experienced units," Bill told him. "I know how it feels, and as a matter of fact, I have to keep talking myself down off the ledge because it's one of mine in danger." Seth nodded his understanding as they started down the long, tree lined driveway toward the house. All the other vehicles pulled in behind them, and once they were out of their cars Bill raised his arm, signaling they were ready to proceed.

The three locals stepped onto the porch as planned. With a closed fist, Patrick banged on the door and announced who they were and of their intentions to search the premises. When he stepped closer he put his ear up to the door, but instead of hearing approaching, or even fleeing footsteps, he heard what he thought was a television blaring, so he pounded harder, and shouted more loudly.

"Riley Ann Wilson, and Billy Flynn, Jr, I am from the Michigan State Police, and we have a lawful order to enter the home and search the residence."

With that obvious show of force, the two agents joined the local officers on the porch and waited for a response. When none came, Jeff got on his radio and asked Steve what, if anything, he saw from the side door.

"The male suspect is lying on the couch," he responded. "No visual on Riley. We heard the pounding and the orders back here. A Bugs Bunny cartoon is blaring on the TV, and it looks like he's asleep. This door is not locked. Please advise how to proceed."

Bill looked at Seth and Patrick, then said, "It is a no-knock order, so we're going to breach. Maureen, I want you to approach the sleeping man because he knows you, and we need to avoid having him freak out when he wakes up to an army of cops marching through his house. We four will scatter and clear the other rooms. It doesn't appear that Riley is here, but we have to check before we turn it over to the crime scene techs."

Jeff keyed his mic and counted down from five, so they could enter from the front and the side at the same time. Maureen turned the handle on the front door, relieved it was unlocked, and headed toward the couch. A Bugs Bunny cartoon was in fact blaring from the television, so as the group fanned out to their designated areas, Maureen turned the volume down, and approached the man she'd always known as Junior. The sudden drop in volume is what woke the sleeping giant, and as he sat up and tried to tame his disheveled hair with his fingers, he became visibly startled when he saw Maureen.

Not sensing any threat of aggression, Maureen quietly greeted the man-child. "Hi, Junior, do you know who I am?"

"I um, you're um, I mean, you are the nice lady from the State Park. Where is my big cousin? I want my hot chocolate."

Maureen sat on top of the coffee table in front of him, and tried to drown out the loud shouts of the group as they announced each room as being clear.

"I can get you some hot chocolate, but we're looking for your cousin. Do you know where she is, Junior?"

Maureen rested her hand on her gun, and rose when Junior stood up from the couch, but instead of approaching her, he took a seat at the kitchen counter and said, "I um, will you, um, can I have tiny marshmallows in my cup?"

Maureen busied herself looking in the cabinets for the Swiss Miss and tiny marshmallows when the rest of the group approached. They'd heard enough to know that he presented no threat, so Bill opened a couple of cabinets until he found an insulated cup with a lid, and quietly told Maureen that they needed to take him down to the station for questions.

"Junior, we need you to come with us, but you can take your cup with you. We need your help finding your cousin."

"Um, okay, but, um, I mean, I want to wait for my cousin to come home because she doesn't let me leave without her. She's been gone a long time."

Maureen took his elbow into her hand and gently guided him off the barstool and toward the door. "It's okay, Junior, we'll take care of you until we find her."

After she got him settled into her squad car, Maureen turned to speak with her brother and the other agents.

"A quick visual didn't turn up anything," Bill said. "In particular: no Jane. I'm going to send Crime Scene in to tear the buildings apart, but Jeff, will you call the DA and explain the situation with Junior? He's clearly of diminished capacity and I don't want anything thrown out due to a technicality, so see if she can get an attorney, or some sort of Guardian Ad Litem to meet us at the station before we question him."

"And be sure she knows that the life of an agent, and quite

possibly a news reporter are at stake," Seth added, "so she needs to act immediately - if not sooner."

Bill walked back to the crime scene vans and told them they were clear as the rest of the group got into their cars and sped off toward the MSP post. Bill and Seth, while excited to be so close to closing the case, had grave concerns about Jane.

"I'm afraid that time is running out for Jane," Bill said, "and getting any helpful information from Junior could prove to be either too time consuming, or ineffective altogether."

"I agree," Seth replied as he backed off from the lead patrol car to allow the cloud of dust to settle, "so we can't just rely on him. We need to get Abbey to dig more into Tia Anderson. Maybe she owns property in that name." Bill agreed and took out his phone to text their technical analyst.

Chapter 53

Day Two – 6:30 PM

Ionia State Penitentiary

Kate had been on prison visits before and was unaffected by the piercing clang that screeched every time they passed through to a different corridor. She was even able to tolerate the invasive search of her body, but never had she felt the anxiety this visit had caused, so she tried to clear away the thought that it related to her best friend and focus on the training she'd had in criminology and the psychopathy of a serial killer. Judy warned her that it would be a grievous error to allow their personal involvement, and concern for Jane to be seen by Wilkins because being the brilliant psychopath that he was he'd see through it, and they wouldn't get the raw, honest reaction they wanted. They made it through the dark and damp arteries into the bowels of the prison by keeping their heads down, and not responding to the vulgar catcalls of the inmates from their cells. By the time they reached the interview room, Kate felt confident in her ability to squash the personal aspect of this meeting and to approach it as she would any other interview.

Kate got her first, in person look at the man she'd spent the last several years calling a crazy bastard when they stepped up and looked through the one-way window at the top of the door. Her first impression was that his appearance matched the moniker she'd given him. His eyes that she'd been told were a dreamy blue, were now a soulless, icy gray that seemed to blend with the stony pallor of his coarse hair and heavily lined face.

"I spoke to the director on the plane, and the warden agreed not to tell him I was coming with you," Judy explained before the guard unlocked the door. "I've been studying this maniac for over 13 years, and I know he thinks he can manipulate and charm you. He's always known I could see right through him, so I'm hoping his surprise at seeing me will give us the upper hand, at least to begin with."

Kate felt almost excited now and looked forward to gauging the monster's visceral reaction to seeing Jane's aunt, and for how she envisioned the meeting would go.

After only one step into the room, she heard the gravelly voice of her team's nemesis. "Well hello, Miss Kate, it is my pleasure and honor to meet my girl's best friend. I so

wish Janey were with you. I miss her more than I can say." Before she had a chance to respond, Judy walked into the room, and had she not been watching for it, she would have missed how his face seemed to register what looked like fear and disappointment, but by the time Judy spoke to him, he seemed to have recovered the emotionless façade he was such a master at conveying.

"Hello, Tad," she said, "surprised to see me?" Kate knew Judy wanted to keep him off balance for as long as possible, so she wasn't surprised when Judy wasted no time in getting to the purpose of the visit.

"I don't even care how you managed to facilitate more abductions and brutal murders to harm my daughter's psyche, I just want to know if your brilliant plans and mind control games counted on Jane becoming one of her victims?"

For the first time, probably in his entire life, Tad Wilkins seemed speechless, and that's how both of the women knew that he had no idea Jane had been taken. Knowing that, they also knew he'd have no knowledge whatsoever as to her whereabouts. Before he found his voice and gained control of his reactions, Judy went on to tell him that if he had a way to contact his newest sheep in the game he so loved playing, that he should do that.

"I don't think you want her harmed. You're finding too much enjoyment in believing that you are somehow able to break her mentally with your sick manipulations, but if you want to keep her as your personal plaything, then you'd be smart to stop the woman who has her because she's as sick and sadistic as you are. You need to imagine what Jane is going through right now, because you know she'll be shown no mercy."

Kate loved that Judy was not only able to get what she needed from Wilkins, but that she'd been able to do it without the creep ever regaining the control he so relished. With their backs to him, the two women stepped up to the door, and called for the guard. Kate was beyond impressed with Judy's blunt and almost clinical articulation of the facts because she knew how hard it was for her to face him again. Jane had been Judy's whole world for a long time, and Tad's brand of poison had been the cause of more anguish and despair than any one person should ever have to endure. Kate knew that Judy had spent countless hours studying his psychopathy and had worked very hard to overcome her personal fears surrounding him. Yet, being the epitome of professional, she was able to tamp down her worry for Jane in order to get the job done and knew there was an invaluable lesson to be learned from the entire five-minute exchange.

The walk back through the depressing hallways to their exit was a quiet one. Kate did notice that Judy's hands were trembling slightly, but she respected the boundary and allowed her to process it in her own way. By the time the car beeped and flashed its lights after Kate pushed the key fob, Judy was fully composed and ready to go.

"I want to come back to Hart with you," she told Kate, "so I can be there when Jane is found."

"Of course," Kate answered. "Since I'm driving, will you text Bill and get an update? As nice as it'd be if Jane was already safe, I have to admit I'm looking forward to kicking that Riley bitch's ass."

Chapter 54

Day Two – 7:30 PM

Shack at the edge of The Manistee National Forest

As Jane continued to work her muscles and her mind in the dark and damp confines of her prison, she heard the even, relaxed breathing of Candace, and knew she was asleep. That's good, she thought, because she's going to need more mental and physical agility than she's ever had to use in order to follow my plan, and there will be no room or time for error. Jane's ultimate goal, of course, was to save them both, but if she could at least get Candace out safe, she'd know she did her job. She signed on for the risks she faced every day on the job and was under no illusions that her plan was a Hail Mary, but it was the only one, given her bound hands and light-deprived senses, she could come up with. Almost as if Kate telepathically read her mind from afar, she heard her training agent and friend's calm but direct voice. "Get your head screwed on straight, rookie, and stop planning on defeat because that is not an option. You are a bad ass, and I know that if anyone can pull this off, it's you."

Jane enjoyed the first smile she'd had since her first drink of coffee at Stella's, and re-started her jumping squats. They were not only good for endurance, but they helped build up her core and the leg muscles she would need for a victorious outcome once the offensive began. Over her own heavy breathing she heard a gasp, and a mew-like sound coming from Candace.

"It's okay Candace, I'm here. We're still good. Take a minute to shake the fog out of your brain and then we'll talk." By the time Jane resumed her workout, Candace was ready to engage and sounded relatively clear headed when she told her that she was awake and ready to hear the plan.

"That's great, and I'll go through it as many times as you need until you're comfortable. I'm not sure how much time we have until Riley gets back, but there is something I must ask before we go over our plan." Candace squeezed the hand Jane had extended in acknowledgement, so she continued, "All those years ago, when I melted down and started beating Tad in the chest, was that your voice I heard?"

Candace gave another squeeze, but this one felt more like compassion than acknowledgement, and then told that it was her and that she was just an intern following her first case which happened to be the Mother Killer Case.

"I was very young, and knew I'd advance further in my career if I stayed on top of, or ahead of, that case. I knew that your Aunt Judy was inside the courtroom fighting to get full custody and permission to change your name when it all went down."

That made sense to Jane because her recent recall still left her mind blank from the time she started whaling on her father's chest until she looked up into her aunt's eyes, but somewhere in the farthest recesses she could hear that tangy voice.

"I wasn't much older than you were, and my heart broke for you. You passed out right there on the sidewalk, so I went up to the guards who surrounded you and told them where your aunt was. They called up there to have her brought down to you."

Try as she might, Jane could not remember what happened after she woke up, and knew it was a topic to add to the conversation she had with Aunt Judy when she saw her. After Kate's last mind invasion, she knew it was a matter of when and not if.

"Ok, thanks for that, and we may get back to it, but right now I need you to listen to the plan because I don't know how much time we have." Candace told her she was as ready as she'd ever be, so Jane took her hands, helped her to her feet, and guided her hands along the wall until they touched the door.

"Ok, that was just two steps from where you're standing, to where the door will open. As soon as we hear the truck, you're going to scoot as close to the door as you can, be sure you're not standing in front of it, it needs to open freely."

"Where will you be?" she asked, and Jane explained that she would be waiting on the other side of the door, so when it opened, she'd be behind it.

"You're going to have that instant of light when she comes in, and she'll be looking for us toward the chair. She will be distracted when she doesn't see us and will probably turn her flashlight on. As soon as you see her looking that way, you have to run through the door, and keep on running. If it's too dark and that's not possible, get into her truck and lock the doors. I'm sure she leaves her keys inside it."

Jane could tell Candace was afraid, which she expected her to be, but stressed again the importance of getting out of the building without hesitating or looking back.

"Don't turn and look for me because I'm going to surprise her from the other side, which will give you a few seconds; so again, do not hesitate or even think about it. Just run like your life depends on it because it does." Jane did not explain how she'd visualized her role, but there was no need. Candace just needed to know her part in the operation.

"On second thought, I want you to stay right where you are because it's a perfect spot, and I'm going to come around and stand in front of you. From this moment on, we cannot speak. I don't know how thick these mud walls are and don't want her to hear us, but mostly we need to hear the truck because as soon as we do, I'm going to squeeze your hands, and get in position on the other side of the door."

Jane got a hand squeeze back in acknowledgment, and then focused her mind on visualizing her ambush on Riley. She felt pumped up after verbalizing her plan, and hoped she didn't have too long of a wait.

Chapter 55

Day Two – 8:00 PM

MSP Command Center – Hart, MI

The team thought the best way to keep Junior calm was to keep him with Maureen, at least until his representative arrived. Bill cautioned her not to ask him any questions about Riley, or anything remotely related to the case, so instead she asked him if he'd seen any of the Bugs Bunny shows with Bug's girlfriend Daisy Rabbit in them. That made him happy, and Maureen noticed that when he engaged with her, the nervous stutter he had at the house was absent. She could see the agents shaking hands with a woman who she presumed to be Junior's representative, so she told him she was leaving the room but that a couple of her friends would be in to speak with him.

"They're really nice people," she told him. "You can trust them. I promise."

When Bill introduced her to Junior's advocate, Ms. Donna Stevens, and she shook her hand, she was reminded of how comforting a warm sugar cookie just out of the oven made her feel. Ms. Donna was a short woman whose gray hair looked like a shiny new nickel, and with the chin length bob, Maureen felt like she was more than likely older than she looked. She seemed to exude a calmness that would be very good moving forward with the simple giant in the interview room.

Maureen told her and the agents that she would make a fresh pot of coffee and left them to discuss their strategy. She paused as she walked out and was happy to hear what Ms. Donna told them.

"Lana, the District Attorney thought that in consideration of what you told her, that Mr. Flynn would benefit more from a Guardian Ad Litem than an attorney. I'm also a licensed social worker, but I have to tell you that at any time if you decide to charge him with a crime, the questions will have to stop until he has legal representation present."

"Understood," Bill told her, "but in the interest of full disclosure, we do have an eyewitness to him leaving the dumpsite of our first victim." Seth stepped up and explained that from what they had seen of the man who called himself Junior, they were not certain he was even aware of the full circumstances, but was acting on the instruction of his cousin.

"From what we've been able to gather, our suspect, Riley, has taken care of him since he was a young boy, so it's not out of the question that he would follow her blindly. As we told Lana, our main objective of this interview is to find out if he can lead us to where she takes the women she abducts. She has one of our agents, and quite possibly a reporter, and their time is running out, so we need some answers-quickly."

"Understood," she told them as Maureen came back with a tray of coffee, and a fresh hot chocolate for Junior.

Jeff turned the audio in the interview room on, so when Patrick and Maureen joined him they were able to see and to hear what was being said. As the introductions inside the room were being made, Judy and Kate walked into the bullpen and joined them. Patrick stepped up to Kate, and after they hugged, she introduced Judy to them all.

"Thanks for all the updates," Kate told them, "and I presume you got the message from Judy on Tad Wilkins? He had no idea that Jane had been abducted but is certainly aware of someone killing in his honor."

Ms. Donna took the seat beside Junior and explained that she was not law enforcement and was there only for him.

"I um, do you, um, I mean, when is my cousin going to get here?"

Bill and Seth were in chairs across the table from him, and Bill, who was known to be the softer, more compassionate of the duo, would be primary for the interview. Seth would interject only if they believed they needed a little bit of a strong arm.

"We're looking for her, Junior, and really need your help." Bill told him. "Does she usually keep you home alone for this long?"

"She um, I was, um, I mean, she told me when I finished with the chickens to go in and eat my tuna sandwich. I um, I did, um, I mean I did what she told me to do but she didn't come back so I turned on Bugs Bunny and had a nap. Um, am I in trouble?" With that, Junior started showing the first signs of agitation since they'd found him asleep at home. He began bouncing his feet, and he interlocked his hands so he could twirl his thumbs like helicopter blades. He bowed his head, and pressed his lips together so tightly they began to turn white.

Donna spoke up then and assured him that he was not in trouble, and that the agents would like to help him find Riley. "Do you know where she might be?"

With his head still hung, he raised his eyes and stammered, "I, um, who's Riley?" Things at the table, and outside the room went silent when they realized he did not know her by that name. Judy was able to get Bill's attention and motioned him out, so after stating for the official record that he was leaving the interview room, Bill excused himself.

"I think I have a way to relax him, and maybe get him to talk. Do you mind if I take a go at it?"

"We'll take all the help we can get, Judy, but keep in mind that you can talk about the women, but you cannot ask him about the crimes. He doesn't have the mental capacity to refuse to answer, and doesn't have an attorney present. Kate, while we're talking with him, will you call Abbey? Get her to search for any property in Tia's name, or any other clue as to where she might take them. We can't count on

Junior. We need another plan." Kate, glad for the chance to get active in the investigation again, went into an empty office to make her call.

Bill and Judy walked back into the quiet interview room, and after he announced himself as re-entering, and included Judy and her title, he indicated she should take his chair and begin.

"Hi Billy," she said. "Do you like to be called Billy, or Junior? I'm Dr. Judy and I'm going to help you figure out where Tia is. Are you up for that?" Not only did his face register recognition, but the feet settled down and his hands relaxed. After a minute, he finally responded.

"I, um, I am, um, I mean, Tia calls me Junior, so I like that better, but she only lets me use her name when we're home. If I go into town with her I am to keep my lips zipped. Tia's momma called me Billy when she was beating me with the belt, so I don't like that name. Tia always made me feel better. She'd make me hot chocolate and promised that she would take care of me. She didn't get mad when her momma whipped her in the back with a belt, though, because she said she deserved it."

What took Judy, and probably the whole group, aback was that he'd made the statement in such a matter of fact way, without any of the bitterness or resentment they'd expect. They had all read the file from Abbey and were outraged at the abuse both he and Tia were subjected to, but hearing it declared with no more emotion than it would take to order a cheeseburger was heart wrenching. Under normal circumstances, Judy would be compelled to dig deeper with him on it, but knowing that Jane was possibly getting whipped, or worse, could be dead already, prodded her to push a little harder with the man-child.

"I know you are a big help to Tia when she has to move one of her ladies around. We think one of our friends is with her now and we really need to find her. Do you know where she takes them?"

Absent any speech impediment, Junior told them that Tia let him drive the girls' cars on Monroe Road to a spot by the swamp.

"I don't have a driving license, so it has to be a secret. I hope Tia isn't mad at me for telling. After I throw their phones into the swamp, I walk back to her truck and wait inside of it until she comes out of the mud hut. I usually fall asleep."

Kate returned to the viewing area in time to hear that information, and like the rest of them, and the agents inside of the room, processed how much information they'd gotten from that statement, one of which was why there was no pinging on cell towers and why they couldn't find the victims' cars. Kate was close enough to the window to cause condensation on the glass from her breath, and while it was only seconds it felt like hours before Judy asked the question burning in everyone's mind.

"Can you take us to the mud hut?" She asked. "We think our friend Jane is there, and we really need to bring her home."

"I, um, did you, um, I mean, did you say Jane? Tia hates Jane more than anything. She said she's the biggest sinner of them all because she forsake her father."

Kate felt like her stomach hit the ground when she heard that, thankful, though, for Judy's ability to remain calm at the horrifying statement, because it did not bode well for them finding her niece alive.

"Junior, I love Jane as much as you love Tia, and I promise you, she is not evil. I really need to find her. Can you take us to the hut? Your cousin is probably there with her and we can bring them both back at the same time."

Kate was pleased with the way Judy phrased that, and while a part of her felt badly about misleading him into thinking they wanted to bring Tia back to him, she put it aside. Lying was a perfectly legitimate tool during an interview and she just wanted her partner back.

"I can take you to the swamp and car place, and then we have to walk, but I know the way even in the dark. You just have to follow." Judy exchanged hopeful glances with Bill and Seth, then told the tamed Goliath to finish his hot chocolate and they'd be back to get him in a few minutes.

When Judy and the agents formally ended the interview and left the room, the whole group was talking at once, each of them offering their opinions on how to handle an approach. Bill left them to it while he spoke with Donna, who confirmed that they did not cross any legal lines, but was concerned with his safety if he accompanied them.

"I take full responsibility for his safety," Bill assured her, "but it may be our only shot at saving one, and more than likely two lives, not to mention stop a serial killer from hunting in your towns. We are going to take him, but if it will make you feel better, you may ride along with us."

Bill nodded his head respectfully, but walked away from the Guardian Ad Litem because he would not accept any kind of rebuttal from her. He had an operation to plan, and not a lot of time to plan it, so he walked over to the team and group of officers to lay out his strategy.

"Kate, it's good to have you back; and Judy, thank you. I am certain we would not have gotten what you were able to get out of him. Did Abbey find us anything, Kate?"

"Yes, she just called me back. She found a small parcel of land that butts up against the Manistee National Forest that is still in the name of Tia and Billy's foster family. She sent me the coordinates for it and it's not too far off of Monroe Road. I think we got her, boss."

"Okay. Steve, I want you to be the lead vehicle with Junior and Donna," Bill directed, "and the rest of us will fall in behind. As usual, no radios – communicate with cell phones if needed. Jeff, once we get in the car, contact a rescue squad and coordinate with them. I want an ambulance on site at that mud hut, so let's get them rolling so we don't have to wait."

The same group that had assembled for the earlier search didn't have to be told twice. Everyone except Kate still had their tactical gear stowed, so she went to the locked ammo supply closet and loaded herself up with what she hoped was more than she'd need. Patrick and Maureen told her they'd see her when they arrived, and then told Mike from Traverse City that he could ride along with them. Kate was thankful for that because she hoped she could get Patrick's read on the detective because her instincts were still pinging about him and his motivations.

Seth told Bill as they ran out of the building and joined the caravan that he'd call Abbey to make sure the location services were engaged on his phone.

"With any luck, she'll be able to find us a path from what Junior called the swamp and car place to the mud hut presumably at the edge of the forest, by vehicle. It'll make this extraction much smoother if we can drive in."

Chapter 56

Day Two

Ionia State Penitentiary – 7:00 PM

The guard took me by the elbow and guided my shuffle steps back to the cell. I usually engaged with the chatty guard because it was a good way to build an alliance, but tonight all I wanted was to be left alone so I could figure out what the hell had happened during that visit.

I was ready for Kate, excited about it to be sure, but never even considered she'd bring Judy with her. With preparation, I'm sure I could have controlled the meeting, even with Judy there, but was completely caught off guard. The driving force behind my banishment of her in Janey's life was because she was probably the only one on the planet who could see through my veil. And when I realized that charming my way through her wall was impossible, and that her influence on Janey would make it hard if not impossible to mold her, I did what I needed to do.

When I sat down on my bed, I was grateful once again that the warden had decreed I have private accommodations with no cellmate. They could never track culpability back to me, but the official's suspicions that I managed to manipulate others into doing my bidding was enough for them to limit my time with others. My solitude today was needed so I could replay the five minutes I spent with the two women.

I'm confident that I covered my surprise at seeing Judy quickly enough that any read they may have been able to get from my reaction was nothing more than a flicker. And when Judy came back so fast with the insinuation that I was aware of and even orchestrating a new wave of kills, I wasn't surprised, but the bombshell that Janey had been taken bowled me over. She referred to the killer as a female, so at least I know who took the bait, but how stupid is she. My last letter was supposed to direct her to Candace because I truly am done with her, but I never indicated any feelings except love and forgiveness toward my daughter, so she should not have interfered with her.

Janey is mine to control, and my plan to drive her from her career and back into my arms is as alive as it ever was. I still believe that given enough time and circumstance, I can make her the killing partner I deserve. But, if there ever comes a time that she needs to be dealt with more harshly, then I will be the one to handle it. It is my right after all, and while I don't believe I'll ever have to initiate plan B, I will if I must.

I wish I could talk with Jacob, but I know he's in Virginia, waiting outside the prison gate to escort Adrian Sanchez to his new life of freedom, which gave me a good laugh because freedom definitely does not mean being free. I need to be able to follow the team's progress, and may have to reach out to another one of my assets. I have a lot of faith in Janey's team, though. They are the best at what they do, and I have no doubt they'll move mountains if necessary, but they will find Janey. She just damned well better be alive when they do.

Chapter 57

Day Two

Shack at the Edge of the Manistee National Forest – 8:00 pm

A part of Jane's training, both at the academy and with her dojo, was recognizing and dealing with sensory deprivation, the process that deprives a human being of normal, external stimuli, such as light or sound. She was thankful she was able to draw from that training, because in certain, short-term situations, it can be a good way to regain focus. A laser focus was critical for her plan to save Candace and herself from the sadistic torture and ultimate murder by the madwoman who held them. As she stood silently with Candace in total darkness, she wondered if that sensory loss was what was helping the woman stand still and quiet, without a stitch of clothing on. Jane realized that the reporter who'd been hounding her since her father was arrested had more grit and fortitude than her public persona revealed, and that her stiletto heels, designer suits, and relentless tracking of a story, was just window dressing. She knew the woman had to be cold and at the very least uncomfortable in her nakedness, but hadn't said a word about it. Jane also remembered seeing the deep and blistered wounds on Alicia and Kristen's tortured backs when she viewed their autopsies, and was thinking of the pain they must've endured. She knew Candace had been whipped, yet she hadn't heard even a whimper. Jane found a new respect for her and vowed to tell her how proud she was once they were free.

Jane's meditation was interrupted by a noise off in the distance that sounded like a revving engine, and when she heard the crunching of gravel she knew it was show time. Candace obviously knew too, because she squeezed Jane's fingers a fraction of an instant before Jane squeezed hers. Jane broke the silence rule when she leaned in, and quietly whispered a reminder to run like hell without hesitation, and not to worry about her. Then, with a final squeeze, Jane took the two steps over to the other side of the door so she'd be behind it when it opened.

When she heard the truck door slam, Jane went down into a squat and balanced herself on the balls of her feet so she'd be ready to leap when it was time. She also offered up a silent prayer that Candace wouldn't lose her nerve and would be able to get out of the building. Riley didn't know it, but with the way she was talking to her two captives she was making it very easy for Jane to track her.

"That damn cow in Mackinaw was a tough old heifer," she mumbled as she worked at the padlock, "and the longer it took her to die, the more excited I got about coming back and whipping the skin right off the backs of both you sinners."

Jane considered Riley's words, and while she knew the likelihood of being the victor in her ambush was grim, she also determined that Riley Ann would not come out of the encounter unscathed. Her captor wasn't without strength, but she was just a scrapper and added no brain to her brawn. Jane's hope that even without a weapon, or use of her hands, her skill in reading her opponent and planning an offensive would yield her enough success that she'd at least have time to get them both to safety. She had little hope that her team would find them in time and figured she was on her own. Oddly enough, after the mind conversations she'd had with Kate, she felt up to the challenge.

Jane felt the familiar rush of adrenaline when she heard the padlock disengage and was ready to pounce the minute Candace's foot touched the threshold. Her training also had her prepare herself for the sudden burst of light after being in the dark for so long because she could not afford even the briefest hesitation. The women remained silent as the heavy door started to open, and light from her flashlight illuminated the opening.

Jane was behind the open door and couldn't see Riley, so she had to be hypervigilant to Candace's cues and where the beam from her captor's flashlight shone. When the torture chair on the back wall lit up, instead of immersing herself in the compassion she felt for the victims, her resolve to stop the inhuman cruelty became more steadfast than ever. Kate's voice told her that it was go time, and she was ready.

As instructed, as soon as Riley's attention was drawn to the empty space at the back of the shack, Candace leapt out through the open door, and as predicted, Riley's attention was drawn toward that movement. Before she had a chance to make chase, Jane dropped her shoulders and rammed the woman from behind in a tackle that would earn her a spot on any NFL team in America. Although Riley went down hard, she quickly recovered, but her first action was to look outside for Candace.

Jane hoped that multiple strikes in quick succession would hinder Riley's ability to recover in time to strike back, so she took that fraction of a second to land a roundhouse kick right below her rib cage, and when Riley doubled over from the shock of it she got close, and with her arms bent, jabbed her in the throat with her right elbow. The throat jab seemed to uncage the beast within, so instead of grabbing her windpipe as expected, Riley made a fist, cocked her right arm back and with a battle cry went for Jane's jaw. She was able to dodge the first attempt, but Riley's second strike hit its mark which was the bridge of Jane's nose. Already off balance because of her bound wrists, and unable to staunch the gushing blood, Jane head butted her hard enough that she heard the bones in Riley's own nose crunch just a second before she too began gushing blood.

Jane continued her forward momentum, and with her fingers laced together to form one fist she extended her arms and, with her enemy's left ear as the target, spun herself around like a pinwheel in a windstorm. Riley was able to halt her motion by grabbing her conjoined wrists, and as Jane had done only seconds before, continued the forward motion and flung her to the ground like a rag doll. Jane's head bounced like a tennis ball on the hard packed ground, which momentarily sent her world back to darkness. To keep her down, Riley held her in place by straddling her with a knee on each side.

As soon as she had the presence of mind to do so, Jane opened her eyes, and through her still foggy brain, saw Riley pull a shiny object out of the orange construction bucket she'd carried in. Although her reaction to it was delayed a fraction of a second, Jane recognized the glinting metal as a knife, and started bucking with her pelvis. Riley's knees were so effective in holding her still, for the briefest of seconds Jane wondered if she was a part time bull rider on the rodeo circuit. Riley's broken nose dripped blood on Jane's neck as she doubled down on her pressure to keep her in place. While she continued to fight against the pin, she realized that the knife in Riley's hand was coming straight down toward her throat.

Jane arched her neck back, and twisted her head to the side in time to deflect the blade from her carotid to her left cheek where the scalpel-sharp dagger sliced through her skin like it was softened butter. The grunting sounds of the battling women ended abruptly when what sounded like a continuous blare from a car's honking horn interrupted their struggle. And when the mud hut lit up with a car's headlights beaming through the open door, Jane gave a quick and silent nod to Candace for thinking of it. Jane used the distraction to her benefit, took a deep breath and rolled to her side, and in the same movement used her joined fists to knock the knife out of Riley's hands. Her hope of getting to her feet were dashed when Riley pulled her focus from the noise, and back to keeping her restrained. Since she'd been relieved of her weapon, Jane knew that when Riley's hands encircled her throat, she'd found a different outlet for her murderous rage. She heard Kate's voice tell her to dig deep and not allow her time to increase the pressure. "You do that, rookie," Jane heard, "and you will lose this battle."

Jane wasn't sure if Riley saw the glint in her eye or the smile on her face when she shouted, "Not today, bitch," but dig deep she did, and with the speed of a cheetah and the power of a bulldozer, head butted the killer in her already broken nose and then shot to her feet and backed away. Riley came up just as quickly, though, and since the knife was out of reach, grabbed her bullwhip from the construction bucket, and prepared for the next face off.

Kate rode with Bill and Seth in the SUV, and with the caravan of police cars racing just as quickly behind them, sent silent mind messages to Jane. She hoped, and for her own sanity had to believe, that like the cavalry they'd arrive in time and put a check in the win column for this gruesome case. She listened in and agreed with her boss at how lucky they'd been that Abbey found the old logging road before they even arrived at the swampy parcel. They didn't even take the time to search the victims' cars, but instead instructed the crime scene unit to secure the scene and then meet them at what they hoped would be the shack where Riley tortured and murdered the women.

With full understanding that an operation such as the one they were about to engage in would more than likely take off on its own legs, they still discussed their plan.

"We should assume there are two victims," Seth noted, "and extracting them is priority. We go after Riley once our objective of getting those women to safety is met. Agreed?"

"Absolutely," Kate said. "No collateral damage to Kate or to Candace. I just hope Steve and all the other cops will maintain the same level head." The three agents in the car stopped talking and looked around, and then at each other.

"Do you hear something off in the distance?" she asked them.

Bill sat up straighter in his seat and without taking his eyes from the thick forest that surrounded them said, "I do. It almost sounds like a horn honking, and doesn't that look like taillights?" When they both agreed, Seth reached to the dashboard to engage the sirens, and the bright red and blue lights in the grill of the truck. The rest of the vehicles in the convoy followed suit, and they all sped toward the lights that seemed to guide them through the darkness of the forest.

To Jane, and even Riley, the continuous blare from the horn became background noise as they faced off with one another. Jane had to admit that when Riley uncoiled her whip, she went a little weak in the knees because seeing it dangle like a snake knowing she was the prey it was ready to strike was frighteningly intimidating; she had nothing in her arsenal that could stop it.

"Have you ever heard a sonic boom?" Riley asked her. "Because the noise from my little friend here will cause you as much pain to your ears as its lashes will cause when it slices through your skin."

Jane's face registered no emotion when she heard, still off in the distance, the sirens that made her believe that backup was forthcoming. Riley's mind seemed to travel to a different plane, one Jane figured was the sadist's happy place, so she registered no awareness of the sirens. Jane knew she couldn't thwart a lash from the whip, but figured she'd try to outwit her with her words and possibly engage her long enough for the help to arrive.

"You know he doesn't want me dead, don't you?" She asked her. "He wants me alive. He is going to be pissed when he learns you've taken me because you're denying him the pleasure of keeping me as his plaything. His whole reason for living is to make me lose my mind and my career."

Riley snapped her whip and shouted, "You know nothing about him. You forsake your own father which is sinful. Tad loves me and it is my honor to punish all the sinners in your name."

Without warning, and so quickly that Jane didn't see it coming, Riley snapped the thong of the whip, striking Jane's left thigh. The sound, combined with the sudden pain of the whip, caused her legs to buckle, but she knew if she went down, even to her knees, that she'd never have the chance to get back up.

Kate thought of a precision dive team as she watched the synchronized procession of the first responders behind them take the sharp right turn toward the honking horn. Their clearing came up quickly, and at the speed they'd been traveling, their abrupt turn felt more like a loop on a roller coaster than a routine turn into a driveway. Kate had her holster unsnapped and was at the suspect's truck by the time the rest of the team exited their vehicles, but stopped sharply when she realized it was Candace who was inside of it. It was dark, but she realized immediately that the threat was inside the shack and raised her arm in a signal to the rest of the force to join her. Over the noise of the fading sirens she told the EMTs they were needed at the truck and to bring a blanket.

Jane knew she was no longer alone because out of the corner of her eye she was able to make out the silhouettes of people forming a perimeter just outside the door. She was grateful that help had arrived because she could feel her body getting weaker and she wasn't sure if she had the strength to continue the physical aspect of a fight. The bright lights from the vehicles shining through the open door was almost blinding so Jane diverted her watery eyes away from them, but knew the first person advancing was Kate. When she heard her order Riley to back away, Jane was thankful that this time her voice was not just a motivational one in her mind, and she drew her first relaxed breath since the door to the shack opened up.

Sadly her relief was short lived because in a ninja-like move, Riley was behind her with the whip wrapped around her throat and was increasing the pressure. Jane knew she could not close her eyes because if she did within three minutes she would lose, and may never regain, consciousness. Without the use of her hands she stood zero chance of loosening the choke hold, so she tried to relax her body enough that Riley would think she was passing out and loosen her grip. Jane knew that as the hostage negotiator on the team, Seth would step in; she just hoped he'd be able to talk Riley off the ledge before it was too late.

"Riley Ann Wilson, my name is Seth, and I'm from the FBI. This entire building is surrounded by police officers and FBI agents and we're going to need you to drop the whip."

When Riley looked out and shouted that she would not drop the whip, that she'd been called upon by God and Tad to mete out a fair and just punishment, she loosened her hold on the whip a little, so Jane was able to fill her deprived lungs with some much needed air.

"From Proverbs, 19:18" she bellowed, "*Whoever curses his father or his mother shall be put to death.*"

Jane could feel the whip around her throat getting tight again as Riley seemed to become more agitated, but despite her light headedness she had faith in her team. Jane added whiplash to her mental list of injuries because Riley's face became redder and blotchier with every Bible verse she shouted, as if her blood pressure was about to explode. The more strident her rant became, the more physical Riley got, almost as if flailing her arms added more passion to her preaching. She could feel the braiding of the whip cut into her skin, but the constant movement of Riley's arms afforded her the opportunity to get some oxygen. As she looked toward Kate, she could see that her team realized the urgency of their action, and when Kate nodded and left the group she knew they had a plan.

Kate never took her eyes off of Jane when she told Bill and Seth that since Riley seemed to have lost all touch with reality they'd stand little to no chance of talking her down on their own, and Jane was running out of time.

"I think we need to bring Junior up so she can see him. By all indications, he is the only thing in this world that she loves. She may settle down enough that we'll be able to get to Jane."

Both of the men nodded their agreement, so Kate ran back to the squad car Junior was in and asked Judy to bring him up. They were all worried about how Junior would react to seeing his protector in her current state, but they were out of options. Firing at Riley needed to be a last resort because just one twitch by either she or Jane, and the wrong female could be struck.

Jane never took her eyes off the group assembled out front, and when she saw Judy rush up with a very large man, she was both shocked and confused. The concern she felt for her aunt having to see her in such a compromised position overwhelmed her enough that she was able to snap her mind to an awareness she'd lost to oxygen deprivation. With her eyes, she tried to convey to the woman who'd become her mother that she would be fine.

Seth got Riley's attention when he stepped forward and said, "You know how this is going to end if you don't release Jane, so I have to ask, do you really want your cousin to see you get gunned down?" And then using the name by which Junior knew her, continued, "He needs you, Tia. Don't let his last memory be of you getting shot."

Riley loosened but did not release her grip when she saw her cousin, and shouted that Junior had nothing to do with the punishments. "He had no idea what was going on, do not harm him."

At the sound of her voice, Junior broke away from the elbow grip that Judy had on him and stepped forward.

"I, um, are you, um, I mean, when are you coming home Tia? I missed my dinner."

Proving she wasn't a total sociopath with absolutely no feelings or compassion, Riley's face softened and she let the whip drop to the ground. As Jeff and Steve rushed in to take her into custody, Jane dropped to her knees and gulped in the first full breaths she'd been able to take since it started, and by the time Kate reached her she felt a little more clearheaded.

"It's about time you showed up, partner. Did you find Candace?"

When Kate embraced her, Jane saw that Maureen, along with

another woman, had taken Junior by the hands and were walking away when Patrick and Judy led the EMTs into the shack.

"You're welcome, rookie. You owe me one. Now, let the paramedics help you; you look like hell and Candace is on her way to the hospital." Jane knew she needed some medical attention but still managed to chuckle when she said to Kate, "You should see the other guy."

Chapter 58

Day Three – 8:00 AM

Spectrum Hospital, Ludington, MI

When Jane woke up and saw the IV pole with bags of fluid attached to a line going into her arm, she recognized the source of the low, steady beeps she'd been hearing all night. Her throat still felt like it did when Riley had the braided whip around it, and when she reached up with her free arm to determine what it was, she heard her Aunt Judy: "You had some pretty nasty abrasions, and bruising from the whip, so they put a medicated salve on it. That's the gauze you're feeling."

Jane took Judy's hand into hers and after telling her how happy she was that she was there, asked her to update her on where they were with the case.

"Kate and the team is on the way, so I'll let them update you on the case. I'll go over your injuries, deal?" Jane nodded her agreement and listened while Judy told her that aside from the neck abrasions, she needed 12 stitches to close up the wound on her cheek from the dagger and that she had a golf ball size bump on the back of her head, but luckily no sign of a concussion.

"The thickness of your khakis saved your thigh from what could've been a much deeper laceration from the whip, and they were able to close that up with just a butterfly patch. Your eyes are both black, but that's from the broken nose, which they re-set while they had you anesthetized last night. The good news is you should be able to leave later today."

Jane felt the bandage on her cheek, and was grateful that at least the scar would be covered up by her hairline, and now she understood the throbbing sensation she felt on the bridge of her nose.

"How is Candace, and Riley?" she asked her aunt.

"I can answer that," Kate said as she walked in and handed Jane an extra-large cup of coffee. "Other than being dehydrated, Candace is doing fine and is asking about you. Her back, of course, is like ground hamburger, but they got to it in time to prevent any major infections. She's lucky Riley didn't get a second go at her." Jane raised the head of her bed so she could take a drink of the heavenly brew Kate brought her and asked how Riley fared in the altercation.

"Oh, you gave as good or better than you got, for sure. Her nose is broken in two places, her bottom two ribs are cracked, and the thyroid cartilage in her neck is fractured. The doctors were amazed that she could speak much less breathe, but for a while, her only form of communication will be a dry-erase board."

Kate paused for a drink of her own coffee and then spoke again as a training agent and mentor when she told Jane how proud they all were, and that Candace was alive because of her actions.

"Kate is right," Bill said as he walked into the room with Seth. "You more than proved your value to this team, and to the Bureau, and thankfully you did it all by the book this time." They all relaxed at the boss's reference to the first case when Jane went rogue. As Patrick and Maureen came into the room with a box of fresh pastry and a tray of coffee from Stella's, Jane ran her fingers down the bandage on her check.

"Don't worry about a scar, Jane," Seth told her. "It just proves that you were stronger than the force that caused it. It tells you where you've been, but in no way has to dictate where you're going." Jane put her hands back in her lap, grateful as always to absorb Seth's wisdom, and asked them to update her on the case.

"You'll get a full briefing once you're back to work," Seth told her, "so for now we'll just give you the footnotes. The shack and truck are still being processed, but there should be enough physical evidence to seal Riley's cage for the rest of her life."

Patrick released the hold he had on Kate's hand and added that even after she'd been read her rights and was advised to stay quiet, Riley didn't stop talking about her kills.

"Her voice was getting pretty gravelly by then, but she prattled on about how they were fair and just punishments, and that the world needed to be cleansed of all the sinners." They all discussed how fortunate they were that the arrest had been by the book because the onboard cameras were engaged and recording what they considered to be her confession in the car.

Jane appreciated the information and had reconciled herself to the knowledge that until the investigation was complete she wouldn't have all the answers, but there was one burning question on her mind.

"Has my father's involvement been discovered yet? We all know he was somehow behind all of this."

Kate fielded that question, and answered because Jane deserved the truth. "They found a locked box of love letters he wrote her, and they were full of scripture and Bible verses, but the common theme of them was the sin of forsaking the father." Jane was aware that prison changed people, but told them that in the years she knew him, he was not at all religious.

"We didn't even own a Bible as far as I know, but why did she think I was the reason for all the punishments, and how did those letters get out of the prison? I thought he was monitored."

"We have Abbey working on that," Seth told her, "but are thinking his attorney had them hand delivered. Junior told us that every once in a while a long black car brought his cousin a big envelope. Regardless, though, somehow that evil son of a bitch will have plausible deniability and we won't be able to tie him to anything."

Judy stepped up to the bedside and told Jane that she had an opportunity last night to study the letters and believee that he was somehow able to convey his evil desires subliminally.

"Riley, or Tia, which was her given name, and Junior, were so badly abused by her parents that I could only read it a little bit at a time because it made me physically sick. The father raped them - brutally and repeatedly - but then the mother whipped them for it. During the beatings, scriptures played on a continuous loop on a tape recorder. Eventually Tia believed she deserved the punishment, but she always looked after her cousin. On the good-news side, though, Donna, the Guardian Ad Litem he has been assigned, has submitted a petition to the court to become his foster parent. He is very comfortable with her, and she reports that the only thing he's asked for is his hot chocolate with tiny marshmallows and hasn't even brought Tia up."

Jane felt sick at what the two children suffered and was happy that the man child was going to be okay, but she still had a hard time connecting herself to the attacks. As if she could read her inner turmoil, Judy continued.

"Tad was not happy to learn you'd been taken because he still believes he can turn your

soul as black as his. I think he may have gone too far when he gushed about his heartbreak over losing his daughter, and it opened up the Pandora's box of hidden evils inside of Riley."

Jane sensed her conversation with Judy was not over, but listened as Bill announced that he'd hired another agent to join their team. Seth didn't seem surprised, but she and Kate immediately started firing questions about who the new agent was.

"The director has been after me for a while to add another agent, and when I met him, it seemed right. He's a U.S. Marshall, currently on an assignment, and will come over to us when it's over. For security reasons, I'm unable to provide you with his name, but know that he's very well qualified and will fit in perfectly."

Jane looked at her family, and knowing they'd been up all night working on the case, she told them that if they went back and rested that she would too.

"Just don't forget to come back for me this afternoon," she said with a laugh.

As they all filtered out, Judy came back to her bedside and told her that she had a lot to share with her about the earlier years because it was time, and because she believed she was ready to hear it.

"Thank you," Jane told her, "I've had a lot of flashbacks lately. I'm ready to put it all together, but I want to assure you that my soul is not up for grabs. Tad Wilkins cannot and will not get the best of me."

"I know that. Get some rest, and I'll see you in a few hours." When Judy walked out of the room, Kate and Patrick came back in.

"I'm going to hook up with you back in Virginia. I invited Patrick and Maureen to come back with us and go to the big ass barbecue I promised my parents we'd have, so I'm going to travel with them." She was still talking to Jane but was looking up and into the Irishman's face when she said, "I need to tell them both a story, and I know I will have their undivided attention during our travel."

Jane smiled at the not-so-hidden message and bid them safe travels, then picked out another cinnamon roll, took a fresh cup of coffee and settled back to quietly reflect on the case. It seemed like she'd lived a lifetime in just three days, but despite her throbbing nose, sliced cheek, and the bullwhip lash on her leg, she'd never felt more alive. Not only did she take pleasure in taking a monster off the street, but she also felt like she'd had a personal growth spurt and truly felt like her mind was cleared of all things Tad Wilkins related.

Jane heard rustling in the hallway when her door opened, and when she looked up, she saw that the detective from Traverse City was walking into her room carrying a motorcycle helmet.

"Hi Jane," he said. "Do you remember me?"

Of course she remembered him. She just couldn't figure out why he was in her hospital room and was a little nervous when he closed the door tightly.

JANE'S PUNISHMENT

"Yes, Mike, I remember you. What can I do for you?" Not really knowing why he was there, and being in the compromised position she was, Jane picked up her call button in case she needed to call for help.

Mike grinned and told her he was not there to hurt her, but that he had some information and a message to share. Jane became even more skeptical because of his vagueness, and without mincing any words, asked, "What the hell is that supposed to mean? Information and a message from who?"

Mike sat down beside the bed, and with a deep breath, gave her the information he promised he'd give.

"The message is from Nick, and he wanted me to tell you that he's sorry for ending it the way he did, but for everyone's safety he had no other choice. He still loves you – a lot."

"Okay, now you're pissing me off," she scolded. "How about you start with telling me who the hell you are, and then, if I believe you, you can tell me about Nick."

"I am actually the marshall assigned to Nick while he's in witness protection. He has followed you and your cases since he left, and when he saw that this current one had all the earmarks of your father, he wanted me nearby to watch out for you so I pulled some strings, got some creds from Traverse City, and here I am."

Jane leaned back in the bed and took a drink of her coffee while she tried processing what the man had just revealed to her. As if he knew what questions she would ask, Mike continued.

"Wilkins threatened him, his family, and you when you applied to the academy. Told him if he didn't talk you out of going, that he'd end you all. We both know how that worked out, but as Wilkins is so apt at doing he told your boyfriend that he'd allow everyone to live, but that he'd have to become one of his assets on the outside. With Nick's background in finance, Tad put him in charge of laundering money through a firm in New York City. After the Mother Killer case, he thought it was a perfect time to turn state's evidence."

All of that rang true to Jane when she remembered their contentious break up, but she had been so focused on getting into the academy at Quantico that she brushed it all aside.

"But that doesn't make sense," she argued, "because the Bureau couldn't find anything to tie Tad to that firm."

"No, and he knew that, but he also knew that he and his family would be put into witness protection and would be safe from Tad. He wasn't too worried about you because you had the force of the entire FBI to protect you, but he could not live with himself any longer. He is not cut out to be a criminal."

Jane had been thinking a lot about Nick lately, to the point where just before the case she admitted to herself that she was probably still in love with him, but had to put it into the "to be dealt with later" compartment to work the case. I guess it's time to open that compartment, she thought, and questioned Mike about where he was, insisting on meeting with him.

He was emphatic when he said, "That is not going to happen, and if you mention this meeting or try to find him, you will be risking not only your life, but his and his family's as well. I did not want to come here and do this, but he threatened to go rogue and come himself if I didn't." Jane's rational brain realized the truth in his words, and knew that with time, her heart would catch up to her brain.

"Why now?" Jane asked him.

"Because he wanted me to warn you that your father is a very cunning, very dangerous man, and he's not done with you yet. Nick told me that the pride and the love you have for the job will make you give your all to every case, every time, with no exceptions, and seeing what I saw in the last 24 hours, I have to agree. He just wants you to keep your eyes open to Tad's games, and stay safe because he wants to see you when this is all over."

Mike stood up to leave, and as he walked out the door told her he'd see her again soon, but Jane didn't have any time to process that comment or even question it, because right behind him, Candace wheeled herself into the room.

Jane didn't think she'd ever be happy to see the reporter, but having gone through what they did together, she was glad she was there.

"I was going to have the nurse take me to you," she told her, "so I'm happy you're here. How are you feeling? Are you doing okay?"

"I am doing as well as I can be, I guess. My back still burns, but they tell me that's from the medicine they have to keep on it to prevent infection. I'm going to have some nasty scars, though, but mostly I needed to thank you for saving my life. You were like an angel sent from heaven. You kept me calm, and made me believe that I could survive, and I will never forget that."

Jane reached out and took Candace's familiar fingers in her own.

"You did an amazing job, Candace. Neither one of us would be here today if you would have veered even a tiny bit from the plan because you provided me with the diversion I needed to do my part. I'll tell you what a very wise man told me about the scars: he said not to worry about them because they were just proof that we were stronger than the force that tried to stop us. Those scars prove that you are a survivor, and I hope you never lose sight of that."

Chapter 59

Ionia State Penitentiary

Three Months Later – August 2011

It's been said that some of life's best lessons are learned on the heels of adversity, and not even a malignant narcissist would refuse to acknowledge that sometimes the original path was no longer viable. At the same time, that same narcissist is smart enough to forge a new path that will provide the same outcome. I diagnosed myself as a narcissistic psychopath when I was nine years old which is even younger than the experts will diagnose it, but as I've said before, I'm smarter than most. After all, it isn't much of a leap to realize that I possess all the qualities of the extreme psychological syndrome of a malignant narcissist. I'm proud to admit that I am a special breed with a perfect mix of sadism, aggression, and the inability to enjoy the company of others, yet am such a good pretender most people don't even realize they're a sheep in my flock until it's too late because I already own them.

In my life, there have only been two people that I've been unable to fool. It pains me to admit it, but Janey, and my biggest nemesis, Judy Newell, have been like the non-stick coating of Teflon to the best efforts of some of my most valued outside assets. I still believe that with the proper manipulation I will realize my goal of entering into a killing partnership with my daughter. The lesson I learned from the debacle that one of my serial killer groupies created during what she considered an homage to me was that the only person with the control and power to make it happen with Janey, was me. It didn't take me long once Janey was rescued to engage Jacob and start the many wheels of my Plan B into motion.

I also know that to be successful I will need to alienate Janey from Judy, and I've considered a couple of different scenarios to make that happen and keeping Judy alive-for now, is my best option. Who knows, maybe she'll be the first of what will be a long and successful partnership. I have another piece of unfinished business I need to personally handle, and I have that weasel, Adrian Sanchez, working on it now that he's been released. So, while someone with a neurotypical brain may look at lessons learned because of failure, I see those lessons as a way to open up a whole new world of opportunity, one that when the time comes, I will be ready to embrace.

Dear Reader,

Thank you for choosing my book. I hope you enjoyed reading it as much as I enjoyed writing it.

The third book in The Mother Killer Series will be another chilling ride through the minds of psychopaths as you follow the twists and turns trying to separate the good guys from the bad. The team you've come to know and love in the first two books will be back on for the most important chase of their careers.

Follow me for updates and sneak previews as Book 3 progresses.
Facebook – jill.wagner-author
Instagram – jill.wagner_author

You can also follow my author page directly, on Amazon where you order my books.

Before you leave, if you would be so kind as to leave an Amazon review, and recommend The Mother Killer Series to other readers. Word of mouth, and Amazon reviews go a long way, and are a tremendous help for other readers to discover my books.

Thanks again,

Jill

Made in the USA
Columbia, SC
26 July 2024